ROGUE'S KISS

SCANDALOUS MISS BRIGHTWELLS (BOOK 2)

BEVERLEY OAKLEY

AUTHOR'S NOTE ABOUT THE SERIES

The Scandalous Miss Brightwells

Welcome to my Scandalous Miss Brightwells series!

Wicked and lively Fanny and Antoinette Brightwell have made spectacular marriages—despite scandals and the treachery of a disappointed suitor determined to besmirch their reputations.

So, who better to play matchmaker when a deserving candidate waltzes into their orbit?

Rake's Redemption is the first in the series of five stories, each of which can be read as stand-alone stories.

Here's a bit about them:

1. Rake's Redemption

The beautiful Brightwells—clever Fanny and her easily-led sister, Antoinette—battle scandal and spurned suitors to achieve gilded marriages against the odds. A love match in Fanny's case and a very satisfactory compromise in Antoinette's.

"Fanny and Fenton's story is full of drama, humor and sizzle." ~ Amazon reader.

Read for FREE in KU

2. Rogue's Kiss

How bold would a potential suitor be if he were told the lie that the young lady he desires has only six months to live?

"A great read - one which will leave you sighing for more." ~ 4 Out Of 5 Hearts From Cariad Books

3. The Wedding Wager (formerly titled Devil's Run)

A rigged horse race - with a marriage and a lost child riding on the outcome.

Can the matchmaking Brightwell sisters avoid scandal and disaster as they try to rescue

two tortured souls and unite their passionate hearts?

"Very intriguing Austen-esque novel with well developed characters and story line. The best historical romance novel I've read in a while." ~ Amazon reader.

Read for Free in Kindle Unlimited.

4. The Accidental Elopement

Thank you for reading! I hope you enjoyed the series as much as I enjoyed writing about these two scandalous sisters and their matchmaking conquests!

Read for free in KU.

ROGUE'S KISS

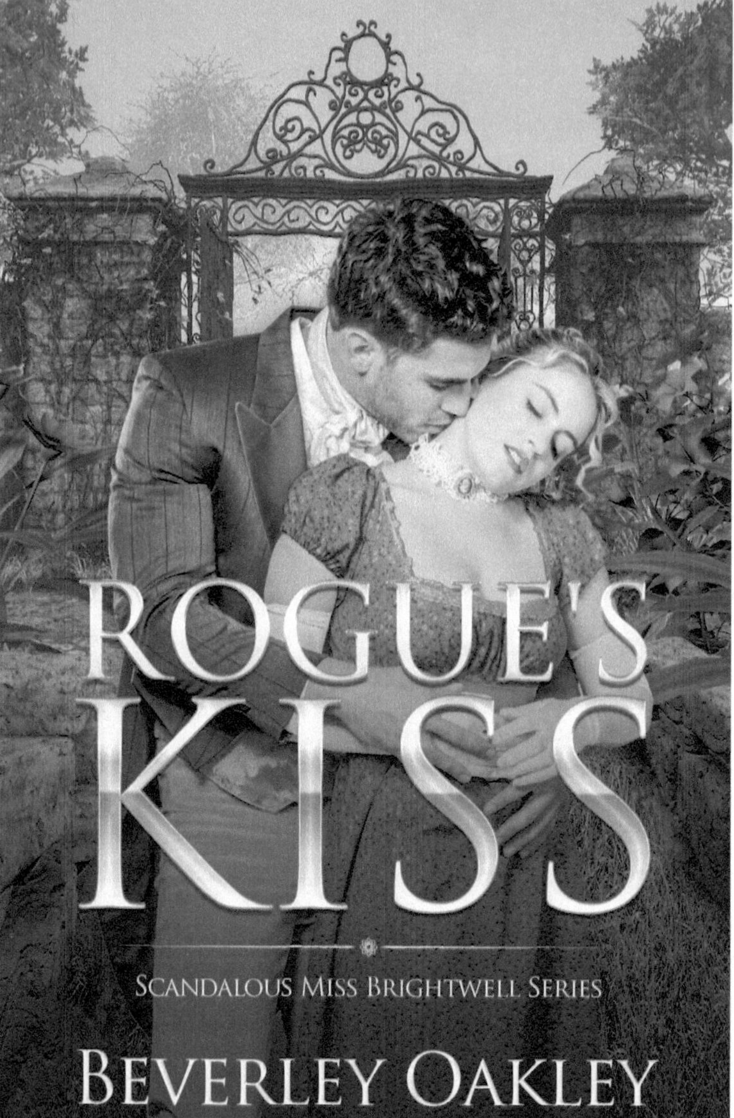

ROGUE'S
KISS
SCANDALOUS MISS BRIGHTWELL SERIES
BEVERLEY OAKLEY

CHAPTER 1

"ARE yer asking to be killed?!"

It might have been a line from the dramatic romance novel Thea was reading to her aunt in the plush confines of their carriage but the fact that the shout was from taciturn John Coachman went *beyond* dramatic.

"What the devil are you playin' at? Off the road, lassie!"

Before Thea had time to see for herself what might have so agitated their normally mute and sullen driver, his next uncharacteristic expletive was cut short by the strangled cry of an unseen woman.

With a screeching of horses and harness, the carriage lurched to a sudden halt, but it was the wail of an infant that really distressed Thea as she picked herself up from the carriage floor, trampling accidentally on the extravagant floral confection she'd dislodged from her aunt's head, which earned her a cuff over the ear.

"Aunt, have you no heart?" she cried, scrambling to look through the window. "A child has been injured!" Her less than gentle benefactress's propensity to lashing out whenever she was displeased was the least of Thea's concerns right now.

"An urchin with a careless mother by the sound of it."

Horrified that her aunt was more interested in the injury to her headdress she was now examining rather than any peasant, Thea put her head out into the drizzling rain, saying anxiously over her shoulder, "If someone has been injured we must offer our assistance!"

"Utter carelessness!" Aunt Minerva rapped on the roof, then leaned across to shout over Thea's shoulder through the open window. "Move along, John, unless we have killed some person."

Another bellow from what could only be a *very* tiny infant was the final straw. Thea pushed open the door but her attempt to leap to the ground was impeded by a meaty hand clapped upon her shoulder.

"Get right back inside, my girl! There could be footpads lurking in the forest."

The suggestion the older woman might be afraid of anything was as out of character as Thea's refusal to obey, but not even a pack of wolves would hold Thea back from assisting a poor little mite, if required.

"It's a child, Aunt. A child!" Tearing herself free, she leapt onto the road and ran to the front of the carriage.

"John! Tell me what's happened?" She halted, staring about her, confused.

Where was the squalling infant? There'd been a woman, too, for Thea had distinctly heard her scream and John had addressed her, directly.

Dusk was falling, and in the gloom, the trees of the nearby surrounding forest appeared ghost-like. A little more than a decade ago, when Thea had been a child visiting her aunt, she'd been chilled to see the bodies of the highwaymen who lurked in these woods hanging at the nearby crossroads. These were safer times but coaches were still fair game in these parts, where they were several miles from the nearest town on a winding stretch of road.

The sudden distinctive mewling of the ghostly child brought Thea's investigations round to the other side of the carriage where John Coachman stood uncertainly a few feet from a young woman weeping as she huddled over a bundle of blankets.

Aunt Minerva put her head out of the window and, perhaps reassured by the strength of the infant's lungs, called out, "It's the woman's own fault if she ran in front of us! Thea, offer her a coin if she looks like she's going to be difficult."

Thea ignored her. If the child had been injured by their carriage, she'd never forgive herself. She leaned forward to put her hand on the woman's shoulder and caught a glimpse of pale skin, shining golden hair and frightened, tearful eyes before the girl—

for she was little more than that—hastily covered her face with her veil.

"Are you injured? Is the baby all right?" Thea asked. There was no carriage in sight yet this was not a young girl from the ranks of the poor and unwashed, judging by the pleasant waft of orange water and the pristine linen worn by both mother and child.

The young woman rose to her feet. Though she was plainly dressed, her half boots and round gown were fashionable and of the highest quality. The baby's blanket was hand embroidered, as was the collar of its frilled lawn shirt.

Ignoring her, the young woman gripped her child closer to her chest while she darted a panicked look in the direction from which she'd come. Thea's attention, meanwhile, was diverted by the tear-filled blue eyes of the tiny tot who gazed at her from his mother's arms. When it raised its little fists, she noticed with a start of surprise a tiny sixth finger on its left hand.

Hesitantly she repeated her offer of help for the young woman looked on the verge of fleeing. Meanwhile Aunt Minerva was rapping once more on the roof of the carriage, demanding in plaintive tones that they'd never get home before nightfall.

Long shadows fell across the road and to Thea's fanciful imagination the landscape was rapidly acquiring the eerie look that came at dusk in places highwaymen frequented.

Only when she followed the direction of the woman's gaze did she notice another veiled woman, older and stouter, on the other side of the road. This female's large hands were placed uncompromisingly on her Pomona green upholstered hips, the bosom of her unfashionable velvet pelisse thrust forward. Thea thought she seemed undecided as to whether to approach from the copse of trees that partly concealed her but when it was clear she'd been observed, she marched across the dusty, rutted road and gripped the elbow of what was apparently her shocked and frightened charge.

"Leave be, Miss Eliza, for it's too late to change your mind and you've only yersel' to blame for all the trouble you've got yerself into."

The young woman pulled away, her face contorted with distress. "I can't leave him yet! He fell from my arms, did you not see? We must consult Dr Raine. Only he can satisfy me that Gideon was not injured."

"Weren't my fault," John the coachman declared in the midst of all this, his serge greatcoat flapping around his legs in the stiff breeze. He looked as frightened as the girl as he pointed a stubby, accusing finger in her direction. "Ran right in front of me, she did, heading for them trees over there, though what she'd find other than footpads, I don't know."

The young woman seemed intent on hiding her identity, holding her shawl up to her face, covering all but her eyes. "I won't do it," she whispered, turning her back on the stout woman who'd made a move to wrest the child away from her. "I won't give him away."

"Are you ladies in distress?"

Thea hadn't been aware of the approaching high-perch phaeton coming from the direction of the town that was their destination. Startled, she looked up at the driver who addressed them from his lofty perch, just as her aunt issued from the carriage and stomped around the front to demand what was going on.

Thea ignored her. If the equipage didn't turn heads, the young man who spoke, peering down at them as he held the reins loosely in one hand, certainly did.

Thea's skin felt suddenly warm and her throat constricted. For a moment she could only stare. The dying rays illuminated a face that was as aesthetically pleasing as it was supremely confident. Lightly curling brown hair was brushed back from a high forehead while a fashionable line of sideburns highlighted sharp cheekbones. The shape of his lips, slightly quirked, was decidedly arresting, Thea thought, as his light grey eyes regarded Thea with similar interest.

"I… I'm not sure." It was rare for Thea to not know what to say. She was generally obedient to her aunt but she also knew her own mind. However, it was so extremely rare to come face-to-face with that almost mythical species, a handsome young man, that she was robbed of speech. Having been to no more than a couple of balls at the local Assembly Rooms near the hamlet where she lodged with her aunt, Thea was used only to being amidst neighbours where the mostly elderly gentlemen were obliged to ask her to dance in order to complete a set. It was quite another matter to address a gentleman —indeed, the most handsome one she'd ever set eyes on—that she was at a complete loss, though she made a valiant attempt to concentrate on the matter at hand.

"This young woman…" Thea glanced to her left and her hand flew to her mouth as she appealed to John. "Where did she go? Panicked, she contemplated the possibility the darling baby might be injured. "Why, she was afraid her child had suffered harm but now they've both gone!" Of the older woman there was also no sign.

John Coachman, still standing at Thea's left, seemed more concerned with defending his driving than worrying about the young woman's disappearance. He wrapped his muffler more tightly around his neck as he adopted a look of moral rectitude. "Ran right in front of me, she did," he repeated, "dropping 'er baby on the ground after she'd 'ad it out wiv that gypsy lass." He stabbed his finger in the direction of the hill opposite the woods, which rose up, overlooking the town.

When Thea squinted into the sun, following the direction of John's stubby finger, she saw a ragged figure on the summit of the hill. Tall and slender and dressed all in black, the young woman appeared to be focused on the gathering on the road below her. A stiff breeze gusted through the trees and the shawl that covered her head fell away, revealing a blaze of copper hair haloed in the rays of the sun just before it dipped below the horizon. The woman turned quickly and the magnificent hair was shrouded again in her black shawl as she slunk into the trees.

"Saw the pair of 'em fightin' over who'd put their poor wee mite in the basket when there's only room for one," John muttered. "Sinners." He sucked on his gums and shook his grizzled head. "Sinners, all of 'em."

"Get back in that carriage, Thea!" Aunt Minerva's command cut the air like a whip as she turned with a curt nod at the gentleman who was yet to introduce himself, and headed back towards the dark confines of her equipage, repeating her demand over her shoulder for Thea to join her.

"Sinners?" Thea repeated, not understanding John until, without stopping to think, she put her hands to her cheeks as she blurted out, "Of course! The new foundling home's just opened and it has a bell to alert the authorities when a baby is placed in the basket." Immediately the words were out, she realised this was not a subject to mention in company with a handsome young man, though she wasn't exactly sure why. She blushed and muttered, "Well, that's what Mary told me this morning, only she didn't say why anyone would want to put a baby into a basket in the woods when surely it can get all the fresh air it needs in its mother's arms."

"Perhaps some babies just need more fresh air than others," suggested the young man with a smile. Tossing aside the reigns, he leapt to the ground.

Thea, with strongly beating heart, was

admiring his magnificence as he rose from a beautifully executed bow before being taken by surprise as she found her hand suddenly in possession of his.

"Mr Sylvester Grayling, at your service," he murmured, his gaze travelling the length of Thea with patent admiration before adding the information that he, too, had witnessed the tussle over whose child would occupy the basket hanging from the post as he'd crested the hill. "I'd have placed bets on the gypsy woman in black. She was infinitely keener to be rid of her burden than the soft, blonde lass who turned tail and ran with her babe, right in front of your carriage."

Thea bit her lip. "I think I'm going to cry," she whispered. "How terribly sad to have to give up one's child."

"Yes, isn't it?" the young man agreed with heavy irony. "Ah well, we all have difficult choices if we're to make the best of the few short years we're given, eh?" He grinned again before executing another flourishing bow. "And now I must leave, for it's late and your companion is understandably anxious to get into town before the sun is well and truly set. Forgive me for casting a pall over the lively but far too short occasion of making of our mutual acquaintance. Nevertheless, it has been diverting to meet under such unusual circumstances." He continued to eye Thea appreciatively before adding with a sigh, "Alas, I must continue my journey in the opposite direction though might I be permitted to know your name, Miss…?" He looked questioningly at Thea.

"Miss Brightwell."

He nodded. "A pleasure to meet you, Miss Brightwell. And I'm sorry for your distress though I'm sure there's no need to concern yourself over the wee babe."

Thea bit her lip and glanced across to make sure her aunt was out of earshot before she confided, "I'm afraid I shan't sleep a wink until I'm satisfied it's all right. I do so love babies." She sighed. "I would love to have a dozen of them some day, you know."

She jumped, her embarrassment that she may have spoken unwisely compounded when her aunt bellowed from not three feet away, "Get inside the carriage this minute,

Thea, and stop conversing like a common trollop in the street!"

Thea sent the young man an apologetic glance as she gathered her dark travelling pelisse about her and called back, "I was just thanking Mr Grayling for stopping to see if we required his assistance, Aunt Minerva."

"The only assistance required by me is from a girl with her head glued on who knows her place. Now get back inside before it's suddenly midnight and we're overrun by highwaymen."

"No highwaymen these days, let me assure you, Madam." Mr Grayling spoke bolsteringly for Aunt Minerva's benefit, his smile and tone causing a most odd and unprecedented mix of feelings surging through Thea. Her brothers had died young and she had only one male cousin. Conversing with anyone of the opposite sex, much less remotely eligible as Mr Grayling assuredly was, judging by his interest, was a breathtaking experience.

"I take it you're headed for Bath?" he added with a nod in the direction they were travelling.

Thea tried to keep her voice steady beneath his steady gaze and hoped she didn't blurt out something completely inappropriate—like what beautiful grey eyes he had. Instead she managed, "My cousin, Lady Quamby, has invited us to lodge with her for several weeks while we take the waters and…and enjoy something of the novelties Bath has to offer."

"Lady Quamby? Indeed?"

Thea had little time to wonder at what sounded almost like heavy sarcasm before the shrill urgency in Aunt Minerva's voice spoiled the moment.

"Thea! Come this moment!"

Reluctantly, Thea nodded at the young man. "It was a pleasure meeting you, Mr Grayling." Boldly, she held out her hand. "I hope business is good in the south."

"Thank you, Miss Brightwell. I hope so too." He gripped her fingers just a little longer than was required, his eyes warm as he replied, "If it's not, it won't be too great a hardship to return early." Relinquishing her hand after a quick kiss on the tips of her fingers, he nodded in farewell. "Enjoy your stay in Bath. I'm sure any time spent with Lady Quamby is guaranteed to be ...*diverting*."

Thea returned to the carriage, her heart turning over like a waterwheel. She wished she'd had the courage to enquire further as to the nature of his business. That might have given her an indication of how soon or otherwise she'd see him again. Clearly her connection to Lady Quamby, her irrepressible cousin Antoinette, interested him.

Thea didn't know why, but her aunt had never spoken well of Thea's two cousins, Antoinette and her older sister Fanny. She'd therefore been highly surprised when Aunt Minerva had accepted the invitation to attend the christening of Lord Quamby's heir, baby George, whom Thea was simply dying to meet. In fact the invitation had been directed to Thea and had only included Aunt Minerva as an afterthought. Cousin Antoinette's careless phraseology had put the old lady into high dudgeon and she'd let loose with a great many nasty things said pertaining to the respective 'loose characters of those girls', as she'd put it.

Nevertheless, after initially roundly refusing to attend the event, Aunt Minerva had changed her mind just the day before and informed her niece, Lady Quamby, by return messenger that she would accept her invitation after all, and that she intended to stay three weeks. Thea, who loved her beautiful, bold and somewhat wild cousins, couldn't wait to see them again.

Though she'd have been even happier if her aunt had chosen to remain behind.

As Thea settled back into her seat, she tried to attend to what her aunt was saying but an image of handsome Mr Grayling bending over her hand, his eyes locked on hers, kept intruding. She tried not to shiver or do anything else that might alert her aunt to her romantic daydreaming; therefore she began to coolly list an inventory based on his obvious attributes.

Probably he was somewhere in his latter twenties. That was a very nice age, she decided. Not too old, like the widowers her aunt liked to suggest would be the only marital prospects a dowerless maiden such as herself could entertain.

Like his name, his eyes had been a cool grey. She decided she very much liked the combination of cool grey eyes and slightly curling light-brown hair.

"Devil's spawn!"

"What? Mr Grayling?" Startled, Thea spoke out loud before she could stop herself.

"If that was the gentleman you were associating with after I ordered you back to the carriage, then I have not the slightest idea since I was not the recipient of his address." Her aunt's nostrils twitched. "I was in fact remarking upon the gathering we just stumbled upon. The devil has done his work and there will be no redemption for those creatures—mothers or babes—here on Earth."

"You can't say that about a baby!" Thea gasped.

"I can if it has the wickedness of both parents coursing through its veins. And as for that young man, Thea, let me tell you that a moonstruck girl is like a beacon advertising her availability." Aunt Minerva's small black eyes bored malevolently into Thea's from beneath a wayward bunch of silk lily-of-the-valley that had come loose from her bonnet. "Your behaviour was most unbecoming. I overheard he was leaving town and not a bad thing, either, my girl. Let me tell you one thing. If he shows you the same flicker of interest once he learns your true situation, you had better beware. A man of good standing, as he clearly is, wants a dowry, Thea, and you have nothing." She sucked on her gums and her nose twitched even more as if something very unsavoury were in the wind. "No, my girl, let me tell you that if he's still interested, it's because he's ferreted out your vulnerability and intends to trade on it.'

Thea pouted, then bravely muttered, "Not everyone is motivated by money or… bad intentions, Aunt."

Her aunt was unimpressed. "In my experience they are, girl, and you're an innocent if you think otherwise."

With a huff, Thea retrieved her tatting

from her reticule and set to work grimly correcting her last mistakes in the cuffs she was hand working. She would not give her aunt the satisfaction of, an answer. So Mr Grayling would not have offered her the time of day if he'd known her true station in life? Well, that was probably true enough but she could dream a little, couldn't she?

As for those babes, their pitiful plight tugged at her heartstrings. How could her aunt speak so about them?

Thea loved babies. She didn't care whether they were the dirty little creatures she sometimes saw in the arms of the working women in town, or the pristine-clad, sweet-smelling infants of her distant relatives. Babies were adorable, regardless.

Aunt Minerva regarded her through beady brown eyes. "No girl is ever too young to understand the dangers to society of the devil's spawn," she muttered. "A child born out of wedlock will forever writhe in the fiery furnace of hell."

'Born out of wedlock?' Thea looked at her aunt steadily. She wasn't exactly sure what being 'born out of wedlock' entailed but she'd heard Aunt Minerva spouting sentiments like this for the seeming eternity she'd been her unpaid companion. "Then it's a harsh world we live in, Aunt, if we are judged on transgressions beyond our control, rather than by our own actions."

Aunt Minerva raised her eyes heavenward. "Perhaps it's a good thing you know so little, though you're unlikely to ever be educated in the dubious joys of marriage. Spinsters forever, you and me both, and you'd best get used to it."

Thea felt her mouth drop open and disappointment wash through her veins. "I'm twenty years old, Aunt Minerva. I mightn't have a dowry but that doesn't mean I must reconcile myself to remaining a spinster for the rest of my days. Why, Mr Grayling—"

She bit her tongue as her aunt rounded on her. "When that Mr Grayling returns to Bath he won't offer you the time of day, I can promise you that! Not when he learns you're a charity case because your impecunious father was more interested in keeping his peagoose of a wife happy with her fripperies and indulging her with a growing brood of children they could not afford to keep."

"Aunt!"

"That was perhaps harsh, and I shall apologise for the reference to your brothers and sisters, struck down through no fault of their own by misfortune."

Through tear-filled eyes, Thea could see her aunt looked a touch remorseful though not nearly enough. How could she say such shocking things about her family?

"But as for being a spinster, I'd say it was a decent enough state of affairs to be in control of one's own fortune, for let me tell you, I've been preyed upon by fortune hunters all my life."

Thea looked at her aunt askance before ducking her head to concentrate once more on her handiwork. She swallowed as she summoned the courage to respond for she was not prepared to let this pass. "So when did you receive your first marriage offer, Aunt?" she murmured.

The older woman shifted in her seat. "I was eighteen when I was courted by a certain gentleman to whom I made clear I had no interest. In the twenty-seven years since I couldn't tell you, there've been so many."

"So you've never wanted to marry, then?"

Aunt Minerva's sudden stillness was telling and it looked as though she was going to take advantage of the reprieve offered by John Coachman, who shouted down from the box at that moment, telling them that Lord Quamby's estate was just beyond the rise.

In the dimness of the carriage interior, Thea saw her aunt's chin wobble as she dabbed at her eyes with a piece of embroidered linen and sniffed. "There was one gentleman, but that was a long time ago. Twenty years ago, in fact."

Thea's heart was easily engaged. She leaned over to pat her aunt's shoulder. "I'm sure he's never stopped thinking of the chance that slipped away, Aunt Minerva," she whispered.

"He ought to be tormented by regret after the dishonourable way he treated me!" her aunt snapped, flicking away her niece's hand. "Now shoulders back, Thea, and sit up straight. You already know how little I think of your cousin and her husband but they're nobility. An earl and his countess can do whatever they like. You, however, need to mind every move you make."

CHAPTER 2

WHAT a relief it was to step beyond the heavy atmosphere of the carriage and be welcomed by first Antoinette's cheerful greeting, and then her sister's, as the cousins gracefully descended the front steps of Lord Quamby's townhouse.

"And you're already here too, Fanny. I'd not expected you!" Thea had always admired Fanny's dark looks and the feisty temperament her cousin hid beneath a veneer of polished sophistication. Now she gazed at her with undisguised admiration as Fanny directed them to a comfortable cluster of seats, as if she were just as much the hostess as her sister, whose home this was.

Antoinette, the younger, could not have been more different from Fanny, with her golden hair and her pink and white complexion. Antoinette exuded innocence. Thea was still trying to decide if her younger cousin was incredibly intelligent but went to great pains to hide the fact, or whether she really was the beautiful little peagoose the family painted, who, despite being a penniless debutante with a dubious reputation, had managed to snare an earl.

Either way, Thea reflected with a pang as refreshments were ordered, the two cousins were shining beacons advertising life's possibilities, compared with dull and dutiful Thea.

"Thought I'd still be lying-in?" Fanny put her hand to her now flat belly while her lips curved into the wicked smile for which she was famed. "I didn't need to spend a whole month staring at the ceiling when I was ready to dance a jig the moment the little monkey was out in the world."

Thea glanced at her aunt and wasn't surprised by her pursed mouth. Aunt Minerva, however, managed to hold her tongue though Thea knew she'd not have hesitated to rebuke her niece when Fanny was unmarried. Now Fanny was a viscountess and she had precedence over Aunt Minerva, who was now just the spinster daughter of a lowly baron, though one would never guess it given her airs. Aunt Minerva had inherited a fortune, though, and that stood for something. Something she did not hesitate to use over Thea as both threat and inducement.

Still, Fanny and Antoinette had managed to acquire both title and fortune. Thea never got tired of hearing the astonishing stories of how Fanny had won the heart of rakish Lord Fenton, and how Antoinette had later happily accepted the hand of the aging Earl of Quamby, who had originally been betrothed to Fanny. She'd learned not to bring up the subject in her aunt's hearing.

"And when can I see the new heir?" Thea asked. "Both of them," she added, for Antoinette's child had been born six weeks earlier than Fanny's.

Antoinette raised her eyes to the ceiling. "Why, Thea, you've only just arrived and already you're talking babies. I hope you won't become a bore, but then you always were fond of the dirty, squalling little things, weren't you? And to be sure, little George has his sweet moments, but he's a tiresome child for the most part who does nothing terribly interesting, unless you consider sleeping, feeding and crying worthy of note."

"Unlike my Katherine, who is as agreeable as her dear father," Fanny interjected with a smile as she smoothed down her skirts. "Antoinette has never been the maternal kind, but fortunately she did recognise the importance of producing a lusty heir for Quamby who, but for her, might have died childless." She pressed her lips together, clearly mindful of not breaking into an unseemly laugh in Aunt Minerva's hearing, causing Thea, who'd heard whispers of some unmentionable scandal, to blush.

"Well, I saved Quamby from having to hand over everything to his awful nephew, George Bramley, didn't I?" Antoinette, reaching across to offer Thea a plate of sugar biscuits, looked smug before she sobered. "A word of warning, though, Thea. I hear Bramley is in town." She nibbled at her biscuit but her expression remained serious. "Once he learns there's another Brightwell on the lookout for a husband, you can be assured he'll do his best to blight your prospects with all sorts of awful rumours. He tried to spoil our chances but Fanny and I were too clever for him. We had the last laugh, didn't we, Fanny?"

Thea noticed that Fanny sent a rather quelling look at her younger sister, whose irrepressible gaiety certainly was at odds with what Thea would have expected of a new mother, and a countess, to boot.

Fanny, for once, appeared to choose her words carefully. "Antoinette is right that you should beware of George Bramley, but that is all I wish to say on the subject. Yes, Thea, you shall visit the nursery in good time, but first you must tell us all your news before you become distracted with our divinely angelic infants. I'm sure you've endless stories with which to divert us of the past six months you've been living with Aunt Minerva, for that is when we last saw you. Six months ago."

"And then tomorrow night we shall go to the Assembly Rooms." Antoinette clapped her hands together, her eyes shining like a child's. "You've never been, have you, Thea? No, Aunt Minerva never takes you anywhere, does she? No offence intended, Aunt Minerva, but you're not one for high revels and that's understandable at your age, but tomorrow we shan't let you sit out an evening when there'll be such wonderful entertainment on hand." She smiled ingenuously at her relative. "You shall enjoy the food and cards, and the rest of us can enjoy the dancing."

"I doubt if we shall have recovered from our journey so soon," Aunt Minerva responded in quelling tones with a sharp look at Thea.

Antoinette looked disappointed before she brightened. "Oh well, but we shall wait and see how you are feeling in the morning, shall we? I know Quamby was looking forward to escorting you, Aunt."

Thea looked sharply between the two. Perhaps Antionette was well aware, contrary to her apparent ingenuousness, that Aunt Minerva would find the idea of being escorted anywhere by an earl—regardless of his reputation—far too great an enticement to resist.

Her aunt, however, was not about to give any of them reason to hope. "Time will tell, Antoinette. If my gouty foot is playing up, Thea will have to remain behind to soothe it with unguents, for though she's a drain on the purse she *is* the best nurse I've had."

Thea studied the pattern on the teacup she was handed while pretending not to notice the horrified looks her cousins exchanged. A pang of misery completely quelled the excitement she'd allowed to build. So this was how it was to be? The much lauded visit to Bath was only so Aunt Minerva could claim she'd been housed by an earl, while she eschewed every other diversion on offer—and kept her niece in proverbial leg irons, attending to her multitude of imaginary ailments.

"Oh, but Aunt, you simply can't stay here. You must go out with us so…we can boast to society we're entertaining a diamond of the first water, knowing how many disappointed suitors you've discarded at your feet." Antoinette's concern was replaced by pleasure at having come up with something so convincing, Thea could tell. She managed to hide her amusement as she noticed the way her aunt puffed up her chest.

"I am in no position to say, today, how I shall feel tomorrow," her aunt nevertheless said crisply. "I am frequently beset by the most debilitating ailments, which visit me entirely without warning."

Or that coincide with when I have an invitation or an opportunity to enjoy some diversion, Thea thought dolefully.

"Besides, Thea might not wish to be in company so much when her wardrobe is so sparse." Aunt Minerva patted the squirrel's tail hairpiece that protruded from her lace cap. "I've not the money to spend on her when her father left her so pitifully unprovided for, and it appears she shuns those clothes of mine which I have so generously sent her way."

This was a painful topic for Thea. The simple muslin and velvet pelisse she wore now had been a generous present from Fanny some months previously, but if they were to attend any social events beyond the christening, she'd be sadly lacking in comparison with not just her own stylishly and expensively garbed cousins, but even the lowliest parson's daughter.

An image of handsome Mr Grayling, whom she'd been dreaming she might meet at some entertainment in Bath once he returned from his business, was replaced by relief that it was just as well she'd not be part of the social whirl, since he'd see from just a glance what she was: a hanger-on. A poor relation. Aunt Minerva had done a fine job the past year in tempering any hopes Thea had ever harboured of entering into holy matrimony. The thought nearly made her weep. Babies. Oh, how she longed to have babies with a loving husband by her side. Her own parents had been so terribly fond of each other and their many children, and Thea had always known that she wanted that same felicity of mutual feeling and a large family, too.

Admittedly, there was some merit in her aunt's criticism of Father's dealings with money, she owned sadly, for he'd taken considerably less care of his somewhat meagre fortune than he had of the beautiful wife upon whom he loved to lavish expensive presents, and who had no idea of the fast-decreasing limits to his funds. Not that Thea would have minded about having no money as long as she could have had her family. But the terrible fever that had swept through the village two years ago had put paid to that.

"You certainly are known for your generosity, Aunt Minerva," Fanny said without a trace of irony, Thea was impressed to note. "Thea wrote to tell me of the fine brown and green velvet round gown you so kindly passed on to her."

Thea's heart leapt into her mouth. Surely Fanny wouldn't divulge the fact she'd likened Aunt Minerva to a toad emerging from a bank of sludge when wearing the supposedly fashionable outfit? She shuddered with fear and accepted that she'd only been receiving her just desserts; for shortly after Thea declared to her cousins that she'd rather deport herself in public wearing nothing but her petticoat than suffer the humiliation of being seen in such an abomination, her aunt gifted her the notable creation.

Aunt Minerva's cloying smile at Fanny's compliment was a glower by the time she swivelled her jewelled throat in Thea's direction. "Perhaps I *shall* attend the Assembly Rooms tomorrow night. It'll give Thea an opportunity to sport the brown and green. I'd been thinking only recently I hadn't seen her wear it, but then reasoned that it was because I've not taken her anywhere it can be seen to advantage. I was surprised when, last Thursday, she did not put it on when I knew how much she harboured hopes of securing the interest of the nice young curate who insisted on coming to tea long after I'd made it clear his hopes were…well, hopeless. Now I realise that it is as you say, Antoinette, and I've been unkind in keeping

Thea at home with me. Even if it's impossible she'll ever marry, given her parlous financial state, it would be a kindness to allow her to attend a few entertainments, though not so many that would stretch her limited wardrobe and make her a subject of unkind gossip for having only the one dress to wear in company."

Thea resolutely drank her tea. Oh my dear Lord, she'd rather die than go forth in the hideous ensemble her aunt would have her wear. She directed a desperate look at Fanny, who said smoothly, all wide-eyed innocence, "Why, Aunt Minerva, that was because she thought the gown so much more flattering to your colouring, she told me. You must have been quite a head-turner with your lovely bronze ringlets, if you don't mind my saying so." Her gaze travelled with clear-eyed scrutiny over Aunt Minerva's visage before fixing upon the somewhat odd length of orange fur that blended with the ginger ringlets that hung in front of her ears. "It is remarkable time has not dulled your assets."

Thea held her breath as Aunt Minerva

narrowed her eyes. Fanny had gone too far this time. But then her aunt put her hand once more to the squirrel's tail hairpiece that supplemented her sparse greying locks, and smiled coyly. "Oh, I have my secrets, even at my age," she simpered. "Let me tell you, when I was young, the gentlemen were fighting over me. One in particular was so distraught by my rejection he shot himself."

'He wanted to marry you?' Antoinette squeaked with such incredulity, Thea and Fanny both sent her the evil eye, so that she added with commendable alacrity, "But of course, what young man would have passed up the opportunity to secure your hand in marriage?"

"Mr John Dempster was his name," Aunt Minerva recalled, gazing moist-eyed into space, apparently mollified by the turn of the conversation. "But I rejected him, and what do you think he did? Rushed off to the continent where, in his mental derange-ment at my rough treatment of his hopes, he shot himself through the heart."

Antoinette tilted her head. "The heart? One doesn't shoot oneself through one's own heart, surely? Is he actually dead, then?"

Aunt Minerva cleared her throat and replied smoothly, "Mercifully, the Good Lord was not yet ready to take him."

"So he's not dead." Antoinette clarified. "I must say, trying to shoot oneself through the heart doesn't sound very efficient if you're intent upon succeeding. Why didn't he put the pistol into his mouth? That's what one does when one really wants to kill oneself."

"Antoinette, that's enough,' her sister warned, turning back to her aunt with a sympathetic *moue*. "Poor Mr Dempster. I'm sure he never got over you, Aunt."

"Indeed he did not. Never married, I hear."

"Never married! What a cruel waste, Aunt," Antoinette went on blithely, "when you could have made him so happy and we'd have had possibly dozens more cousins and not just poor Thea, who is all alone." She clapped her hand to her mouth at a fierce look from her sister, no doubt recalling that Thea had once been the eldest of six before the scarlet fever.

Thea forced her mind onto other matters as she pushed away the pain.

"Mr Dempster sounds a particularly foolish and unworthy suitor, Aunt Minerva." Fanny took over smoothly. "Perhaps you had a special admirer amongst them all?"

For a moment Aunt Minerva stared into space as if recalling something very intense. Her lips worked and her head shuddered slightly on its well upholstered stem. She opened her mouth to speak before shutting it abruptly, her eyes narrowing into slits of malice.

"I think it's high time you took Thea off to the nursery," she muttered. "I can see the children later when they're clean and ready for company."

As soon as the girls reached the nursery, after a promise to bring young George and Katherine down to see their great-aunt later, they broke into convulsive laughter.

"Oh, Thea, if it weren't that you had to live with her the year through, we'd be looking forward to the old gorgon's annual visit with the greatest anticipation." Antoinette hiccupped. "Did you see the evil look she sent some unknown past would-be lover? If she could just have put a hex on him, he'd have been writhing on the floor in front of us, spitting out green smoke as he slowly turned into a toad."

"Hush! Not in front of the servants," Fanny admonished, waving away the nursemaid as she picked up young Katherine and cuddled her. "You say you were courted by the curate?" she asked Thea.

"But a lowly curate?" Antoinette clarified. "Please say you didn't entertain the idea for a minute."

Sadly, Thea forced her longing gaze away from Fanny and her baby to look at her feet. "He was a very sweet young man. I was fond enough of him that if he'd asked me I'd have consented to be his wife for I couldn't imagine I'd receive an offer from anyone else, but Aunt Minerva said it was out of the question."

"Of course it was," Antoinette said roundly. "You'd be subjecting yourself to a life of penury from which there'd be no return. For once Aunt Minerva did you a service."

Fanny, now bending over the pristine coverings of her baby's crib to tuck Katherine back into the warmth, harrumphed. "That was no service. That was simply *self*-serving. Aunt Minerva will not sanction any marriage for you, Thea, as she has you in mind for far more important things." She kissed her baby's plump little fist, which remained wrapped around her finger, adding, "Yes, indeed, as her handmaiden into old age. No, there really is a great urgency to find you a husband in the next couple of weeks. But of course you'll need clothes. Antoinette and I have already discussed it. Aunt Minerva would far rather see you step out looking like last season's sludge, all but announcing to the world that you're as poor as a church mouse. But Antoinette and I were, too, only last season— and aren't we a stellar advertisement of how one's star can rise in such a short time?"

Thea felt a surge of such gratitude she didn't know how to adequately respond.

When she'd thanked her cousins, who now declared they'd take her directly to their dressing rooms, she remained in the doorway.

"Can we play with the babies a little longer? See, George doesn't want to go to sleep just yet."

They stared at her, open-mouthed.

"You mean, instead of going to look at clothes?" Antoinette asked with a frown.

Thea nodded. "I've been dying to hold both little George and Katherine in my arms all the way here and I don't think I can wait another minute."

Her cousins exchanged glances. "Well, you're an odd one, Thea," Fanny remarked, "but you're so pretty, so your future will be assured if Antoinette and I have anything to do with it. And it certainly won't include rubbing unguents into gouty feet. If I have my way, you'll be outranking Aunt Minerva before the end of the season."

"And then," said Antoinette as she returned to her youngster and picked him up, "you can start having all the babies you want, though *why* you'd want to, I don't know. I mean, the beginning part is highly entertaining but everything else after that—"

She broke off at an unusually fierce look from her sister.

THEA COULDN'T BELIEVE HOW MUCH FUN she'd had. Trying on her cousin's clothes, which they insisted she might borrow, had been like having the keys to some wondrous palace, but playing with the babies had been the most fun of all.

Now, as she waited in the drawing room to leave for the Assembly Rooms, giggling with Fanny and Antoinette, it was like the old days when she'd giggled with her sisters in a home filled with warmth and love and laughter.

More fun was in store when Fanny and Antoinette's brother made his appearance, looking surprisingly elegant in a pink and gold striped waistcoat beneath his coat of navy superfine for his night on the town.

"Oh, Cousin Thea!" he declared,

bringing his hand to his heart as he stood before her in the centre of the Aubusson carpet beneath the chandelier. "What a celestial vision! May I have this dance?"

Thea giggled as her cousin Bertram executed an elaborate bow before her. "What a paragon!" he went on as Thea rose then curtsied, fluttering her eyelids for Bertram's benefit as she played along. "Aunt Gorgonia will just have to accept by the end of this visit that she will be losing you to the highest in the land. Why, I declare that the richest and the handsomest of men will come to blows trying to prove themselves worthy of you."

Fanny and Antoinette laughed and Bertram added more soberly as he leaned against the mantelpiece, "Fact is, you look extremely fetching in that sparkling creation Fanny's lent you. And it fits you a good deal better than it did Fanny last time she wore it."

"Which was three days after I'd given birth and you burst unceremoniously into my room when I was seeing how many of my clothes I could still wear," Fanny defended herself coolly as she reclined upon the chaise longue.

"Ah yes, weeping, if I recall. Fenton told me to get out using the coarsest language."

"Well, of course he did! He was comforting me and reassuring me that I'd soon regain my figure and that I'd—"

"Always be the most exquisite creature in the entire world."

They all turned at the caramel tones of Fanny's husband, the incomparably handsome Lord Fenton, who appeared in the doorway like a sleek and supremely confident black cat.

With Aunt Minerva clinging to his arm.

Thea dropped back into her seat, head lowered, and waited nervously for her aunt's reaction.

The laughter stopped, the general good humour in the room replaced by a tense anticipation. Aunt Minerva narrowed her eyes as she took in Thea's appearance, her mouth a thin, tight line. "Thea, go upstairs and change." Her voice was low and warning.

"But Aunt Minerva, I'm happy to lend Thea my gown," Fanny began before her aunt cut her off, ignoring her as she prepared to speak once more to her niece. A pin could have been heard to drop in the uncomfortable silence as she held up her hand.

"Do it now, or we'll hold everyone else up. If I'm good enough to lend you the clothes you need, you'll show the gratitude I deserve. Now go!"

A very subdued Thea returned shortly afterwards wearing the brown and green velvet, stiffened with its monstrous padding around the hem, which made her feel like a burgher's wife, parodied by fashion, her natural shape distorted with roulettes that encircled her upper arms. It would have been impossible to have appeared graceful, even if she were the most accomplished opera dancer in Covent Garden.

Silence greeted her as she self-consciously moved past the gathered assembly and reseated herself opposite Aunt Minerva with becoming meekness.

Antoinette sent her a silent, horrified look while Fanny pretended to be engaged in quiet chatter with her husband.

Bertram, who was playing with the lid of a snuff box as he continued to lounge by the fireplace, turned as she took her seat to remark, "That's a mighty fetching object you have on your head, Cousin Thea. Might I ask what it is?"

"It's a toque, of course!" snapped Aunt Minerva. "My finest, too, which I've gifted to Thea since it was made for that gown."

"Yes, yes, of course." Bertram looked apologetic but he continued to stare at the toque with a concentrated frown while the rest of the party clearly forced themselves to chatter as they might before they were off to any diverting entertainment.

Thea simply sat on her chair, all pleasure at the possibilities the evening had previously held completely sucked from her, wondering how she could possibly contrive to develop some life-threatening ailment in the next two minutes. Anything would be better than having to actually appear in public wearing so painfully the advertisement of her leg-shacklement to her hateful aunt. Tears threatened, so when Fanny asked kindly, "Have you danced much in the past, Thea?" she could only shake her head.

"Oh, that doesn't matter," Antoinette broke in. "Some of the young men who ask you will have two left feet, anyway."

Bertram, continued to frown, his gaze still riveted on Thea's ensemble. Gravely, he said, "I'll dance with you if no one else asks."

"Bertram!" Fanny rounded on him. "Cousin Thea will be swamped with offers."

Thea could see that her lively, inventive, enthusiastic cousins didn't know what else to say. Her shoulders slumped even more and she felt her Aunt's gown about her as if it were a living thing, sucking the life out of her. "That's very kind of you, Cousin Bertram."

Lord Fenton rose. "Shall we go?"

Thea sent a longing look at the door that led towards the passage that wound ultimately past her bedchamber. Perhaps if she clutched her stomach and claimed a sudden bilious attack, she could contrive to stay at home. She didn't care if that was what Aunt Minerva intended—for clearly her aunt intended either that or an evening of total humiliation.

"Oh good Lord!"

Thea clutched her belly in preparation for her charade but not before Cousin Bertram's expletive literally rained down on her, together with a good quantity of the contents of his generous glass of Madeira.

"Oh Cousin Thea, how clumsy of me!" he exclaimed, brandishing a snowy handkerchief and dabbing at the sticky wine that was all down the front of her dress, scarring the velvet and pooling onto the floor.

"Gracious, such a lovely dress! Ruined!" Fanny cried, rushing forward and attempting to help Bertram mop up the mess, yet managing to smear the damage to an even greater extent. "Can it be saved?"

"Of course it can't. Well, not in time for this evening, at any rate." Lord Fenton remained calmly in the doorway where he'd stopped, turning to watch the fuss. "Fanny, please go upstairs and find Cousin Thea something suitable of yours so we don't hold up the party. My apologies, Miss Brightwell, for keeping you waiting." He turned from where Aunt

Minerva was staring at the scene with an expression of horrified outrage while Thea felt her dismay blossom into hope and happiness.

With an almost indiscernible wink, Lord Fenton was indicating the doorway through which Thea had almost condemned herself to a lonely, miserable night on account of Aunt Minerva's poisoned chalice, or rather her gift of a dress, before darling Cousin Bertram had hit upon salvation.

Upstairs, already laid out upon her bed, Thea found a gloriously simple but elegant white muslin gown together with all the necessary accessories: long satin gloves, pearl-encrusted hair combs and a thin gold chain to wear around her neck. It did not take Thea long to dress.

"Oh Cousin Fanny, thank you! How clever of you to think of such a reprieve and to plan it all with Cousin Bertram. I don't know what to say!"

"We'll have to credit Bertram with a rare moment of genius, for he came up with that all on his own." Fanny finished doing up the tiny pearl buttons on the back of Thea's dress then stepped in front of her with a smile. "Now, are you ready?"

Thea took her cousin's arm with a grateful smile. "I'm ready."

"And are you nervous?"

"I've never been more so." Thea gazed at her cousin with a mixture of trepidation and hope. Cousin Fanny looked utterly ravishing yet once Thea had thought her merely lovely. Now Fanny had been imbued with the gloss of happiness and riches since her astonishing marriage. And Fanny claimed the same could happen for Thea. Could it? She barely dared hope, yet the truth was, all she wanted was a husband who would love her, and enough money to feed a large family.

"A touch of nervousness isn't the end of the world. You look utterly charming." Fanny sent Thea a satisfied look as she led her down the stairs. "Just remember," she added over her shoulder, "Antoinette and I want only your happiness. If you do everything we tell you, I believe you have every reason to hope you'll not die a dried-up old spinster having sacrificed your youth and happiness to Aunt Minerva."

Her words reverberated in Thea's head all the way down the remaining steps, clanging with greater force as she faced the patent disapproval of Aunt Minerva in the lobby, the only one of the company who did not compliment her when she was suddenly feeling like a princess.

Could it really be true that Aunt Minerva wanted to keep Thea unmarried for her own convenience?

Thea shuddered at an image of her venerable relative's misshapen ankles and none too sweet-smelling feet.

Taking Cousin Bertram's arm she smiled up at him, determined not to let a crotchety old woman spoil what now promised to be a thrilling evening.

"Cousin Thea, you are a vision," he murmured, and Thea tingled all over with happiness.

Right now it seemed no risk was too great if it meant not having to massage Aunt Minerva's corns and bunions until the end of time.

CHAPTER 3

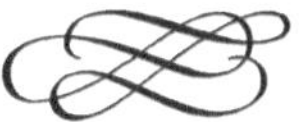

*T*HE music and gaiety as they entered the Assembly Rooms hit Thea in the face like a draught of fear and trepidation, mixed with the promise of so much. Now her stomach really did clench. She felt sick and lightheaded.

Fanny nudged her. "Smile," she admonished in a whisper. "Always remember to smile, no matter how afraid or how excited or otherwise you are. Ah, Mr Ponsonby, of course I remember you. How delightful."

Despite the fact Fanny was clinging to her handsome husband's arm, Thea was astonished by the attention she and Antoinette received from gentlemen from all walks of life. Lord Fenton didn't seem to mind. Thea gazed dreamily at him. He was the epitome of any girl's wistful fancies, she decided, with his devilish good looks, his nonchalance and, above all, his obvious devotion to his wife.

Lord Quamby was not here this evening but Antoinette did not seem to miss her husband and Thea was quick to notice the disapproval in her aunt's eye as she watched her niece flirt with a great many clearly entranced young men.

Forming a rather regal group, the Brightwells and Lord Fenton progressed through the room, greeting friends and causing more than a ripple of interest from those on the sidelines, Thea noticed self-consciously. She was of course aware of the whispers of scandal—thanks to Aunt Minerva's information—that surrounded her cousins, but she could also see it had not been to their detriment and that indeed a well connected husband made up for any amount of prior scandal.

Still, Thea acknowledged she wasn't a risk-taker like Fanny and Antoinette even if she wouldn't have minded an opportunity to at least be *temped* to do something scandalous.

Antoinette, who'd linked arms with her as they made their progress, suddenly gripped her wrist and Thea heard her slight intake of breath. Surprised, she raised her head as her cousin stopped to address a dark-haired man with the most arresting eyes Thea had ever seen; though not in a handsome way, she quickly noted, for they rather resembled coals glowing in his pale face. Meanwhile his lips were curved in a thin line and his expression as he gazed at Antoinette was decidedly dangerous.

Of middle height and neither slender nor portly, he was exquisitely turned out and yet Thea had the impression his coat of superfine would have looked better on a lowly footman or coal lugger. She shuddered inwardly. There was something decidedly off about this young man who, though he smiled and enquired after her health in an apparently congenial manner, continued to look at Antoinette as if he'd like to do her a great deal of damage.

"Dear Mr Bramley, it is always delightful to see you but I really must not keep you from your friends…though perhaps you'd like me to tell you about young George."

Once Antoinette had dispensed with the introductions, Thea had imagined she'd move on in the face of such blatant hostility dressed up as social nicety, but her cousin remained, telling Mr Bramley, almost co-quettishly, "The lad is so strong and lusty these days. You'd be very welcome to pay us a visit before the christening next week. Lord Quamby thinks baby George has *his* nose, but indeed it is just like yours, my darling boy's own beloved Uncle George." She turned to Thea. "Do you not think baby George has a nose just like Mr Bramley's? Or perhaps, Mr Bramley, I can call you 'nephew' and we can be on more familiar terms, now that we are related. Well, by marriage at any rate."

Thea didn't know what to say. There seemed some odd, almost dangerous subtext behind her cousin's words.

George Bramley glowered but Fanny arrived at that moment, draped over her husband's arm. Taking her sister's wrist, she gave it a little tug, saying with a smile and a nod at Mr Bramley, "There are so many charming people to greet tonight, I'm afraid we really must proceed. Come, Antoinette. So delightful to see you again after so long, Mr Bramley."

Carried along in their wake, Thea stretched around to look over her shoulder and was surprised—and a little daunted—to observe the fulminating look in Mr Bramley's eye as he stared after them.

"Have I missed something?" she asked, once they were gathered around the refreshments table. Antoinette was helping herself to ham and chattering to a fair-haired gentlemen—though flirting was perhaps a more apt description.

In a discreet undertone, Fanny whispered, "Mr George Bramley is the nephew of Lord Quamby."

"I know," said Thea.

"He's also the father of little George."

Thea nearly dropped her plate. "No!" Wide-eyed, she stared at Fanny. "But...how?"

Fanny sent her a considering look. "One day I shall tell you exactly how but perhaps here is not the place or time. Just one word of warning…" Her look became serious. "I can't say this too many times, Thea. You must beware of Mr Bramley. He has no love of the Brightwells. Fortunately Antoinette and I survived the scandalous things he put about regarding us last season that would have ruined our entire family's prospects. I just don't want him doing the same to you."

Nodding, Thea was about to spear a thin piece of buttered bread when now it was her turn to gasp.

"What is it?"

Thea knew she was beginning to resemble the strawberries garnishing the syllabub. She was ever one to show her heart on her sleeve, and even though she shook her head to deny anything was the matter, she could not fool Fanny, who immediately deduced the truth.

"He must be quite the Corinthian to have elicited such a reaction." Grinning, she rescued Thea's teetering plate and put it on the table. "I first thought you'd seen a gown you covet but indeed that gasp was uttered in such tones it soon became clear a young man was more likely. Well, do point him out." There was laughter in Fanny's voice before she sobered, not yet looking in the direction in which Thea was staring, wide-eyed. "First, though, a word of advice. Take a deep breath, pull back your shoulders and look away. That's right. You must learn to temper your emotions a little better, Thea, if you are at least to fool Aunt Minerva." Now Fanny squinted in the direction where, a second before, Thea's attention had been riveted. "Ah… I think I know who he is, or at least Bertram does, so I can orchestrate an introduction but if you show how much you're dying to dance with him in front of Aunt Gorgonia, you know you've damned your chances."

Thea nodded miserably. "I know, and I also know it's perfectly pointless. Please don't say anything to Bertram. Just let me look at Mr Grayling from afar. I can at least pretend there is some prospect of hope." She put her hand on Fanny's sleeve and added urgently, "Promise you won't say anything to anyone?"

Fanny shrugged lightly as she loaded her plate. "If that's how you want it, Cousin Thea. But remember, you'll never get anywhere in life if you don't put the wheels in motion, so to speak."

Thea stared at the array of ham and thinly sliced bread and butter spread out upon the table. She had been ravenous when she'd arrived but suddenly she had no appetite. Mr Grayling might have made an unexpected appearance and given her heart a tremendous jolt of pleasure but, in truth, there was no possibility of Aunt Minerva countenancing anything between them. Not even a dance.

Despite Fanny's bolstering, Thea's own gloomy predictions seemed destined to win the day. Seated on her aunt's left side a little later, she responded as required—in the affirmative—each time Aunt Minerva made a comment, such as, "What a charming toque Lady Milton is wearing."

"Indeed it is." Obediently, Thea picked up the refrain.

"Her daughter certainly has a face that would push up mushrooms."

"Hmmm." This, she uttered in vague tones.

"Well, doesn't she?"

"Yes."

"Well, Thea, it's not nice to always agree that something is bad or wanting. In fact, it is tiresome for me to hear it. What about something that shows a little more imagination, such as: 'Indeed she has and that's because she has a proboscis that could launch a ship.' You're very dull company, I'm afraid. Ah, here's a young man passing by. Let us try again but this time with a response from you that's a little more diverting." Aunt Minerva looked at Thea to see she understood the game, then settled herself more comfortably upon the cushion of her chair. "Ready?"

Thea nodded.

"A handsome man this one is, to be sure, but too handsome for a lady to trust. Why, just behold the way he's looking at you, Thea. As if he'd like to gobble you up!"

The last was begun with quelling opprobrium and finished upon a squeak, for, to Thea's astonishment, the gentleman, whom she'd just identified as Mr Grayling, was now bowing before Aunt Minerva, asking her venerable relative if he might be permitted the pleasure of the next dance with her young companion. And Thea, squirming in her seat, a smile spreading across her face, could only despair at the response.

"Miss Brightwell does not dance."

Aunt Minerva's clipped tones brooked no argument, imperiously drowning out the eager acceptance that had sprung to Thea's lips as she raised hopeful eyes to the handsome, brown-haired young man before her.

"I'm so sorry," she murmured, disappointment threatening to overwhelm her. Mr Grayling inclined his head as he now turned upon Thea an enquiring look, as if she might have the power to sway her aunt.

Thea glanced at Aunt Minerva but the old lady had her eyes raised to the ceiling and was fanning herself as if she'd lost all interest in the conversation.

"My niece doesn't dance so there's no

point in hoping she'll suddenly grow dancing shoes," she snapped, swinging round to lance the young man with a terrifying scowl.

"Aunt Minerva," Thea whispered, horrified at her aunt's rudeness.

But Aunt Minerva's word was final.

And in the crowded Assembly Rooms, the sprung boards of the dance floor groaning under the weight of everyone else in the room who did dance, Thea knew this was unlikely to be the only pleasure snatched away before the night was over.

Prolonging his look of enquiry, Mr Grayling's beautiful grey eyes seemed to drink in every last detail of the lady whom he hoped to honour but he received nothing from Thea who could only blush, she was so mortified. With a final, regretful smile he turned on his heel and disappeared into the crowd.

In an irony to compound Thea's devastation, Aunt Minerva's sudden need of the chamber pot was not timely enough to recall Mr Grayling but her aunt's replacement by Fanny and Bertram was a welcome relief.

"I had not thought that being Aunt Minerva's companion meant I must cut myself off from *every* pleasure," Thea said sadly. "I've met Mr Grayling before. He's a most charming gentleman, and when he asked me to dance, Aunt Minerva sent him away." Choking back tears, she fiddled with her ivory fan in her lap, grateful for her cousins' obvious sympathy when she looked up. "Aunt Minerva declares no gentleman is interested in a dowerless young lady but even so, she won't let anyone remotely eligible slip past her guard. I thought she'd be *glad* if I made a good match."

Fanning herself furiously to match her roiling emotion now that sorrow and self pity had given way to anger, she cast a surreptitious look in the direction of the handsome gentleman who'd been given such short shrift moments ago. Mr Grayling was lingering just near a knot of revelers a few yards away.

"He does seem taken," Fanny murmured as she sipped her champagne, seated demurely beside Thea. "I shall have to ask Antoinette what she knows of him. She's far more active in courting diverting society than I am these days. Oh look, Thea, he's staring right at you."

Thea's heart rate doubled. Buoyed by the thrill of the interest she saw reflected in his direct gaze, she nearly snapped one of the little ivory points of her fan with her sudden burst of energy.

"A match would take me off Aunt Minerva's hands," she declared with a toss of her head.

"More fool you, Thea, for such silly daydreams." Unfortunately for Thea, her aunt had chosen this moment to return. Smiling equably at everyone's embarrassment as Bertram and Fanny rose hastily, the older woman settled her bulk across the space on the settee they'd just vacated, tapping her charge upon her shoulder with her lorgnette.

She patted her side curls and raised one eyebrow. "An illustrious match would of course be desirable but bear in mind, Thea, that most girls aren't as lucky as your Brightwell cousins. Fanny's viscount and Antoinette's earl were lured very cunningly, but you are not so clever. Neither is your cousin Bertram," she added with a quelling look at her young nephew who shifted in the chair opposite which he'd just commandeered, no doubt wondering if Thea had revealed the fact he'd lost another five hundred at Hazard only minutes before.

Aunt Minerva's features settled into an expression of prune-like rectitude. "No doubt, you think I'm a mean-spirited creature who wants to deny you happiness in order to tend to my wants and vagaries. Is that not right, Thea?"

This was so on the money that silence greeted this pronouncement. Aunt Minerva's chin wobbled and then her mouth started working as if caught in the current. To Thea's surprise, she actually discerned moisture in the corner of her aunt's drooping eyelids as the venerable creature went on with considerable emotion, "The truth of the matter, my dear, is that I will not see your heart broken as mine was when I was your age, all on account of a heartless fortune hunter. Yes, a fortune hunter just like that—" she stabbed the point of her fan in the direction of a debonair, greying gentleman holding court with a couple of simpering matrons, her eyes pinpricks of malice—"so-called gentleman."

Snapping her head round, she glared at Thea. "If you came with anything even remotely substantial, you'd have the young men tripping over themselves to charm you down the aisle. As it is, they're all wondering if I'll make you my beneficiary, and who knows but that I may choose to reward you over my good-for-nothing nephew. My dear, you must know that I have only your interests at heart when I turn your potential suitors away."

Thea pressed her lips together. "So…it's not that you don't want me to marry, it's that you're afraid I'll marry the wrong man. That I'll allow my head to be turned by a fortune hunter." She knew her combative tone was not wise but after mouldering away under the same roof as her father's sister for what seemed like eternity, the little patience she had left was at snapping point. Thea's nature was retiring and she knew the importance of keeping her head low but she did have a good deal of pride, and spirit, and this had led to the occasional burst of pique. Had she and Aunt Minerva been born male, they'd have certainly come to blows before now.

Of course, had she and Aunt Minerva been born male, Thea certainly would not be playing housemaid to anyone, for she'd have been educated and given a meaningful role in life and Aunt Minerva would probably be running the Bank of England, cheese-paring miser that she was.

Bertram cleared his voice. "I think Aunt Minerva means that your best interests are her chief concern."

"I know how to say what I mean to say," Aunt Minerva snapped. "And I couldn't have said it more clearly than I did. That man," she went on with another vicious stab with her fan in the direction of the silver-haired gentleman in the yellow striped waistcoat, "was under no illusions that I would have laid my heart at his feet had he merely crooked his finger at me—but did he come running?"

Thea hoped the glances she and her cousins sent in her aunt's direction did not indicate their astonishment that the gentleman in question might ever have been in danger of responding to Aunt Minerva's lures.

Bravely, Bertram persisted in his self-appointed role of peacemaker. "I'm sure the gentleman must have been distraught to have lost his opportunity with you, Aunt," he murmured.

"Perhaps you were not direct enough," suggested Fanny, and Thea had to stifle her snigger. Her cousin's sense of irony was acute.

"Oh, Mr Granville had every opportunity. I smiled at him, I wore my most becoming gowns, I engaged him in diverting chatter...but he returned my interest only after I inherited my fortune."

"Mr Granville asked you to marry him?" Fanny sounded intrigued while Thea glanced at her aunt's goblet and wondered if the Madeira had gone to her relative's head.

Aunt Minerva sniffed. "He did and I refused him," she said self-righteously. "I wanted to give him the set-down he deserved."

There was an awkward silence in the face of her clearly profound agitation. It was Fanny who bravely ventured, "And…what happened?"

Aunt Minerva cleared her throat. "Of course, he was supposed to repeat his offer the next day."

"And he didn't?" Thea glanced from her aunt to the silver-haired scion of sophistication who, she noticed, was sending very interested looks in their direction. He was handsome, she decided, if one liked older men; though not nearly as handsome as the young man who'd asked her to dance earlier.

Resigned to her fate, now, she tried to persuade herself that her lovely Mr Grayling was no doubt just as her aunt painted him: a designing rogue who'd lose interest the moment he learned she had not a penny to her name.

CHAPTER 4

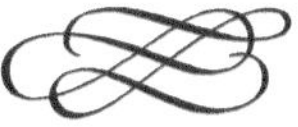

SYLVESTER Grayling rubbed his chin thoughtfully as he listened to everything his new acquaintance, George Bramley, was telling him about the illustrious throng which pulsed around them.

He'd left Bath several days previously on the business of negotiating a fine piece of horseflesh but that had been expedited faster than he'd anticipated and now he was enjoying an evening at the Assembly Rooms, even though he'd promised to drive to London to see his friend, Starky Willis. But the possibility that he might see the charming chit he'd met on the road amidst all that baby palaver was more enticing.

He thought she'd melt into his arms after he'd honoured her with a dance offer but that gorgon of a relative had proved an effective gate-keeper. His pride was still smarting that an old woman in oyster velvet should have the power to make him feel like a schoolboy again.

Nevertheless, there was some pleasure in the shy smiles the young lady sent him each time he caught her eye from across the room. Sylvester was determined that, if for no other reason than he would not endure a repeat of the four years his own horrendous Great-Aunt Phillida had taken his rearing in hand, he *would* contrive to dance with Miss Brightwell.

Again he noticed the girl's bright eyes on him. He flashed a smile at her, delighted by the coy blush that spread across her cheeks, before he turned back to George Bramley who chuckled. "Ah, behold, yet another bold and beautiful Brightwell. But take care. They're all penniless. Nevertheless, they're exceedingly clever at drawing you into their orbit before singeing your wings on their flames." Bramley patted Sylvester on the back and turned him to face another cluster of chattering young ladies. "Miss Amelia Huntingdon is far easier prey. She is pretty, with a sizeable portion, and I've noticed the glances she's been sending you. Engage her for this dance and see if I'm right."

So Sylvester did and although it was pleasurable to hold her slender form against his during the daring waltz, his mind continued to be diverted by thoughts of Miss Brightwell's curves moulding his own.

MEANWHILE, THEA WAS FOLLOWING HIS movements like a love-crazed schoolroom chit, her dismay at seeing him in the arms of the pale and insipid Miss Huntingdon as dampening as being caught in sleet.

Bertram and Cousin Antoinette found her standing disconsolately at the depleted food table in the anteroom.

"Why so low, cuz?" Bertram pinched her cheek. "You're free for the next five minutes at any rate. Aunt Minerva has captured an audience, and anyone to whom she can give an earful on the subject of Prinny's shameful treatment of his rightful queen is unlikely to escape quickly or lightly." The previous week the former Prince Regent, now George IV, had divided public opinion by refusing his consort, Queen Caroline of Brunswick's admission to his Coronation at Westminster Abbey, a matter on which Aunt Minerva had decided views not very flattering to the new king.

Thea tried to take comfort from Bertram's cousinly bolstering but it was hard to feel anything but hopeless despair at a lot she was sure held no pleasure for her ever again. Thanks to the generosity of Cousin Fanny, who was her size, she had clothes to wear that Aunt Minerva would never have paid for, but it was heart-breaking to know that while she might have access to public events while looking like a lady, every potential suitor was going to be fobbed off by Aunt Minerva.

"I'm doomed to be an old maid," she replied, knowing her lip trembled and that she was being overly dramatic, for there were others far worse off than she. "I shall know no joy, and my happiness will be confined to the amusements I can provide myself."

"That sounds no fun at all," Antoinette sympathised. "I'd hate to be responsible for my own pleasure." She gave a wicked smile. "If it's as dire as all that, I might have to give you a lesson in what I think you know nothing about. Ah, speak of the devil, here is your handsome Mr Grayling. Good evening sir, I believe you have already met my cousin, Miss Thea Brightwell."

Mr Grayling bowed low over her hand, and when he rose, Thea could barely draw in a breath, she was so thrilled by the flattery and intensity in her erstwhile admirer's lingering gaze.

"An absolute pleasure, Miss Brightwell," he murmured, and Thea had barely time to choke out a reply before her aunt's stentorian demands to know where her niece was echoed throughout the room.

Thea had sworn to remain sentinel at the gilt sofa her aunt had abandoned but she was torn. This might be her only chance to speak to Mr Grayling but if she crossed her aunt so publicly, tonight might also be her only evening of entertainment during the entire time she was a guest of her cousin.

She hesitated, her gaze riveted on the handsome man before her. He had the most exquisite, noble nose, she thought. And his lips… oh, but how she longed to tenderly contour them with her fingers. Warmth surged through her and she blinked rapidly, shocked. No, not her fingers, her lips. Unconsciously, she ran the tip of her tongue over them, as if priming them, before realizing with embarrassment how transparent she was. How wicked to even entertain thoughts like that!

"Thea Brightwell!"

With weary acquiescence Thea inclined her head. "A pleasure to meet you, too, Mr Grayling." It would be counter-productive to push for aunt too far. She'd pay for her rebellion with interest. She had to obey. "Pray excuse me, sir."

SYLVESTER STARED AFTER HER IN GENUINE

bemusement and, to avoid looking like a fool, half-heartedly speared a slice of nearly transparent ham from the sad looking display before him and deposited it on his plate. This was not the way he'd expected matters to proceed.

Surely the scorching looks Miss Brightwell had sent him could not have been misconstrued? Yet no sooner had he contrived to present himself once more to her when she was no longer in company with the oyster-velvet-clad gorgon, than she'd run off like a frightened rabbit...or a coquette. Which was it? Could she really have been playing games?

"Charming chit, ain't she?" Bertram Brightwell's bluff laugh cut into Sylvester's musings and he turned to raise an eyebrow at the young man accompanied by his beautiful sister, the youngest, blonde—not to mention, scandalous—Miss Antoinette, who'd snared an earl and whose supposed antics behind closed doors titillated society.

He'd met Lady Quamby—though he could only think of her as Miss Antoinette—at the earl's birthday celebration earlier that year, just weeks after she'd given birth, in fact. Not that one could tell. The girl was exquisite in pale pink silk with silver trimmings, and her bearing was confident, almost conspiratorial, yet when he glanced over her creamy bared shoulder towards the far corner of the room, where her lovely, chestnut-haired but less flamboyant cousin had just jilted him by the food table, she paled into insignificance.

"More of a charming enigma," Sylvester responded.

"Pray enlarge?" Miss Antoinette's blue eyes danced with mischief. There was nothing maternal about her, he thought. She was as flirtatious as he imagined she must have been before she'd become Lord Quamby's countess. Forcing his gaze away from the more sober but more enticing—to his eyes, at least—Miss Brightwell he tried not to stare, but the stories he'd heard about Quamby's wife were incredible; that the earl gave her complete licence to seek out pleasure discreetly as her reward for silence regarding his own peccadilloes. Dangerous ones, he understood, that courted the death penalty.

Before he had a chance to respond, Bertram said, with an intense frown, "No telling what a gel will do if she's only got six months to live."

"What?"

It tumbled from Miss Antoinette's lips with an expletive and Sylvester's own as a gasp of dismay. "Six months?"

Miss Antoinette looked shocked. "What are you saying, Bertram?" she demanded.

Bertram sighed heavily. "I overheard Dr Horne telling Cousin Thea the terrible news. Don't you wonder why she looks so sad and won't dance? Her heart cannot be exposed to sudden shocks...although," he looked contemplative, "I did also hear the doctor say that gentle pleasures and mild, controlled excitement might well prolong her life." He cleared his throat, adding, "That is, by a couple of months or so only."

Sylvester shook his head, his horror echoing Miss Antoinette's, who clearly had not been privy to the news of her lovely cousin's imminent demise. "Poor young woman," he murmured. "So lovely and so…"

"Doomed," Bertram supplied with a sigh. "Still," he brightened, "she is to be commended on her stoic acceptance of her miserable lot. Her aunt has brought her to Bath to take the waters but sadly is so concerned for her niece's health, she will allow Miss Brightwell no pleasure whatsoever."

"She would not allow me to even dance with her," Sylvester recalled, the rejection taking on a different hue. "Is she…so reduced in health?"

"Oh, Miss Brightwell would dance a jig if she were allowed. She simply craves something that will draw her out of the unhappy final few months she's been allotted." He shrugged before fixing Sylvester with a long and meaningful stare. "But what chance is there of that?"

CHAPTER 5

$\mathcal{A}$NTOINETTE swung round the moment a contemplative Mr Grayling had made his excuses and departed.

"What on earth—"

"Clever, eh?" Bertram asked, clearly pleased with himself as he leaned against the door lintel that separated the supper room from the ballroom. "Thea needs a husband and Mr Grayling is clearly entranced. Haven't I just aided her prospects if he thinks he won't be saddled with a wife with no financial prospects? Well, not beyond four months at most, if they elope soon enough."

Antoinette looked admiring. "Goodness, that is inspired, Bertram."

Her brother grinned. "And soon our dear sister, Fanny, will be saying it, too." He tossed back his drink and wiped his mouth with the back of his hand. "Aunt Minerva thinks I'm not too bright, sis, but let me tell you, the whole Brightwell clan will soon be thanking me for providing Cousin Thea with more than just the husband of her dreams. Mr Grayling is worth a pretty penny, I've heard."

DEEP IN THOUGHT, SYLVESTER WOVE HIS WAY across the crowded Assembly Room, all the while keeping the lovely…dying…Miss Brightwell in his sights. He observed how well she attended her aunt and her air of quiet acceptance touched his heart and stirred his admiration. What would he feel if he had been given only six months to live?

A great melancholy descended upon him as he contemplated the question. Why, he'd want to live life to the fullest, he decided, locking eyes at that moment with the chestnut haired beauty. Her dazzling smile sent a surge of excitement to his loins, arresting his progress. Lord, she was breathtaking. Her sheath of a gown followed the lush curves of her willowy body like a wicked enticement. Yet there she was, a prisoner at her aunt's side, her smooth, lovely face a beautiful mask hiding her hopes and desires; a prisoner of her death sentence and the strictures of her relative.

Sylvester continued to observe her covertly. He'd not missed the disappointment in her expression when she thought he'd passed out of her orbit. Ah, but she'd have no chance of learning of the passions she inspired; a beautiful young woman like herself, so coy and modest. To think that she'd die a virgin, denied the pleasure of a man's kiss…a man's possession. He closed his eyes against images of Miss Brightwell pressed against his chest, the pair of them standing alone in a dense forest as they gazed into one another's eyes.

But at the memory of her longing looks, her very clear interest, the forest was suddenly replaced by a large four poster bed, Miss Brightwell beneath him and, what's more, responding with all the passion and ardour he'd hopefully imagined would be displayed by the young lady he'd choose as his bride upon their nuptials.

An unexpected vision indeed and not at all the kind of thoughts he should be entertaining if he were to maintain a bearing of respectability wearing such tight trousers in a public place.

Turning, he nearly collided with a footman holding aloft a tray.

What a fool he was! Miss Thea was an invalid and she would die a virgin, for if he followed through on his desires, he'd not only ruin her, he'd quite possibly reduce even further her remaining few months.

But then, he thought, sipping his champagne, if he played the caring suitor, he could contrive to give them both pleasure without damaging her health or limited prospects.

He brought himself up short. No, he was self aware enough to know that he was a bull in a china shop with no sense of delicacy once his passions were aroused. Indeed, he was the last man who could be trusted to safeguard Miss Brightwell's delicate constitution the moment she allowed him past a certain threshold.

So intent was he on focussing his gaze upon Miss Brightwell's serene visage while she was engaged in conversation with her aunt that when her name was borne upon the lips of a gentleman in conversation only a foot from him, he leapt as if stung. He strained to listen.

"Miss Brightwell is well aware of the dangers. If only she'd heed her doctor's advice."

Sylvester eased a little closer to the ginger-whiskered gentleman who spoke with such authority.

"It was you who advised her to take the waters, was it not, Dr Horne?" His rotund companion tilted his head. "Aye, she does not always take your advice, does she?"

"She'd live a good deal longer if she only did, but stubbornness has served her well thus far. I'd have predicted she'd be in her eternity box a good many years ago."

As soon as the rotund gentleman had moved away Sylvester took his opportunity. He couldn't believe his luck.

Introducing himself, he cleared his throat and frowned, giving the appearance of trying to tackle a difficult topic, which indeed it was. "Excuse me…Dr Horne? Ah yes, I hoped I was right. You're the eminent physician whose fine reputation I've heard so much about."

The gentleman's wary look was replaced by one of smug acquiescence of the compliment. He stroked his whispers and puffed out his chest. "There are some ladies who greatly inflate the value of my contributions to the health of this town but I can't help but admit it pleases me to hear it, sir."

Sylvester smiled. "While I would not dream of mentioning names, sir, I would appreciate a word of advice from you on how I might tackle the delicate health of a person who…means a great deal to me."

Dr Horne inclined his head, a little more guarded now. "I'm afraid I cannot discuss matters of a personal nature."

"Nor would I expect it," Sylvester assured him hastily, "but it's on account of wishing to *prolong* Miss Brightwell's good health—oh dear! I did not intend to name her— that I've sought you out."

Dr Horne looked surprised. "You have an interest in...that eminent woman's good health?"

Sylvester floundered a little here. "It is in fact...er...a friend who has an interest and who has asked me, on his behalf, to ascertain what he might do to facilitate the...individual in question's...er...pleasure during the remaining time allotted to her."

Dr Horne's eyes nearly popped out of his head. "Your friend is an *admirer*?"

Sylvester nodded. "Yes, my friend has in fact admired her from afar, and unbeknownst to her, for many a year. Now that word has filtered through to him of her delicate health, he confided to me that if he only knew how to please her, he would do it. But he is driven distracted by worry that he will make a blunder of it. He's not declared himself and he fears that if he should surprise her too greatly, it may be fatal. My friend demanded of *me*, how far he could go before his attentions become dangerous to her health but I know nothing of such matters. And then I overheard that you were the eminent physician, Dr Horne."

Dr Horne pulled at his ginger moustache. Words seemed to have failed him. "I am flattered that you should have heard of me. But…you say your friend wishes to pay his attentions to *Miss Brightwell?*" He blinked rapidly before saying in a rush, "I did not mean to mention names, sir."

"Of course not." Sylvester nodded, understandingly.

Dr Horne's expression became cynical. "The person of which we speak has no desire to marry."

"Indeed, marriage was not what my friend had in mind. He wished merely to extend to her the hand of friendship, to offer her the admiration he has long kept secret. Would she be amenable to receiving such declarations? Or would they cause perhaps palpitations of the heart, which would have the opposite effect of that desired by my friend? That is what my friend has asked me to ascertain." Sylvester waited hopefully.

Dr Horne contemplated him through narrowed eyes. "My patient is stronger than she looks. If she felt the recipient worthy of her regard, I've no doubt she could entertain him with no risk to her health whatsoever."

"Perhaps you would be so good as to broach the matter with her," Sylvester suggested cautiously.

Dr Horne raised his chin. "Your friend ought to do his own work rather than send someone else. Certainly not her physician."

Sylvester sighed. "Alas, his acute shyness has been the reason the gentleman of whom I speak has never found the courage to address Miss Brightwell but has instead held a candle to her charms for many a year. That is why I offered myself as proxy. I would hope to see some happy resolution to his unfortunate situation."

Dr Horne continued to stroke his whiskers and look contemplative. After a long pause he said, cautiously, "This is an interesting situation I had not considered.

Perhaps such unexpected admiration would be conducive to an altering in my patient's disposition." He tapped his fingers upon the side of the glass he held, his frown deepening as he added, "Indeed, perhaps what you suggest *could* in fact work in favour of her health."

Sylvester allowed himself to hope. "I assure you, my friend would hate to cause offence. His motivations are entirely honourable."

Dr Horne nodded and pursed his lips. "All right then. If appropriate, I shall endeavour to elicit the good lady's feelings on being approached by a secret admirer who has held a candle to her since she was barely out of the schoolroom, as you seem to infer."

Sylvester gave a silent sigh of satisfaction. He'd been deeply shaken by the dire prognosis Bertram Brightwell had issued regarding Miss Brightwell's health, but if she could be encouraged to accept his attentions—or if her aunt could be persuaded by Dr Horne that his attentions were in lovely young Miss Brightwell's best interests—

Sylvester was more than amenable to doing what he could to facilitate her…pleasure, as Bertram called it. Pleasure? The gleam in that other young gentleman's eye had conveyed a broad interpretation of the word, though Sylvester could see that poor Miss Thea Brightwell enjoyed very little pleasure of any kind with that terrible relative forever rattling the keys of her incarceration by her ear.

Helping himself to another champagne from a passing tray, he tried to reconcile the image of sweet-faced Miss Brightwell, the lively smile she'd shone on him fading like a rose as the next few weeks passed. A sweet, gentle creature who'd be quite dead in six months. That is, unless he could coax some more life into her for her remaining earthly tenure and thereby extend her existence by even a few weeks.

Pleasure? Again he mulled over the word and its meaning. He was a gentleman who'd not dream of sullying a lady's reputation but of course Miss Brightwell would not be contemplating marriage in her delicate condition.

So, what could pleasure entail in such a scenario?

Bertram Brightwell had rolled the word across his tongue with such salacious pleasure suggesting a far lewder interpretation than Sylvester's. But was Miss Brightwell the innocent she appeared? Sylvester had recently been treated to a comprehensive summation of the Brightwells' collective virtues—or lack of—and indeed, pleasure was high on the family agenda. He'd heard it from many sources.

The Brightwells, Mr Bramley had told him, were like glorious weeds, climbing inexorably over walls while strangulating the more gently reared blooms that stood in their way, in order to push their beautiful heads ever closer to the sun.

Miss Thea Brightwell might be a shyer version of her bold and beautiful cousins but she was just like they had been barely a season before: penniless and no doubt seeking to reclaim the once exalted position lost by her father through carelessness. By no means was that her fault but Sylvester did wonder whether the knowledge she had only six months to live would make her more amenable to taking risks.

Bowing as he excused himself, he made his way towards the card room as he went over his recent conversation with the doctor. Sylvester would never manage to contrive a meeting with the girl if her aunt was always in attendance, but if he could get poor Miss Brightwell's personal physician onside to encourage gentle outings that did not include the old gorgon, Sylvester imagined he could anticipate the following few weeks in Bath with a great deal of hope.

CHAPTER 6

THE following evening, Dr Horne was still shaking his head over his extraordinary exchange with the friend of his patient's anonymous but nevertheless unlikely admirer as he was ushered into the venerable Miss Brightwell's drawing room.

One of his regular patients and his wife had uprooted themselves from the country to take the medicinal spa waters, and had paid for Dr Horne's removal to Bath for the next few weeks. Of course, Miss Brightwell was far too cheese paring to fund her physician's relocation but she certainly enjoyed his daily attendance.

Less enamored of the prospect of attending his most difficult patient on a daily basis, Dr Horne acknowledged a certain frisson, almost thrilling, at tending to the exacting and impossible Minerva Brightwell while she was resident at Lord Quamby's rambling estate just outside the town.

As usual, the fire was crackling, heating the room to almost insufferable temperatures, as was Miss Brightwell's wont, even on such a warm evening. Reclining in an armchair and wearing a round dress of Pomona green with a matching bejewelled toque, she was snoring gently while her young companion stitched quietly in the corner.

He glanced at the niece and felt a pang of sympathy, for the girl was a beauty. He knew she'd been orphaned several years previously and had been left financially vulnerable until the formidable Miss Minerva Brightwell had obviously seen it was to her advantage to offer the girl a roof over her head. From his daily observances, it appeared there was little respite for the poor unpaid companion.

"Dr Horne," Miss Thea exclaimed softly

as he was shown in. "How glad we are that you could come so quickly. Aunt Minerva is asleep now, as you can see, but not twenty minutes ago she quite had it in her head that her dying hour was upon her."

Dr Horne pulled at his moustache, ridiculously gratified at the pleasure he'd clearly precipitated in the young niece's breast, his cheeks suddenly burning, though not from the heat of the fire. "It's always a fortuitous thing to bring good tidings to one's patient, so perhaps Miss Brightwell's constitution will be fortified at the knowledge that her untimely demise would cause great sadness to a certain...gentleman," he murmured with a wink.

"What's all this whispering behind my back? Why, it's the height of rudeness! What nonsense is this you're muttering about, doctor?"

There was nothing to suggest the ailing invalid about Miss Brightwell as she leaned forward and cast her fulminating gaze upon her personal physician. "Playing games, are you? How dare you encourage him, Thea!"

Dr Horne held up his hand to defend

himself; or rather to defend the poor young lady, who was no doubt a regular recipient of such accusations.

"Pray calm yourself, Miss Brightwell. I was merely alluding to a conversation with a certain…ah…admirer of yours. Had I known you were awake, I would have approached the matter with more consideration for your delicacy. I certainly would not wish to see you overset…and nor would the gentleman in question, who seeks reassurance of your good health."

Miss Brightwell looked suspiciously at him. "A gentleman, you say? Seeking reassurance of my good health?" She stroked her whiskered chin as she looked first at the doctor and then into the merrily crackling fire. "If he's sincere, it assuredly is not my nephew, who is in daily contact to gauge how soon or likely it is he will be in receipt of my fortune. Greedy, money-grubbing slug," she muttered. She jerked her head round. "So why would someone wish for my good health if he has nothing to gain by it?"

Dr Horne stepped further from the fire.

Sweat prickled the back of his neck and he noticed that the heat was affecting Miss Thea too, judging by her flushed cheeks and décolletage. The sight was curiously affecting and he struggled to return the young woman's guileless smile with no indication of the sinful thoughts chasing themselves round his head. "At the Assembly Rooms yesterday evening," he managed, returning his attention to his patient, "I was approached by a gentleman who wished me to pass on the felicitations of an old admirer of yours who—"

"An admirer?" Miss Brightwell's eyes widened before she assumed a pose of glorious abandon. Her fat ankles resting on the footstool were now crossed and her incredible chest thrown forward, offering him an unimpeded view down the valley between her enormous bosoms; a disturbing sight, which immediately conjured up an image of Miss Brightwell's unfortunate admirer gasping his last in her smothering embrace.

Adopting a languid air, Miss Minerva Brightwell went on, "And why should I not have an admirer? Beauty is timeless and I was considered a rare beauty in my day." She raised an eyebrow at a noise from Miss Thea, who appeared to be struggling to keep a steady hand as she worked the needle through the white linen of her embroidery project.

When Dr Horne caught the girl's eye in a sudden moment of conspiracy, he was unprepared for the charge of sensation that nearly unbalanced him. Why, for months he'd been in almost daily contact with Miss Brightwell's niece as required by her demanding benefactress but tonight it was as if he noticed her for the first time. He cast another surreptitious glance in her direction. There was a definite bloom to her cheeks he'd not noticed before, and a dewy tenderness in her expression when she looked at him. She'd changed as if overnight, he thought.

Shocked that he, widowed for twenty years, should be visited by such inappropriately lustful fancies, he forced his attention back to his patient.

"Clearly your admirer retains an image of you untarnished by the passage of the years,' he murmured. He reordered his expression into one of suitable solemnity and tried not to allow Miss Thea's sweet profile to distract him. "Indeed, I have been charged with the task of acting as his emissary in order to ascertain whether the, er… inimitable Miss Brightwell would receive his attentions." He cleared his throat again, still reeling from the unlikely possibility that Miss Brightwell's admirer was not motivated by something other than his patient's tenuous claims to beauty and grace.

For a long moment Miss Brightwell appeared lost in wistful contemplation of the dancing flames. Suddenly she swung round, her bulbous brown eyes fired with the savagery of a bull dog as she demanded, "Why has he not come himself?" And her tone so bristled with aggression that Dr Horne wondered if he had sufficient reserves of tact to convey Miss Brightwell's response in the proper manner to the interested gentleman. Or should he indeed make it clear that Miss Brightwell's admirer was in danger of having his throat torn out if he put a foot wrong in the event that he followed through on his dangerous amorous impulses?

Bravely he stood his ground, saying evenly, as he'd promised, "Your admirer is aware of your delicate constitution, Miss Brightwell. Indeed, it is his fear that his attentions might compromise your health that he solicited my advice." He paused. "I assured him that if he took matters…gently, then your health would only be improved."

"Good man." Miss Brightwell leaned back and looked at him approvingly. With a coquettish smile, she twirled around her finger a chestnut curl which Dr Horne, on closer inspection, suspected was the squirrel's tail hairpiece of which she was so fond. Indeed, she refused to be seen without it, even during examinations, when his entrance was clearly preceded by a hasty donning of the said appendage, and not always quite straight.

Daringly, he darted another glance at the lovely Miss Thea, whose plight he found curiously affecting. Poor child. To be subject to the shifting vagaries of such an old tartar would try the patience of a saint. Yet throughout all, Miss Thea had maintained a calm and dignified demeanour, punctuated by a charmingly girlish response to the most extreme of her aunt's retorts. The young woman must have patience in abundance. As she quietly stitched away at her tambour he contemplated her plight. This was no life for a pure and beautiful young woman, though of course with little or no dowry it might well be her lot for many years to come with the older Miss Brightwell's supposedly palpitating heart looking likely to carry her into her ninth decade.

So captivated was he by the graceful movement of Miss Thea's slender fingers as they plied her needle and thread that he lost all sense of where he was, imagining those same fingers massaging his brow at the end of a long day, tracing the line of his jaw, trailing the length of his chest.

He swallowed, suddenly breathless. The importance of a handsome marriage portion paled in significance compared with the pleasures a lonely widower might enjoy at the hands of such a paragon of beauty and virtue.

Miss Minerva Brightwell broke the silence with a rasping sigh. Her features had relaxed as she continued to stare into the fire, her drooping jowls echoing the pouches beneath her eyes, which were softened by nostalgia. "So my darling has finally realised the error of his ways," she murmured. "Well, Dr Horne!" She levelled a decisive look upon him. "You may tell my…admirer…that I eagerly await more concrete signs of his regard."

A GENTLE WALK AT NOON, AND ONLY IF THE weather was exceptional, was Aunt Minerva's only concession to improving her health through the exercise Dr Horne continually suggested. However, her struggle to put one leg past the other as she leaned heavily on Thea had filled her niece with a morbid aversion to doing anything outdoorsy with her aunt, despite her natural love of nature and fresh air.

Two mornings after the dance at the Assembly Rooms, Thea was again struggling under the weight of her demanding bene-factress, dreaming of handsome Mr Grayling, whom she'd have little occasion to see and none to entertain, when she spied Dr Horne advancing purposely along the path toward them.

With relief she greeted him, for now her aunt would be required to halt a few moments and so reduce the painful pressure on Thea's shoulder.

"Good morning, Dr Horne," she said with more pleasure than she usually reserved for the pale, ginger-haired and awkward gentleman, whose hands always felt so clammy, though there was nothing she could particularly object to about him. "What a beautiful day it is, isn't it?" She smiled warmly, wishing to prolong the break from her duties, for she was exhausted by her exertions on behalf of her aunt.

Dr Horne returned her greeting with a look of concern. "My dear Miss Thea, are you quite all right? You appear excessively fatigued and your colour is high." Frowning at Aunt Minerva as he took Thea's hand, he muttered with professional solicitude, "Let me feel your pulse, my dear. I fear you may be unwell."

"Yes, I am a little…fatigued," Thea said faintly, swaying against Dr Horne as she played upon the possibility of a reprieve.

"You were perfectly well when you set out this morning," her aunt responded acidly.

Thea fluttered her lids and exhaled upon a sigh. "Fatigue seems to have got the better of me… Oh, Cousin Antoinette!" She suddenly noticed the barouche that had drawn level with them on the gravel path. "No, I am not feeling quite the thing. A lovely morning, Cousin. I was just asking Dr Horne if he wouldn't mind accompanying Aunt Minerva the last few hundred yards home and I can travel in the carriage with you."

Hiding her huge relief at her unexpected escape, she climbed into the dim interior and it was only then she realised her cousin was not alone. Opposite, sat Antoinette and, beside her, Bertram. And with a final start of excited astonishment, she saw that on the seat upon which she'd settled herself, Mr Grayling was reclining languidly.

He straightened when she entered the confined space, brushing his hair back from his high forehead, his beautiful grey eyes assessing her with surprise, as if he'd not been aware they'd stopped beside her and her aunt.

"What a delightful pleasure," he said, kissing the back of her hand, which sent tingles of pleasure fizzing throughout her entire being. His tone and the gesture were so familiar it was all she could do to stammer something equating a reasonable response, for in truth her heart was thundering and heat burned her cheeks. A brief glance at her aunt and Dr Horne whom she'd abandoned on the gravel path made it very clear that she would pay dearly for her truancy, but any price was worth paying right now if she could enjoy such proximity to the handsome gentleman she'd believed she'd never set eyes on again.

And, on the subject of eyes, his never left hers as the carriage jolted gently over the rutted path. With each jolt Mr Grayling somehow seemed to inch a little nearer until, by the time they reached the house, his thigh was touching hers, resulting in the most exciting, intimate sensation she'd ever experienced. That is, until he surreptitiously reached for her hand. While the siblings opposite studiously trained their interest out of the window, Thea could only stare between her hand caged in his, and his kindling gaze still trained upon her face.

Mr Grayling liked her.

Of all the vast array of lovely ladies in Bath, he'd clearly singled her out for his attentions. That is, if you didn't count Miss Huntingdon with whom he'd danced twice at the Assembly ball.

And as he handed her down from the carriage minutes later there was no mistaking the sincerity in his tone when he said, "I wonder to what lengths you'd go to dance the waltz with me, Miss Brightwell, for I declare my visit to Bath will be a wasted one if your aunt's strictures triumph over my desire to—" He dropped his voice, adding meaningfully, "take you in my arms."

Thea thought she would swoon upon the spot.

A little later, over tea in the conservatory of Lord Quamby's handsome townhouse and with Mr Grayling no longer a part of the company, Antoinette and Fanny immediately launched in upon the topic of this gentleman.

"I believe Mr Grayling has a difficult choice to make," Fanny remarked with a sly look from beneath her thick fringe of lashes.

Thea squirmed for Mr Grayling's words still echoed with thrilling intensity in her head making it difficult to attend to her cousin who went on, "Of course, there are other gentlemen far richer than he to interest Miss Huntingdon, but he is handsome and he is second in line to inherit rather a fine estate." She stirred her tea thoughtfully. "If I were a gambling girl, I'd consider it quite worth the risk."

"Well, I am hardly in a position to make either wagers or take risks." Thea forced a smile as the crushing reality was brought home to her. Mr Grayling would no more choose her for a wife than he would an actress from Drury Lane. Her shoulders slumped. "Miss Huntingdon is pretty and she comes with a fortune. What do I have to offer?"

Fanny nodded thoughtfully. "Miss Huntingdon might be comely and rich but she is also insipid. Extremely insipid. Would she be someone with whom Mr Grayling wishes to spend his future? Sometimes a little fire to stir a man's senses can encourage him to take actions that are quite…unexpected."

Thea jerked her head around at Antoinette's giggle, unsure if her cousins were making fun of her. She certainly didn't know what the cause of their amusement could be.

"Oh really, Thea, you can't be quite so obtuse," Fanny said, her tone now changed to a mixture of amusement and annoyance.

Thea frowned, for if she wasn't being obtuse, all she could imagine they were suggesting was the antithesis of how a young lady concerned for her future would behave.

"Aunt Minerva would cast me out if a hint of scandal attached to my name," she said stiffly. "I cannot see Mr Grayling again. I certainly cannot see him alone."

Fanny put her head to one side and appeared to contemplate the matter. "Certainly not if anyone knew about it. Ah, Fenton…" With a beatific smile she greeted her devilishly handsome husband who'd entered the room. "We were just discussing Thea's future."

He looked surprised. "So your Aunt Minerva is willing to give you up and allow you one? A future, that is?" Lord Fenton strode across the Aubusson carpet and lowered his impressive frame onto the settee by his wife, immediately taking her hand and caressing it with such blatant wanting in his eyes, Thea felt the jolt all the way to her lower belly. She'd never seen raw desire like that in all her life.

Though when she came to think about it, the look in Lord Fenton's eye could be said to equate to the unmasked desire she'd read in Mr Grayling's face as she'd sat beside him in the carriage. She swallowed. Her throat felt thick, her skim clammy and at the same time a feeling of such longing seemed to invade her whole being she had to look away.

"Indeed Aunt Minerva would not give Thea up, but that is not at issue here," Fanny said, with a touch of asperity, as if her husband were being perfectly stupid. "Thea is a beauty and she has caught the eye of Mr Grayling, for whom she feels a considerable degree of…affection." She patted her husband's hand, smiling at him before transferring her gaze to Thea. "What we need to deduce is how to ensure Mr Grayling comes to value the strength of Thea's feelings for him."

The equable tone of Fenton's response would have been surprising, had Thea not observed that he held his wife's intelligence in the highest regard. "I'm sure you've already hit upon the perfect cunning plan." He transferred his fond gaze from his wife's lively countenance to study Thea with considered concern. "That is, provided Thea has no objections."

"No objections to what?" Confused by

the sense of shared understanding between everyone else, Thea scanned each face. Antoinette's full mouth was turned up by the wickedest pucker and her eyes danced; Fanny looked serenely self-satisfied; and Fenton looked…well, as handsome and devoted a husband as Thea longed to make of…Mr Grayling?

All of a sudden she was trembling, the kernel of hope growing within her that perhaps some day she, too, like her cousins, could orchestrate a future more fulfilling than any she could hope for in her current circumstances.

"Thea, I think you should come to my room before lunch," Fanny told her, while Fenton continued to surreptitiously fondle her ungloved hand on the sofa between them. On the surface she appeared as dignified as her position required but Thea did not miss the colluding look she and Antoinette exchanged.

Then Fanny returned her attention to Thea, her eyes dancing with merriment before she sobered. "Of course, Lord Fenton is right to be concerned. Once—you may have heard—my darling Fenton was London's most notorious rake, so he's the first to know how easily an innocent young woman, untutored in the ways of this wicked world, can come to grief. Happily, he is now a reformed rake," she looked smug, "and you can rest assured that with a little help and tuition from your Brightwell cousins, all of us are only too ready to ensure you make a success of this rare opportunity to snare a man's interest from under your aunt's nose."

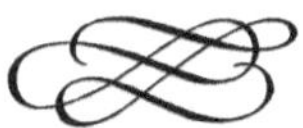

ALL that was needed was a plan. A cunning plan, and no one had mastered the cunning plan better than Fanny.

Fanny had nearly lost Fenton after she'd surrendered her all, assuming that as a gentleman he would do the honourable thing. Then Fanny's nemesis, the odious George Bramley, had whipped up the vilest rumours about Fanny's suitability as a wife, so that Fenton had in fact offered Fanny a secret little bower and her own carriage rather than a ring and a title.

Well, Fanny had won her position as Lady Fenton through some very clever maneuvering. Not only had she secured her position in society as Fenton's wife, she'd secured his affection, too.

Such marital success was just what she had in mind for her cousin. Thea was the most deserving candidate but she also provided Fanny with excellent material to work with. The girl was lovely in both looks and nature, and she was intelligent and pliant, too. She wanted marital success and to give up her parsimonious existence as Aunt Brightwell's companion, and Fanny had no doubt Thea would prove obedient to all Fanny's ministrations and instruction.

Not that Fanny intended Thea to know every detail of how she and her siblings planned to orchestrate her fate. That wasn't necessary at all and, in fact, would be most unhelpful. Thea was less daring than Fanny, and a lot less outrageous and immoral than Antoinette. She'd be a reluctant protégé if she knew what her cousins intended. No, Thea would have to be managed like a slightly temperamental thoroughbred, but no doubt that delicacy of temperament was more likely to appeal to Mr Grayling. Fanny's investigations had revealed a man who did not favour the bold and the brash but rather the beautiful and bashful.

So on a crisp June morning, when the flower beds by the castle walls were in full bloom, Fanny persuaded Thea to accompany her riding at an hour considerably earlier than Fanny, certainly, was inclined to take her exercise. Lolling in bed with Fenton was decidedly the best way to while away the morning hours, but Fanny was never one to shirk her duty when it came to furthering the collective interests of the once maligned Brightwells. Yes, she was definitely prepared to endure a degree of sacrifice for the satisfaction of seeing her cunning plan bear fruit in the shortest possible time. Fanny in fact was determined to hear wedding bells peal by the end of July at the very latest.

"I never took you for a sportswoman, Fanny," Thea panted as they crested a hill and brought their mounts to a halt. The valley spread out before them: a patchwork of variegated greens interspersed with woodland. Thea sighed. "What an utterly charming vista. I could live here forever."

"Then you're far more the country bumpkin than I am, Thea." Fanny smiled. "Give me the hustle and bustle of the city any day. I immerse myself in the country for a short time on a regular basis so that when desperation hits its peak, I can throw myself back into what I truly love, and enjoy it all the more."

Her cousin looked at her in astonishment. "I thought people only lived in town when they had no other choice. Why, I grew up in the country and it's the only place I'd choose to be. Even Bath is too bustling for me."

"Then we'll have to find a nice quiet country barrister with a self-deprecating demeanour to fall in love with you, Thea, for any man of ambition is going to want to live in the city."

Thea raised her eyes to the skies, where a weak sun was attempting to punch through the thick cloud cover. "Oh, I'm prepared to make compromises, Cousin Fanny," she murmured. "Perhaps I'm not so fond of town because I'm always perceived as the poor relation, and believe me, there's nothing worse than that. I just wanted to crawl under the bed every time mama tried to entice me to attend an entertainment with her, both of us dressed in the fashions of three seasons ago."

Fanny could see how this was a likely contributor to Thea's jaundiced views on living in London. "Don't imagine I was in a better financial position, dearest. It was my mama's ambition that saw us fitted out in the latest. She gambled every last penny on outfitting Antoinette and me for our final season. I can tell you, the pressure was considerable, knowing that if we failed to secure the wealth and titles Mama desired for us, we were destined to spend our days like you, mouldering in the country as unpaid companions to Aunt Brightwell."

Thea levelled a half-envious, half-desperate look upon her cousin. "Goodness, so I'm the one living the life you'd have lived had your courageous efforts not won Fenton over." With the reins slung loosely over one wrist, she clasped her hands and pleaded, "If you have any suggestions as to how I might win Mr Grayling's high regard, do tell me, Fanny. I really am all at sea when it comes to knowing how to behave with a gentleman. Especially one like Mr Grayling, who sends my heart into such palpitations I can barely force out a sentence."

Fanny felt a great surge of satisfaction at hearing this. Securing Thea's marital aspirations was going to be far easier than she'd thought since her cousin was clearly proving so malleable.

"Why, good lord, I do believe that's Mr Grayling himself coming towards us!" Fanny exclaimed. The girls shaded their eyes, squinting into the distance as a dark-clad, indistinct figure on horseback assumed all the right proportions, emerging through a final copse of trees as...Mr Grayling.

Fanny leaned across the small space that separated them to say to her cousin, "I suggest you appear interested but not too bright and eager. A certain whimsical lethargy might be in order as you feel your way with any unknown gentleman." She hesitated, adding, "That is, before you know what they're truly after."

Thea nodded.

"What a delightful surprise it is to see you, ladies."

Mr Grayling doffed his hat and as he focused his pleasure upon Thea, Fanny was pleased to observe that while the planes of his angular face indicated a determined character, she could discern no suggestion of cruelty. She'd made such studies a feature of her sizing up of the male contingent ever since her painful encounter with Lord Slyther, the disgusting libertine her mother had chosen to foist upon her if Fanny failed to secure an acceptable match. Fenton often whispered stories of a man's true character, his predilection for certain activities that were demeaning or demoralizing to those weaker than himself, and Fanny was always assiduous, when meeting the said gentleman in a social setting, in ascertaining whether an unguarded look, or faint grooves about the mouth might bear up such an undesirable streak.

Fortunately, Fenton had heard only good regarding Mr Grayling and now, as Fanny studied him, she saw only determination, ambition and a very decided interest as he narrowed his eyes and, studying Thea closely, asked, "You are not worn out after your ride, Miss Brightwell? From a distance I saw both of you fair galloping up the hill." He smiled. "You're very flushed."

Thea blinked and opened her mouth to speak but Fanny said quickly but with bolstering sympathy, "Darling Thea will prove to us all just how...*robust* she is. Yet she *is* worn out—aren't you, dearest? —while I am just itching to put Major through his paces." She tilted her head and looked enquiringly at her cousin. "Why don't you allow Mr Grayling to take you for a gentle stroll over to that fallen log, where you can rest for a few minutes while I give Major his head?"

"Really, Cousin Fanny, I don't think I—" Thea began, but Fanny brushed away her objections with a blithe wave of her hand.

"What difference are a few minutes with or without a chaperone? I'm sure I could trust an honourable man like Mr Grayling with my life as well as your reputation, Thea." Fanny chuckled as Thea dubiously dismounted in response to Fanny's imperative indication; then she leaned across to address Mr Grayling in a collaborative manner.

"I hope you have no objection, initiating my cousin in the art of conversing with a gentleman. I'm sure she'll be quite tongue-tied but," she dropped her eyes and affected great sorrow, "Thea's time is limited and I am fond of her." She smiled a meaningful, colluding smile. "As I think she is fond of you, Mr Grayling. You are just the kind of gentleman to whom I would entrust darling Thea—" She broke off as she was aware of Thea taking a step closer and looking en-quiringly at them. "Carry on, Thea. Mr Grayling will join you in a moment, so that you both may enjoy the view from the top of the hill. I shall be back in twenty minutes. No need to look at me like I've cast you into the lion's den."

"Cousin Fanny!" Thea gasped in embar-rassment, putting her hands to her face as she glanced from Fanny to Mr Grayling.

Fanny was glad the gentleman shared her amusement at Thea's reaction. He really was charmed by the girl's charm and innocence, she thought.

Resuming her conversation as Thea began to trail obediently towards the fallen log, she indicated her cousin with a nod of her head. "You understand that under normal circumstances I would never consider leaving Thea unchaperoned."

Mr Grayling nodded, his expression suitably grave. "Rest assured, Lady Fenton, you have no cause to fear that I shall say or do anything that might remotely tax Miss Brightwell, or that may be cause for scandal."

Fanny raised her eyes heavenward. Perhaps he wasn't as understanding as she'd assumed. It seemed she really must spell it out. "But that is exactly what you *must* do, Mr Grayling. I am charging you with the task of introducing Thea to the pleasures that she will all too soon be denied when her sweet young life is cruelly cut short just months from now." She sent him a meaningful look, hoping he really did have the intelligence to follow what she was implying.

Dawning gratification crossed his face, quickly followed by alarm. "But what if she—"

"Unexpectedly...expire? There is no danger *now*, I assure you, Mr Grayling. Her doctor says that while she is well and robust, she must enjoy every amusement she can. He recommends gentle stimulation and mild exertion. When she starts to decline in another four months or so, why, *then* we must take every care with her."

She was about to say more, only Thea, who was already a few feet across the grassy turf, turned. Fanny saluted her and curtailed her advice with a smile. "Can I leave my cousin's...education in pleasure...to you, Mr Grayling? As long as there are no whispers surrounding the pair of you, I shall be only too pleased to think that you've so kindly stepped in to shoulder the burden of caring for Thea in a way only a gentleman for whom I can tell she has feelings could do."

WITH HIS THOUGHTS IN TURMOIL, SYLVESTER led his horse towards Thea, who was stroking the nose of her docile mare as it cropped the sweet grass on the hilltop. Lady Fenton's parting words had been a licence for anything, it seemed, but the lust that had coursed through him a few moments ago was tempered now with a curious mixture of emotions he couldn't quite identify. He certainly must not let the girl down by feeling pity. Didn't she deserve to feel what her cousin believed she ought before she went to her grave: pleasure and passion? Delivering upon that was what he'd been charged with.

"What a beautiful morning it is, Miss Brightwell," he murmured. For the first time in his life he wasn't sure how to approach a lady. Their very aloneness was highly irregular, and she'd know it. Sylvester, by contrast, was used to secret assignations and, on occasion, fast and furious lovemaking with highly experienced women who had looked to him to deliver a mutually satisfying experience. Bored married women and voracious widows had been his usual fare until now.

A shy—dying—virgin with a reputation to be protected was entirely out of his league.

Gad, but she was lovely, he thought as he approached, raising her head to regard him with a look of unsettling intensity. He was unexpectedly assailed by a wave of tenderness coupled with a charge of feeling to his groin.

"I'm sorry you've been saddled with me while Cousin Fanny takes her exercise." Her voice was lilting and musical and he noticed the slightest upturn to her lips, suggesting humour as she added, "Fanny is very impulsive and she does like to seize the moment when she can."

Sylvester lay his handkerchief over the fallen log. "Are you so unlike?" he asked, offering his hand so he could help her to sit.

"As Aunt Minerva's companion—and unlike Cousin Fanny—I have few moments to seize."

And so little time left in which to seize them, Sylvester thought with a pang as he sat next to her, careful that his thigh did not rest against hers—yet.

"Your aunt is…somewhat exacting, I'm led to believe. But let's not talk about that. Let's talk about you."

"Me?"

It was almost a squeal of surprise. Amused, he touched her cheek, very briefly, then carefully clasped his hands in his lap as he gazed into her eyes. The flare of response in their blue depths was gratifying and he was just congratulating himself on how well he was conducting this gentle prelude to the greater intimacy with which he'd been charged, when she said abruptly, "I am totally dependent on my aunt, Mr Grayling. My father left me penniless some years ago. That's really all there is to know about me."

He took her hand. "Should I be shocked by your candour or full of admiration for your honesty?" Admittedly, he was surprised by her revelation, which for the moment hindered what he had in mind, but perhaps needed to be dealt with. "You are a very lovely young woman." He hesitated. "And I should like to know you better, having observed you from," he smiled as he added with emphasis, "*across* the Assembly Rooms."

Rising, he drew her to her feet. "Come, let us walk the path that skirts the cliff face. Do you see your cousin over there?"

He pointed to a speck in the distance, which he assumed was Fanny galloping hell for leather over the downs. Lord, but Lady Fenton, as she had become, had inspired the lustful fantasies of half of London. He well recalled the whispers and innuendo that had swirled around her regarding her suitability as a wife. Some of the more scandalous suggested she'd had a raging affair with Viscount Fenton before they were married, and that he'd even proposed to set her up as his mistress. But then Earl Quamby had made her an honest offer, which soon had Fenton begging her on his knees to pledge her troth to him. The whole world knew that part, followed by the shock of the season when Miss Fanny Brightwell did indeed succumb to Lord Fenton's avowals of love and in fact broke off her betrothal to Lord Quamby to wed the man who'd stolen her heart. Jaws had barely been put back into place when the younger Miss Antoinette wed Lord Quamby not one week later, producing for him a son and heir after supposedly nine months and five minutes—though it was whispered the babe was vastly overcooked.

Miss Thea was a meek lamb to her cousins' fire and daring, which was fine by Sylvester, as he had no interest in a jezebel who'd lead him a merry dance before conferring her favours upon him. While the girl's tragic plight both touched his heart and made it thrill with forbidden opportunities—well, forbidden under any other circumstance—normally he was not drawn to the weak and helpless. But perhaps he was of a more altruistic and philanthropic nature than he'd supposed. He'd be rendering her the greatest service if he could wean her ever so gently into a world of forbidden pleasures before her time on earth was at an end. It's what Lady Fenton explicitly wished of him, and what he was relishing—even more now that he realised he'd have to be more creative about his wooing—

Miss Brightwell shaded her eyes. "She is a very long way away," she said doubtfully.

"Then let us take a shortcut through the woods to cut her off at the pass." Sylvester placed her hand in the crook of his arm, patting it firmly to keep it there, and increased his pace until they were well camouflaged by the wooded terrain.

Aware of her increased breathing, he glanced down at her. "Would you like to stop a moment, Miss Brightwell? The exertion is perhaps not good for you."

She touched her bosom—full and rising with increasing rapidity he couldn't help but notice—and looked up at him with real fear in her eyes.

"Mr Grayling, we shouldn't be alone," she whispered, stepping back and finding a solid tree trunk behind her, regarding him as if he were suddenly the devil incarnate and seeking her first opportunity to flee.

What choice did he have but to arrest her flight with what he was sure would have her in raptures?

Closing the distance before she could say another word, he brought his lips down to hers in a deep and resounding kiss, wrapping her in his arms as he pulled her to him, the hardening of his member almost painful as he anticipated how quickly her shock would turn to ecstasy.

It did not. An unprovoked kick upon the shins as she tore out of his embrace was instead her unexpected reaction, and dumbfounded, he watched as she picked up her skirts and ran towards the clearing as if the hounds of hell were nipping at her heels.

"Miss Thea, stop!" This was unprecedented. No woman had ever run screaming from his arms. He only ever initiated intimacies when he was confident of his reception, and the shy, interested looks this young woman had been sending him had given him every reassurance.

He caught up with her when she was back on the bridle path, hailing the distant figure on horseback as if she were in the most desperate plight.

"Miss Thea, forgive me!"

"You had no right to take such liberties, sir!" She swung round, her face suffused with anger before she presented him once more with her back, stumbling in her haste to reach her approaching cousin.

Mortified, Sylvester was by Miss Brightwell's side by the time Lady Fenton reined in, her expression a picture of both guilt and confusion.

"Thea, dearest, what's happened?"

Miss Brightwell shook her head and Sylvester experienced a great wave of embarrassment as she cried, "I can't tell you here, Cousin Fanny! Please, let us return home immediately." With a sideways glance at Sylvester, she added, "There's been a terrible misunderstanding. I'm sorry if I gave you a false impression of the kind of young woman I am, sir. Clearly I am at fault for you to have behaved with such…liberality."

This was begun in a tone of uncertainty and finished on one of great irony, before she dismissed him roundly with, "And now I must bid you good day."

IN a fog of mystification, Fanny rode with Thea back to the estate. Only when Thea was met by Antoinette and Bertram in the drawing room, and they refused to release her until she explained the reason for her disordered spirits, did Fanny get to the bottom of the matter.

"I don't know what I could have said to have made him behave in such an ungentlemanly manner," Thea wept as she collapsed onto the chaise longue. Raising her head to untie the ribbons of her bonnet, which she tossed upon the floor, she buried her face in the crook of her elbow. "Oh, the indignity! I thought he was the most charming and gentlemanly of gentlemen but he was nothing but a rogue!"

"Because he tried to kiss you?" Antoinette enquired, looking as mystified as Fanny felt.

"Because he did kiss me!" Thea's body shook.

"And you didn't enjoy it?" Antoinette asked.

"That's beside the point!" Thea responded, jerking her head up angrily. "I told him I had not a penny to my name."

"Why would you say that?" Bertram's eyebrows shot up into his hair. "Why would anyone tell anyone else they had not a penny to their name?"

Fanny turned to him. "Men must bluff about such things but for women, it's a different matter. But Thea, my dear," she turned back to her cousin, "why do you think he kissed you for any other reason than he thought you most charming? Are you not delighted you've gained his interest?"

"He saw me as an easy target. A man with honourable intentions would never behave with such impropriety. I thought he was a gentleman but he merely saw an opportunity to take advantage."

She began to cry in earnest now. The three siblings shook their heads. Fanny cleared her throat and moved to take a seat beside Thea.

"I'm afraid I'm more deserving of your rage than poor Mr Grayling, who consulted me on how best to go about winning your regard." She sighed as if for Thea's benefit when really her irritation was centred on herself. Oh dear, this had not gone to plan. "Thea, Mr Grayling already knew you had nothing, before you told him, for I informed him of the same in the very conversation when I, er…warned him to be mindful of that fact and not proceed if his intentions were…er…not honourable."

Fanny knew it was wrong to lie outright, but Thea's precious sensibilities were not going to be satisfied with anything but some serious creativity with regard to the erstwhile object of interest's motivation in her charms.

Thea slanted a suspicious look up at her. "You did?"

Fanny nodded. "I was quite emphatic that Mr Grayling be under no misapprehension as to how matters stood."

"And...what did he say?"

"He told me that was immaterial, as he'd been won over by your sweet charm. He said he merely wished to know you better to gain a clearer ideas as to..."

She cleared her throat and proceeded with what she knew to be a very wicked untruth, but goodness, she had only the girl's best intentions at heart. Thea and Mr Grayling were ideally matched, and if Thea had only a modestly acceptable dowry he'd be proceeding with a marriage offer. All he needed was a little prod to reinforce the fact that the unfortunate lack of dowry meant nothing when compared with her cousin's abundant charms. Charms he'd never know unless he was persuaded to discover them.

She straightened and launched into her lie without a backward look. "He wanted to know whether you were possessed of passions that were aligned to his."

"Cousin Fanny!"

"Don't sound so shocked, cuz, these things are important," Antoinette chimed in. Fanny was not surprised this would be a point of great interest to her wickedly daring sister. Antoinette had a wondrous love of the opposite sex and a vast desire to help any of her collective sisters who might benefit from a little matchmaking assistance from herself. "Poor Mr Grayling." Antoinette shook her head sadly. "After his last disastrous foray into love, you can imagine he'd be very careful to ascertain he was courting the right kind of potential wife."

"What do you mean 'poor Mr Grayling'? I don't understand." Thea looked in perplexity from one cousin to the other.

Fanny had no idea what Antoinette had in mind, but Antoinette could credit fair success, so she let her sister continue. Of course, Antoinette had not Fanny's keen intellect but she could be creative when it came to matters of the heart. Or anything of a sensual nature. Antoinette didn't usually let either her heart or her head get in the way when it came to matters of the flesh.

Fanny supposed she was simply a woman who took what she wanted without thought for the consequences—so it was a good thing she had an elder sister like Fanny to ensure she got away with what she did.

Though right now, Fanny was quite happy to defer to the younger, who went on, "Some years ago, Mr Grayling married a French woman. A beautiful French woman who showed every sign of loving him deeply but who turned cold the moment his ring was upon her finger." Antoinette raised her eyes heavenward in a gesture of great sorrow.

"Mr Grayling is a widower?"

Antoinette nodded. "But do not ever speak of his late wife. It was a disastrous marriage, and a secret one, too, for she had no money and he knew his family would cut him off without a penny should they discover what he'd done."

Fanny watched Thea's eyes grow large while she herself wondered where this story was going.

"They need not have worried, for there was no unworthy heir resulting from the match." Antoinette shook her head. "The couple lived in France, where this beautiful but cold French woman, who had no tender feelings for him whatsoever and wanted only his money, refused him her bed for the entire year they were wed."

Fanny saw the fiery hue that swept from Thea's bosom upwards. She put her hand on the girl's shoulder. "Do you understand what Antoinette is saying, Thea?" she murmured. After all, most young women didn't have the liberal education in carnal matters mother had ensured they'd had. Fanny and Antoinette had been trained to use their bodies as lures for prospective suitors, to go as far as might entice a marriage offer, but on no circumstances to sully the sanctity of their greatest and perhaps only asset apart from beauty: their virtue. The fact that both girls had taken a great leap of faith and had succeeded in their marital aspiration was a reflection on circumstances and a liberal dose of luck—though cunning on Fanny's part had been crucial, she reflected, while Antoinette had simply been fortunate.

In this instance, however, Fanny felt it

necessary that Thea take that important next step. The girl probably didn't even know the effects a passionate kiss or a little sensual exploration would have upon her, but the only way to draw Mr Grayling into her orbit was if she loosened up a little.

Thea was avoiding her cousins' eyes—and little wonder, for Fanny was conscious of the undercurrent of prurient interest overlaid with suppressed amusement that must emanate from them.

Antoinette giggled as she settled herself on the arm of the settee. "What has Aunt Minerva told you to expect when you get married, Thea?"

Thea's cornflower-blue eyes flickered away before returning to her cousin's face. "Aunt Minerva told me nothing because she doesn't ever intend that I shall get married," she said crisply. "But I always remember Mama telling me before she died that after the marriage, the babies come before one knows it."

"And why do you suppose the babies come?" Antoinette asked. "Your family kept a cow and some pigs and a couple of horses. Don't pretend you don't know, Thea."

Thea looked away. "If having a baby requires doing what I've seen in the farmyard then I think I should prefer to remain unmarried." Her shoulders shook and she began to cry. "Oh, I can't believe that I let Mr Grayling think I should entertain feelings for him when I know I could never bring myself to do a thing like…that!"

Her dismay was so genuine that Fanny, who usually was the first to behave with an appropriately cool head, hushed her with a sympathetic hand on the girl's back. "Well, you do know you cannot have a baby from just a kiss, Thea," she told her. "And it's wrong of you to blame yourself, for it was not you who let Mr Grayling kiss you. He was the one who instigated it through his feelings of passion. He told me of his overwhelming feelings for you when he sought permission to…get to know you better."

"That's right, because he wanted to ensure you weren't like the cold, frigid, and loveless piece he married."

Bertram whistled. "Gad, what a nobleman. To be married a whole year and to let one's wife dictate whether one can get into her bed, much less into her—"

"Bertram!" Fanny held up a warning hand with a meaningful look at Thea who had raised herself and whose luminous, teary eyes looked as if they might pop out of her head.

"So Mr Grayling's wife agreed to marry him but wouldn't let him…?"

She trailed off and Antoinette asked wickedly, "Wouldn't let him what, Cousin Thea? What do you think he wouldn't let her do?" She put her arm about her cousin's shoulders and grew serious. "Oh, we're shameless and you must think we're making the most terrible fun of you but we truly do want what's best for you."

"Indeed, we do," Fanny agreed. "But as you're an innocent, and because we're shameless, we also feel it's important to make you more aware of what was explained, or perhaps not explained, to you by your dear Mama and Aunt Minerva."

"And the farm animals," Bertram added.

Thea looked more nervous than grateful.

"I know it's necessary to lie in the same bed." She shivered as if the thought appalled her. "It's a woman's duty, I suppose."

Antoinette giggled. "There's more to lying in the same bed to get a baby! Oh, do let me tell her, Fanny!"

Fanny glanced at Bertram and then Thea. "You can hardly do so with Bertram in the room." She indicated the door to her brother with a nod. "Sorry, brother dearest, but there are some things a lady can't share with a man."

"Something of an irony, wouldn't you say, when it's the very essence of what a man and a woman do together when the moon is high in the sky and a man's body is on fire."

"And hopefully a woman's too, Bertram." Fanny said, warningly. "I hope you ensure that's the case every time. Now go! Right, my dear Thea," Fanny said, once it was just the three of them. "I don't know if you've ever experimented with the way your body feels when it's touched a certain way...?" She looked enquiringly at her cousin, who simply looked blank.

Antoinette squealed, "Dear Lord, can she really be related to us?"

"Now, now, Antoinette, there was no call for that. It just means that Thea will find herself completely overwhelmed when she allows herself to relax a little more with Mr Grayling, and if he happens to be sufficiently encouraged to be allowed a little licence to be…exploratory."

Thea bit her lip and closed her eyes. "I couldn't possibly," she whispered. "Not if you're talking about things that only married people can do. And even then a woman has to steel herself to…"

"To what, Cousin Thea?" Antoinette whispered. "Allow him to lie next to her, to feel the line of his muscled thigh as it tapers up to his manly buttocks and, oh, my dear, you really do need to find out what else a well-endowed gentleman has in store for you."

Fanny took Thea's hands in hers and began to chafe them as she directed a fond look into her cousin's eyes. "No need to look so horrified. You don't have to do anything you're not comfortable with. All we're saying is that Mr Grayling is actively seeking a wife who will love him with a little passion. Try not to be too buttoned-up, is really what I mean. Sink into his embrace and let his hands stroke you into wondrous pleasure. That's my main advice to you."

"Stroke me?" Thea shook her head as she experimentally held out her arms and began to stroke one with the other. "It is a very pleasant sensation," she said dubiously.

"Not there!"

Fanny stifled her amusement at the shock on Thea's face when Antoinette twisted round and clapped her hand to her cousin's breast.

"There!"

"Surely not!"

Thea jerked away and Antoinette dropped her hand, giving her a quick embrace. "I can assure you, it doesn't feel the same way when the hand belongs to a very handsome, desirable gentleman."

Thea dropped her eyes to her hands, now clasped demurely in her lap, and mumbled, "Aunt Minerva will make absolutely certain I'm never placed in such a situation."

Antoinette sighed. "Then we shall just have to ensure that you are, Cousin Thea, if you are to have any pleasure in this world."

Thea's head snapped up. "I'm sorry to be a disappointment, but I'm not pleasure-seeking at the cost of long-term future happiness, Cousin Antoinette." She sighed and her shoulders slumped, though she managed a wavering smile. "Please don't be cross or frustrated with me. We're very different. I just couldn't bear to tarnish my dear mama and papa's memories with behaviour they'd consider lax or improper."

Fanny tried to think of a suitable response. Thea's intractability could be more of a problem than she'd thought. "An honourable marriage—and a happy one—should be a young woman's greatest pursuit, for it is through her ability to control her husband that she gains power."

Thea blinked as if this was a surprise, and Fanny let out her breath in a heartfelt sigh. "The world is vastly unfair to women. We are completely beholden to our closest male relative or anyone else who can provide a meagre living and who manipulates the purse strings so that we perform just as they would wish." She brushed Thea's cheek with the back of her hand and felt a genuine rush of tenderness for the girl whose innocence and determination to do what was right was so different from Fanny's.

"I don't want to lead you astray, Cousin Thea, or to contradict any of the good advice you've been given by your worthy late parents, but just think on this: What do you think would most please them if they could look down upon you from the heavens above? To see you ten years from now—perhaps even twenty or thirty if Aunt Minerva lives to a great age—pandering to her every whim, rubbing her swollen limbs, bearing the lash of her tongue? For that will be your lot if you don't have the courage to take a stand for your own happiness."

Thea looked close to tears. "But I can't compromise myself in my pursuit of happiness."

"You can at least be clever about it," Antoinette all but snapped. Clearly she was not as sympathetic and understanding of her cousin's conflicts as Fanny was. "What Fanny's saying is that if you don't let Mr Grayling kiss and fondle you at least a little bit so he can reassure himself that you're not going to lead him into such unhappiness as his awful late French wife, you'll be looking after Aunt Minerva for the rest of your life." She sniffed. "And under such circumstances, I'd wager she'd outlive you, too!" she added with venom.

Thea covered her eyes and let out a whimper while Fanny put her arms around her. "There, there, no need to cry about it. Who knows what the future will bring? All we're saying is that it might be a good idea —if the opportunity presented itself—to be a little more relaxed and to take perhaps just a little risk in order to reassure Mr Grayling that you do in fact like him. I doubt Miss Huntingdon would have slapped his face if she'd been in your situation."

"She wouldn't?" Thea's mouth dropped open, then she said as if in explanation, "But she comes with a dowry and not a hint of scandal has ever attached to her name."

Fanny frowned. "Are you suggesting you're behaving with even more circumspection than you otherwise might because you've heard that Antoinette and I were somewhat daring in our pursuit of happiness?" She couldn't help bristling. "Have we somehow tainted you with our liberality?"

"Oh no, no, Cousin Fanny, that's not it at all," Thea hastily assured her. "I just want to be careful. Mr Grayling is the first gentleman—dashing gentleman, that is, because the curate doesn't really count, if one is only counting handsome gentlemen with the means to keep a wife—who's shown the slightest bit of interest, and I can't bear the thought it might only be on account of him thinking he can take advantage."

"Well, let him!" cried Antoinette. "Let him take at least some advantage so he comes back desperate for more. Make him desire you so much that he can't live without you!"

"But only as his wife, dearest Thea," Fanny added with a cautionary look at her sister. "Respectable marriage is all that we're advocating as the end result. It'll just require a bit more encouragement from you than a slap across the face if he ever is brave enough to try to kiss you again."

It was hard to tell what impact her words had on Thea but Fanny was a little more relieved by the flare of bravado reflected in the girl's eyes by the time they rose to bid each other good night.

CHAPTER 9

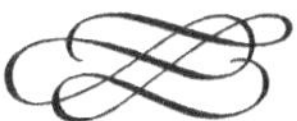

I T was only by the sixth draft that Sylvester felt his letter came close to saying what he truly felt with the right degree of humility and artfulness.

Like a schoolboy squirming with mortification, he'd slunk home after his disastrous encounter with Miss Brightwell, paced the library like a caged tiger, then finally resorted to the inkwell and a sheet of parchment. The written word was not the manner in which he felt most comfortable expressing himself, but he certainly wasn't going to get a chance to put his feelings into words in a face-to-face encounter.

Dorcas, the housemaid, clanked around

the fireplace, building it up and making a dreadful clatter with the fire irons until his concentration was so shot to pieces he had no choice but to cry out, "Will you stop that infernal noise!" Looking up at the pregnant pause that followed, he locked glances with her shocked face, whereupon she brought her apron up to her face and ran, weeping loudly, from the room.

"Gad's teeth!" he muttered. Had he completely lost his artful touch with the feminine species? Could he do nothing to melt a susceptible heart with finesse, or at least not send them all fleeing from him, and in tears?

Stifling the urge to run after the maidservant and make some attempt to appease her before she informed the entire household of his devil incarnate ways, he sighed instead and read through, for the final time, his agonisingly crafted sentences. Then, sprinkling sand upon the wet ink, he stood up and stretched his arms as high as he could without tearing the seams of his nearly new superfine coat as he contemplated how he might proceed with the task

Lady Fenton had set him—purely for the good of her cousin, he hastily reassured himself.

Miss Brightwell was like a nervous thoroughbred. While he'd been assured she was for the moment robust enough in body to accept his overtures, she had still the sensibility of the untutored virgin, which he should have understood. She also clearly had no idea of her cousins' desires to see her exit into the afterlife a little worldlier and, he hoped, a little happier than the virginal miss she currently was.

If guilt nagged at him for deceiving her, it was only for a moment, as he fully endorsed her generous and well-meaning cousins' desires for her happiness, which he would discharge with all the care and thoughtfulness of which he was capable.

He'd started off like a bull in a china shop but he was not going to make the same mistake twice. His letter would make it clear that he felt abject and cast down by his impulsiveness and, if she would accept his apologies, he hoped they might start again.

The thought she might dismiss him altogether was difficult for one of his pride to entertain and as he paced before the fire, waiting for the servant he'd summoned to ensure delivery of his letter, he was buoyed up with hope one minute, but filled with doubt the next. What if she rejected his offer of forgiveness? What else could he do?

An image of her sweet, shocked face kept intruding on his consciousness. She was so innocent, so lovely, so…

The memory of her cousin Bertram's doleful voice chimed in at this point: 'doomed'.

He would not think of that now. He would think only of her innocent charms and the fact that Lady Fenton had charged him with the task of…well, moulding them into something more sophisticated.

He would be doing her a kindness, and that's all this was ever about.

The trouble was, the kindness he might render for an elderly aunt, who liked the company when he found time to dash in and see her before the theatre, did not play havoc with his heart in the way that doing Miss Brightwell a kindness did.

Not that he was in danger of harbouring any inconvenient feelings for the girl. She was sweet and lovely, granted. But she was also dying, and he was if not actually a rake, he was, when it came to practical matters, a gentleman who required a wife with something of a dowry.

Nevertheless, it was a matter of honour that he render Miss Brightwell the kind of service that would see her go to her grave having experienced something wonderful of life.

***

Thea closed her eyes to summon the fortitude she needed to get through this evening. What a torment it was having to untangle Aunt Minerva's skeins of wool and listen to her homilies on good behaviour and everything wicked she'd observed in her nieces. Aunt Minerva had, however, reserved most criticism for Thea, chastising her for everything from her 'roving eye' to her all but throwing herself at 'that unconscionable rake, Mr Grayling'.

Thea accepted all this in silence while inside her rage and injured dignity grew.

Not for one moment was she tempted to defend herself much less mention that she'd displayed every feminine outrage that her aunt would have expected had she had an inkling of what had occurred.

"Thea, what's the matter with you? There's no time to waste in foolish daydreaming when you have work to do! I think the sooner we remove from Bath, the better. In fact, I've decided we shall return to Heskett tomorrow." With a click of her tongue, her aunt communicated her displeasure, tugging at the skein of wool that Thea had in her lap so it jerked up and rolled across the floor.

Thea crawled across the carpet to retrieve it, careful to keep her sour expression averted. It was true she'd been daydreaming, though her thoughts were more akin to nightmares as she relived the ghastly, humiliating images her two cousins had gleefully recounted to her only this morning on what husbands and wives were forced to do when the marriage contract was signed and in order to procreate. Little wonder that a woman would only submit when she was under such an obligation. The idea of flesh touching flesh, much less a man's…oh dear God, the idea that a man had a sword-like appendage that he pushed inside his wife in order to sow the seed of future life was utterly abhorrent. Yet apparently a man gained far more pleasure from his thrusting for the entertainment of it than the serious business of making a child.

And what of the woman who must bear such indignity? Little wonder Mr Grayling's poor French wife had not been up to the task. There must be so very many women in this world who gritted their teeth and lay back staring at the ceiling while they hoped this would be the last time they'd have to suffer such humiliation, hoping that a child had indeed been created within them. She shuddered once more. Were they teasing her? Was this really what marriage was all about, for what Antoinette and Fanny had explained mentioned nothing about love. Only this terrible brutality.

"Thea, what's this sniffling about? You've been like Polly when she has the earache, and you know how I can't abide invalids."

Such admonishments were usually like water off a duck's back, but when her aunt unwisely added, "I hope you're not mooning over your Mr Grayling, for you know nothing will come of that!" Thea couldn't help wailing.

Of course Thea had no intention of telling her anything but somehow Aunt Minerva must have suspected that her niece had had an encounter of some sort with the gentleman in question for soon she was barking questions like a Spanish Inquisitor and Thea, never a good liar to begin with, went to pieces. "Please, Aunt Minerva, you really have no need to be concerned for I kicked Mr Grayling in the shins and ran away. I can assure you that I don't ever want to see him again. Ever!"

Aunt Minerva raised an eyebrow and her look of horror turned to satisfaction. "No doubt he thought he could take any liberty he liked, considering you'd be in the workhouse if it weren't for me, eh, girl?" Her unsympathetic relative returned to her stitching, rocking gently. "We'll be two old maids together, and happy to keep one another company as the years go by. Perhaps it's not a bad thing you've discovered for yourself how quick handsome men are to take advantage of innocence."

The horror of such an endless future with her aunt was at that moment on par with Thea's horror at the specific nature of conjugal rights.

"Dr Horne's here to see you, ma'am." Polly put her head round the door.

Thea, having regained her composure with difficulty, glanced at her aunt with a sympathetic look she hoped would help banish her dissatisfaction with her. "Are you feeling poorly again, Aunt Minerva?"

"An unexpected pleasure, Dr Horne," her aunt said, waving aside Thea's concern as she invited her visitor to sit. "You've come with my liver pills, I take it."

"That…amongst other things."

Thea was conscious of the doctor's particularly intense glance across at her and wondered if she should leave. On the one hand, Aunt Minerva loved an audience when her ailments were discussed, but judging by the doctor's apparent discomfort in Thea's company—for he really had gone a peculiar colour, which to her surprise suggested acute embarrassment—the nature of his visit might be more personal.

"Where are you going, Thea?" her Aunt barked as Thea rose to her feet and began to discreetly quit the room. "I may have to rely on you to ensure my medicinals are properly administered."

Thea's cheeks began to burn. "Of course. Aunt. I merely thought Dr Horne might wish me to leave."

"Good Lord, no, child!"

A surprised glance at the doctor told her he was as taken aback by the vehemence of his denial as she was. Clearly the matter that had brought him here was one of truly great potential embarrassment. Thea narrowed her eyes. The doctor's nose and cheeks were a matching puce rather than crimson. Realisation dawned and Thea, never able to keep her emotions in check, had to pretend her gasp was a cough.

Why, the doctor had designs on Aunt Minerva, she thought. Earlier, when he'd informed Aunt Minerva that an old "friend" wished to pay court to her, Thea could not reconcile the idea of the handsome, urbane, silver-haired gentleman her aunt had pointed out at the Assembly Rooms possibly having any interest in her. Suddenly, realization dawned. Dr Horne, with his red button nose like a cherry atop a Christmas pudding, and his wispy ginger hair and beard, was a far more likely candidate.

Clearly, though, he was feeling his way.

Catching his eye, Thea grinned in collusion, which caused him to drop what he had in his hands and, with much wheezing and puffing, reach down to pick it up.

"Ah yes, the liver pills," he said, though that's not what he'd picked up. Thea took a seat opposite her aunt as she noticed the doctor lean across to hand her aunt an elegant piece of parchment addressed to Miss Brightwell.

"Oh, Dr Horne," she whispered before she could stop the words, and he jerked his head round to stare at her, reminding her of a frightened rabbit caught in the headlights of a coach on a dark night. She gave him an understanding nod and then another smile.

If she could encourage him sufficiently to make Aunt Minerva an offer she couldn't refuse, Thea would be free. She'd still be poor, but someone else would have to take her in.

And anything else was better than having to live with Aunt Minerva.

Provided she still had her reputation intact, she amended, though that wouldn't be difficult. Not after the horrors Antoinette and Fanny had described in ruining one.

With raised eyebrows, her aunt sliced off the seal with her fingernail. It sailed through the air and landed with a hiss in the fire as the old woman impatiently unfolded the paper and scanned it.

She gasped and scanned it again, this time with her hand resting upon her palpitating bosom.

Intrigued, Thea craned her neck to see if she could catch a glimpse of what was written. She caught the words *crave your forgiveness* before Dr Horne rose, blocking her view and asking, clearly agitated, "A simple yes or a no is all that's required, ma'am."

Thea couldn't stop the secretive smile

that tugged at the corners of her mouth as she watched the doctor battle his emotions. Goodness! He wanted to establish if Aunt Minerva was open to the idea of having an amour. Perhaps he'd heard of her aunt's distress over the erstwhile object of her affections who'd not even acknowledged her at the Assembly Rooms the other night and the incident had emboldened him.

Unbidden, an image thrust itself into her mind of the disgusting acts she now knew men and women indulged in under cover of darkness. Dr Horne and Aunt Minerva? She shuddered before remembering that this act was primarily to make babies, or if the man were of a particularly violent and selfish nature. Dr Horne would of course get none of that kind of business where her Aunt was concerned. Which must mean that after treating her as his patient all these years, he'd formed a genuine and inexplicable *tendre* for her.

And now he was asking for her forgiveness? She shook her head. Life was full of surprises. Perhaps he'd been indiscreet about his feelings. Perhaps Aunt Minerva had slapped his face. Surely not, though, for if Aunt Minerva had been outraged she'd have dismissed Dr Horne as her physician.

She gazed at the pair, each as unprepossessing as the other: Dr Horne with his bulbous red nose and wispy ginger moustache and Aunt Minerva with her squirrel's tail forever threatening to dislodge itself. Surely they were far too advanced in age for courting?

Thea brought herself up short. She should be more charitable. Age was no barrier to love. Of course it wasn't. The old dears were quite right to want a little romance and excitement.

A tremor of self-pity ran through her before reasserting itself as something nobler. Since she was not going to experience either romance or excitement herself, why not help facilitate a union between the pair? A little matchmaking could be quite a tonic to enliven her dull, dull days.

Before her aunt could respond, Thea reminded her, "Did you not say we were returning to Heskett tomorrow, Aunt Minerva?"

She was secretly delighted when her aunt turned on her indignantly. "I said no such thing, Thea. Why, trust you to mix up dates and turn my intentions on their head." Aunt Minerva fanned her heated face with the parchment and seemed to be silently doing some sort of experiment with her lips.

Thea would have been perfectly happy to return to Heskett. In fact she'd have preferred it. The fear she might see Mr Grayling again was positively mortifying. To think she'd once been entranced by his mop of light brown curls and intrigued by the elegant line of his side whiskers. She was no better than an easily beguiled schoolroom miss.

She watched the elderly lovebirds out of the corner of her eye as she picked up some abandoned work and began to stitch away at the little garment she was embroidering for baby George, and which she'd present to him before his christening. Dr Horne was examining Aunt Minerva's fat ankles, which her aunt said were too swollen for her to take her morning walk in comfort. The doctor was being extremely charitable as to his reasons why this could be when Thea was fairly sure if her aunt reduced her consumption of chocolate eclairs and sugar biscuits before luncheon, she might well find her ankles strong enough to carry her reduced weight.

"The pain's a little higher, Dr Horne."

Thea jerked her head around to see the doctor massaging Aunt Minerva's calf and her stomach turned over in revulsion. Regardless of what her cousins said, she most definitely did not intend ever to let a gentleman do more than hold her to dance.

But watching her Aunt and the doctor conduct their odd little courtship could be quite entertaining.

"See what Dr Horne is doing, Thea?" Aunt Minerva's called across the room. "You must learn to do the massage just like that. It's a good thing you're here."

"A very good thing, Miss Thea," said Dr Horne. "And so delightful you are staying in town longer. Why, things are just starting to get lively in Bath. We would miss your company." He stared meaningfully at her and

Thea almost winked; and although she didn't, her mouth twitched once more as she smiled at him and murmured, "And the company of my aunt, of course, Dr Horne."

"Most assuredly, Miss Thea. Most assuredly."

"Well, Thea, what did I tell you?" her aunt demanded, tapping the letter she'd received once the doctor had been farewelled. "After all these years Mr Granville has seen the error of his ways. He begs my forgiveness and evinces the strong hope that I will receive him with at least a touch of kindness after our last disastrous parting."

Thea frowned. Surely her aunt was mistaken. "Mr Granville?" Puzzled, she clarified, "So he signed his name?"

"His initials, SG, in case the letter fell into the wrong hands, no doubt." Aunt Minerva sighed and several of her chins wobbled. Thea meanwhile felt merely foolish for having jumped to the wrong conclusion. So Dr Horne really had been delivering a letter on behalf of Aunt Minerva's former swain, though really, the idea of the urbane Mr Granville having designs on her aunt stretched the bounds of credulity.

Unless of course there was some other motivation behind Mr Granville's request. Perhaps he was a confidence trickster who wanted to ultimately lay his hands on her aunt's fortune, just as he'd wanted to do all those years before.

She checked herself. Only a foolish girl would jump to two wrong conclusions in the space of five minutes. Thea must do what she did best: simply observe quietly what was going on around her...and try to come up with better-informed conclusions.

She glanced up when her aunt made some strange noise and with a start, observed that her benefactress was staring into space, sucking on her teeth.

"Aunt?" she asked, though her concern brought Aunt Minerva's head round like a spinning top with the usual rebuke spilling from her lips.

"Why look at you, lazy girl. You're sitting in idleness when I've a whole basket that needs sorting. Who do you think pays a fortune to feed and clothe you?"

Sighing, Thea rose to her feet. "I'm suddenly very tired, Aunt Minerva. I think I shall have an afternoon rest."

"You will not." Her aunt glared at her. "Not until you've finished re-rolling the wool in that whole basket like I asked you this morning. Goodness me, girl. It is I who is off to rest."

CHAPTER 10

BEFORE before either had a chance to carry the discussion further—although Aunt Minerva was always assured the last word—a commotion in the corridor just outside Aunt Minerva's apartments was followed by the sound of girlish laughter and masculine jollity.

"Aunt Minerva, what a pleasure to see you!" Antoinette gushed as she swept across the Aubusson carpet of Aunt Minerva's private sitting room to deliver a smacking kiss on her relative's cheek.

Bertram followed suit, the pair of siblings taking a seat uninvited and gazing at

Aunt Minerva with a degree of pleasure Thea considered most extraordinary. Antoinette looked flushed and lovely, as usual. Thea felt an unexpected stab of jealousy. Her cousin was only a year older, yet she was now a countess and mother of the future Earl of Quamby. Thea didn't care that Antoinette was a countess but she cared greatly that she was the mother of an infant who seemed to interfere little in his mother's quest for pleasure.

Thea longed to be a mother but the possibility seemed increasingly remote. A husband with only a moderate annuity would not be in a position to afford a penniless wife, while a gentleman with more would be in the market for an heiresses or at least a beauty who'd submit to his carnal desires with sufficient enthusiasm to compensate for her pecuniary deficiencies. And Thea knew now she could never do that.

"Your private apartments are so far from ours and we were just remarking that we'd not seen you since our outing to the Assembly Rooms and that you'd soon be charging us with neglect, so here we are." Antoinette smiled beatifically at her aunt as she twirled a golden ringlet around her forefinger.

"I think a good deal of time might have passed before that was likely to happen," Aunt Minerva remarked drily.

"And we also have a proposition for you, Aunt." Bertram grinned and slanted a meaningful look at Thea. He winked. "We thought we'd take you on a grand outing tomorrow, Aunt Minerva." He paused, adding more as an afterthought. "And Thea, if she wants to come."

"And why do you suppose I have either the time or inclination to go on a grand outing?" Aunt Minerva demanded. "Moreover, Thea is fully engaged with a list of duties I need carried out in order to clear my head."

Antoinette leaned forward. "Oh, but Aunt, your presence has been requested for a very worthy philanthropic duty, and I've been charged by Lady Umbrage to pass the message on to you."

Aunt Minerva's squirrel's tail bobbed beneath her lace cap as she twisted her head to pierce her niece with a look of astonishment that quickly turned to excitement. "Lady Umbrage has requested my presence?" Her eyes were suddenly bright. "I'm sure I'd not let Lady Umbrage down if I could help it. What does she wish of me?"

"The opening ceremony at the new Foundling Hospital is tomorrow." Antoinette smoothed her sprigged muslin skirts over her knees and offered her sweetest smile. "Knowing how much you love babies, Aunt Minerva, and owing to the fact that Lady Umbrage's sister is unable to attend due to a chest ailment, her ladyship hoped you'd graciously agree to do the honours with her."

"Oh, my! And what an honour it is, indeed." Aunt Minerva hesitated. "What, exactly, am I required to do?"

"Well, there are five babies whom the governors have chosen to be specially honoured and who shall have bestowed upon them the name of a noble benefactor."

Aunt Minerva's hands which had been cupping her shining face dropped suddenly to her lap as her excitement turned to horror. Her nostrils twitched. "What? Give my name to some dirty, puling little bastard dropped in the basket at the gates by the Foundling Hospital?"

Antoinette and her brother exchanged glances, almost as if they'd expected something along these lines. Stoically, Antoinette did not allow her smile to falter.

Bertram cleared his throat. "Proceedings won't take long and will be followed by a lavish breakfast at Lady Umbrage's estate. I believe a rare and most sumptuous pudding will be served for those with a sweet tooth."

"And of course there'll be champagne."

"Champagne?" Aunt Minerva's eyes narrowed. "For breakfast?"

"There's bound to be," Antoinette said, cheerfully. "It's a christening."

"Lady Umbrage is mighty anxious you'll say yes." Bertram slapped his thighs. "And I promised I'd not let her down. What do you say, Aunt Minerva?"

Thea was watching proceedings with interest. She had no idea why Bertram and Antoinette was so anxious for their aunt's cooperation, though she guessed they were concocting some plan.

Suddenly Aunt Minerva smiled. "Oh, well, I'm sure the child will be dead before long so what does it matter if I have such a namesake?" She looked as if this were happily to her satisfaction causing Thea to stare at her open-mouthed while anger made the back of her neck prickle.

"Well, I'm not going," she muttered.

Antoinette looked aghast. "But…but you have to," she cried.

"Surely I'm not required?" Thea didn't care what Bertram and Antoientte's plan might be. The thought of those darling babies being used for the pleasure and vanity of people like Aunt Minerva, who didn't care tuppence if they lived or died, was too terrible to countenance.

"Of course you are!"

"Why?"

"So…so that you…"

Antoinete looked helplessly at her brother, who supplied smoothly, "So you can ensure Aunt Minerva's dress isn't soiled by the puling little creature she'll be holding in her arms as it's christened."

"Holding in my arms?" cried Aunt Minerva with evident distaste. "Will I have to hold it for very long?" She shuddered. "Someone else's …byblow? I can tell you, my dear Thea, that you most certainly *will* be attending with me.'

There was no use arguing but Thea didn't at all like the prospect of having to gaze upon those poor, destitute children. Her heart would break, she knew it.

Stony faced, she listened to the arrangements made regarding time and transport and was trailing up the stairs to her room when she turned to find Antoinette at her heels.

"You must wear something charming tomorrow," her cousin whispered hastily. "What about the jonquil pelisse over your white muslin? That'll set off your hair nicely and it's very…alluringly innocent."

Thea stared at her over her shoulder. The pleasure of Antoinette's visit had palled. "What does it matter what I wear?" She gave a gusty sigh. "It's not as if anyone will be looking at me and besides, I don't want to go." A lineup of unwanted children would be like a cruel reminder that she herself was doomed to die childless and—she nearly choked on the thought—a spinster assisting her aunt increasingly into old age.

"But Aunt Minerva wants you to go and that's all that counts."

"Why, thank you for reminding me."

Antoinette touched her arm to detain her. "You'll be doing those babies a great service." Her tone was wheedling. "Besides, think how nice it would be if you at least provided one tender heart during the whole charade. Afterwards you could cuddle them to your heart's content."

This stopped her in her tracks and she turned abruptly at the top of the staircase as a great lump rose up in her throat. What Antoinette said was absolutely true.

Antoinette, arriving at the top of the stairs, blinked as if suddenly realising her cousin's distress. "Whatever is the matter?" she asked. "Oh! Thea darling, you really do care, don't you?"

"Yes, I really do," Thea whispered. "I

passed the Foundling Hospital the day after it opened and I saw…" She closed her eyes as she gripped the newel post. "Near the road, some distance from the hospital, there's a basket where unwanted babies can be placed without anyone knowing. There were two mothers fighting over who would put their baby in it." The memory came back to her in all its awfulness and had to grip the bannister even more tightly to stop herself from swaying.

"But…they're just babies," Antoinette said, frowning as if she were trying to establish the real source of Thea's tender heartedness. "They just feed and cry. I'm sure they aren't…well, aware of anything else going on around them. They'd not miss their mothers for they'd never have known them."

Thea couldn't believe her cousin. "But *you* have a child who sleeps and feeds and cries. Surely you have feelings of tenderness for him?"

Antoinette appeared about to dismiss this, but suddenly she smiled. "You know, Thea, I never thought I'd grow so fond of young George. After all, his father—" She stopped abruptly and changed tangent. "I could have sworn the little mite called me mama this morning and my heart quite melted."

"I wish I could see him more but you're always out and about and never want to take me up to the nursery." Thea sniffed. "I do love babies and, it breaks my heart to think I'll never have one of my own."

Antoinette looked affronted, stepping up beside her cousin to put her hand on her shoulder. "What do you think I've been working day and night to achieve, Thea? You will find yourself a husband worthy of you. Certainly Fanny and Bertram and I fully intend that to happen. We like you too much to see you lose your looks and to moulder away as Aunt Minerva's handmaiden." She bit her lip and looked worried. "That's why time is of the essence. In a couple of years you'll be well and truly an old maid. As for babies, don't you worry about the ones you can't help and the ones you want, or my little George. He wants for nothing." She put her head on one side. "You're not suggesting I'm at fault for not being as maternal as you think I should be, are you?"

Thea fidgeted, finding it hard to look at her. "Well, the truth is that until you admitted you were beginning to like him just a little, I thought you might as well not have a baby, Antoinette, so I didn't think you understood what it feels like to so desperately want one." She shuddered as she met Antoinette's look. "I'd even suffer through all those terrible things you told me about with the right, honourably motivated, worthy husband if that's the only way to have a baby, only what man is going to take me as his wife when I have so little to offer?"

"What horrible things?" Antoinette gasped. "I told you only the good things. The horrible part is getting the baby out!"

Thea glanced around to ensure no servants were about then whispered, "I'm talking about all those horrible things about the man nearly ripping a woman in half to achieve his…his pleasure," she muttered. A wave of nausea rose up in her and she closed her eyes. Had she really spoken about such matters in a public place, much less at all?

Surprisingly, Antoinette's good humour appeared suddenly restored. She even sounded relieved. "Well, that's why I'm on hand. First of all, I can't imagine why you should think all those things I described are terrible." Raising her eyes to the ceiling, she clasped her hands together. "The truth is, the right man with the right touch can transport a woman into ecstasy. Why, if I told you—" She stopped, narrowed her eyes at Thea, then changed the subject. "So Mr Grayling's kiss was like a terrible brand of shame, was it?"

Thea looked away. "I…I knew it was wrong," she whispered as she started to make her way along the corridor towards her room. She couldn't possible confess such things in public.

"What, exactly, did you think was wrong?"

Thea stopped and turned. "The moment he put his arms around me, and then tried to kiss me, I knew I simply had to flee if I was to retain my honour and that of the family," she said in a rush.

Antoinette looked interested. "So in fact you didn't really think about what you felt when he did have his arms around you and his lips on yours, and he was kissing you? All you thought about was shame and dishonour? You know that he's told Fanny he thinks you're the most glorious creature who's ever crossed his orbit and that he just died with mortification when he realised you held him in the same aversion as his French wife did?" Antoinette sighed and looked sad. "Poor Mr Grayling, I feel so terribly sorry for him. He pretends to be such a rake but that's purely to compensate for the crushing blow to his manliness he experienced at the hands of that dreadful, unfeeling foreign wife of his."

Guilt flooded Thea at the idea of causing anyone such distress. She cleared her throat. "What was her name?"

"Whose name?"

"Mr Grayling's French wife, of course."

"Oh…um, Minette. But don't you ever mention her name, as I said, for it will shred him of any strength of character that has returned to him. Few men can suffer the humiliation dealt out by a woman, and now, just when he encounters a sweet, pure and blameless creature like you, who suddenly has given him hope for some happiness in his future, you go and kick him in the shins."

"He never used those words!" Thea gasped. Still, an unexplained excitement rippled through her. Could Mr Grayling really have been sincere in his feelings, rather than seeing her as ripe for exploitation?

"Why, didn't we tell you that was so?" A gurgle of laughter rose up in Antoinette's throat. "You're blushing, Thea! See, you do think he's a charming young man. Handsome, too, isn't he? Yes, rather rakish, which is just the way I like them, too, though I'm perfectly content with my lovely…er…companion for the moment."

"Lord Quamby?" Thea brought her hand up to her lips as she realised the horrified disbelief with which she'd imbued those words.

Antoinette was staring as if Thea had

lost her mind. "Lord Quamby is my *husband*. Of course I don't mean him, though he's utterly darling, I'll grant you that, even if he does prefer playing whist to conversing with me. He likes talking to Fanny, though. Their minds are far more attuned, however he does humour me when I talk about all the fun I'm having."

Thea decided, right then and there, that she had completely missed something vital to understanding in the conversation. Antoinette's description of marital relations was akin to describing a society that lived on some unknown planet. A man and a woman pledged utter fidelity to one another, had children, and devoted their love and attention to their offspring.

"And don't think I'm unnatural, dearest," Antoinette went on, voicing exactly what Thea was thinking right at that moment. "I'm worth my weight in gold to darling Quamby. I've provided him with an heir, and so managed to ensure he's well and truly cut out that odious, conniving, dastardly nephew of his, Mr George Bramley." She shuddered. "Now there's a villain if ever

I knew one. And he hates the Brightwells, so just let me repeat our warnings of earlier. If you ever think someone in your midst is trying to blacken your name or destroy your happiness or your reputation, Mr Bramley is the first person you should think of." She brightened once more. "Not that I think you're in any danger. You're too sweet and innocent for him to consider a threat. However, if you look like you're on the path to success, just watch your back and be very, very careful of villainous Mr George Bramley."

Thea blinked and her head reeled. Bath and the high society with whom Thea rubbed shoulders was far from the harmonious, pleasure-seeking environment she imagined as the antithesis to the dreary existence she'd been living.

Antoinette patted her arm. "So, you'll come to the name-bearing and wear what I told you? And with your new bonnet, which I think you should trim with daisies? Very fresh and fetching."

Thea nodded and Antoinette gripped her hand and pulled her back towards the stairs. "Be sure you're ready when we come by in the carriage tomorrow to fetch you and Aunt Minerva. It's going to be a very important day for all of us…I promise you! And now, let's go and visit young George in the nursery, shall we?'

TWO carriages were supposed to be on hand but as Fenton's was undergoing repairs, Thea and her aunt and all three cousins squeezed into the plush but cramped interior of the Earl of Quamby's. When Thea asked what interest Bertram had in the proceedings, he looked affronted.

"I just adore babies, like you," he said. Shifting in the tight space, he added in a contrived offhand tone but so Aunt Minerva couldn't hear, "Actually, my good friend Mr Grayling is one of those whom Lady Umbrage asked to confer their name on these unfortunates, and he called on my expertise as an uncle twice over to stand in as his second—or at least perform the duty you're rendering our worthy aunt, in providing the necessary assistance should the whole experience prove too much for one person."

"But it's just holding a baby for a few minutes," Thea said as equably as she could, wishing her thigh wasn't pressed so close to his. "What could possibly be onerous in holding a baby?" What she really was wondering was how on earth Bertram was suddenly on such friendly terms with Mr Grayling. Though she'd managed to sound offhand, the mention of Mr Grayling's name had sent tremors right through her of something she couldn't quite identify.

"Well, Mr Grayling is somewhat daunted by the prospect." He gave Thea a friendly slap on the knee, adding, "You'll show him how easy it is, though, won't you?"

"There's nothing pleasant or easy about babies." Aunt Minerva, who'd caught the last part of this, sniffed as she leaned back on Thea's other side. "Keep them in the nursery until they're at least of schooling age and can obey orders, I say."

"Yes, Aunt," said Thea, well and truly weary of having to agree with her aunt to avoid an argument. What risks would she take to be free of the yoke of servitude? An image of herself running barefoot through a field, hair streaming behind her, was suddenly appropriated by Mr Grayling chasing her and wearing a look of passionate desire. Feeling hot and bothered, she immediately tried to close down such a thought by telling herself that she'd never indulge in such freedom if it meant countenancing any of the risks Fanny and Antoinette urged her to take.

Indeed, Mr Grayling's kiss the other day had reaffirmed that.

And yet…

She touched her fingers to her lips and stared out of the window as she steeled herself to feel what she knew she ought.

No! From now on she must ever be on her guard for the tricks any of her cousins might play in order to facilitate a closer union with Mr Grayling.

The carriage drew up at the chapel on Lady Umbrage's estate where the naming ceremony was to be conducted but to Thea's dismay it appeared they were late, for the churchyard was deserted.

Hastily Thea took Bertram's extended hand and descended gracefully to the ground in the wake of her two cousins. Impatiently she waited for Aunt Minerva, who'd shuffled her bulk to the open door where Bertram was waiting to help her down, but when her aunt lost her footing on the top step, Bertram was nearly crushed as a result. Thea was fearful and horrified, expecting severe injuries, though Fanny and Antoinette looked as if they were about to explode with hilarity, even before they could be reassured that no one had come to any harm.

With Aunt Minerva declared unharmed with only her good humour dented, they all hurried into the chapel, whispering their apologies as they bustled up the aisle. Or rather, Antoinette, Fanny and Bertram trooped up through the assembled congregation while Thea slunk behind, ready to sink into the ground in the wake of her Aunt, who simply looked down her long nose at everyone else as if they were the interlopers.

Before Thea knew what was happening, she was wedged between Aunt Minerva and, oh dear God, Mr Grayling. Then the vicar was intoning something and out of nowhere, five babies, two of them squalling, wriggling bundles, were placed into the arms of Aunt Minerva, Lady Umbrage, Antoinette and another fierce-looking noblewoman whose allotted infant immediately began to wail.

It was soon joined by the infant Mr Grayling was holding with, it had to be said, commendable calm. Of all of them, Aunt Minerva seemed the most ill at ease. Thea saw the child had white-blonde hair and pale blue eyes. It was a beautiful baby, but it clearly wasn't a happy one.

A few gulps of air did nothing to calm the child and after the third gasp, it promptly regurgitated the watery contents of its stomach all down Aunt Minerva's puce velvet spencer.

With a cry of horror, her aunt nearly dropped the little creature who would have landed on the cold stone floor had Thea not leapt forward and arrested its fall. The feeling of the baby against her chest was nearly too much. She'd have liked to have held the little darling forever but dutifully she tucked its loosened swaddling cloths about its rigid little body and held it out to her aunt.

The reaction was not what Thea was expecting for Aunt Minerva stepped back, palms outwards as she hissed, "I don't want it! You hold it!"

Thea was only too glad to oblige; and indeed, the moment the child was cradled against her chest it calmed instantly. It even began to coo. Thea grinned, turning her face to find herself looking directly into—her heart hitched—Mr Grayling's beautiful eyes. His interested gaze completely robbed her of breath away and a strange curdling sensation in her lower belly was followed by an unnerving clutch between her legs—a feeling so alien to Thea, she feared that she herself might drop the poor little mite she now held. It smiled a toothless grin and gripped Thea's finger with its tiny fist, and instantly Thea felt her whole being relax as she gazed down at the little foundling who soon would have her aunt's name bestowed upon her.

Now that the infant had quietened, Aunt Minerva jabbed Thea's shoulder and reached out for it. Reluctantly Thea relinquished the child.

Silence descended upon the congregation and the vicar had just begun to speak when his words were drowned out by a tremendous squalling from Aunt Minerva's temporary charge. Clearly the cherubic creature had enormous objections to its chosen benefactress and a pair of lungs that would rival those of a bellowing bull—or Aunt Minerva when she had a bone to pick with Thea.

Thea sent a panicked look at her aunt who now jabbed Cousin Antoinette in the ribs in order to effect a hasty swap of her unsavoury charge with Antoinette's placid, dark-haired child.

"Looks like a gypsy but at least it's quiet," she muttered as she carried out the trade.

Antoinette shrugged, smiling at Thea,

who transferred her glance to Mr Grayling. His close proximity continued to send powerful tingles of awareness through her. Very strange, she thought, confused, when she'd convinced herself she never wanted to see him again.

The white-haired child in his arms was sleeping peacefully, and when Thea saw its tiny sixth finger, she nearly gasped out loud. It was the child of the woman they'd nearly run over on their way into Bath.

Shocked, she transferred her attention to the child held by the gentleman beside him, struck by its head covering of fiery copper down. Indeed, *that* was the child of the willowy, black-clad mother standing on top of the hill who'd apparently been determined that her child should occupy the foundling basket at the expense of the well-dressed child with the sixth finger.

Tears pricked at her eyelids. She'd seen these two children with their mothers at the moment of separation. She'd watched as the one broken-hearted mother, clearly from a good family, had been forced to part with her baby while the other mother had been

prepared to use whatever aggression necessary to foster out her own.

No, Thea could never do that. Give up
her infant. Oh, she understood a single
mother had no chance of supporting a baby,
though the shame of such a thing happening
to her would be enough to kill her she was
sure.

It went without saying that the proce-
dure necessary to create a babe was bad
enough but as a single young woman she
was confident there was not the remotest
possibility of anything like a child out of
wedlock happening to her.

THE NAMING CEREMONY WAS A HASTY AFFAIR.
Clearly the noble patrons were not expected
to suffer the contaminated children for
long, and after the event had been recorded
in the ministerial book, the assembled party
proceeded to the lawns outside Lady Umbrage's Queen Anne style manor where several tables beneath the trees were laden
with a selection of pies and tarts and fruit.

Aunt Minerva was overjoyed to be invited to converse with her ladyship while Fanny and Antoinette made themselves scarce, leaving Thea standing awkwardly beside a plate of strawberries.

Usually Aunt Minerva had her niece at her beck and call, so it was rare for Thea to enjoy a moment's freedom. Bertram and Mr Grayling were deep in conversation and when she caught the latter gentleman's eye, he looked away, as if he were remembering their last embarrassing encounter.

Prickles of self-consciousness stole up her bare arms and she rubbed her gloved hands together and turned to walk sedately along the gravel path towards a copse of trees nearby. She'd made a proper mull of things and she regretted everything that had happened—including her response—but, she told herself, it was best that he be under no illusions as to her character.

No, Thea was in fact *glad* that Mr Grayling knew she was not a young woman to trifle with. It was all very well for Antoinette and Fanny to say he was looking for a wife of passion after his first disappointing experience with matrimony, but Thea clearly wasn't going to answer to his needs. She was simply not the passionate type.

And she was as poor as a church mouse. Mr Grayling had no reason to be interested in her at all.

She soon lost herself amongst the trees, the voices from the invited guests carried on the breeze. It was so pleasant to be alone like this. No Aunt Minerva with her demands. No Fanny or Antoinette or Bertram with their expectations.

As the sun warmed her cheeks she took a seat on a large, dry flat rock and leaned over to stare at her reflection in the still waters of a pond surrounded by an ornamental rock garden. Fanny had gifted her one of her old gowns and Thea had recently trimmed her poke bonnet with a floral profusion of which she was rather proud. She looked well enough and supposed it was as Bertram had said; that some respectable clerk might be in a position to one day offer for her and so release her from her dreary existence with Aunt Minerva.

She shifted a little and the gold locket her aunt had lent her swung forward over the water. Fearful it might snap, Thea snatched at it, but her sudden movement was obviously too much for a weak link.

With a gasp, Thea watched helplessly as it plopped into the water.

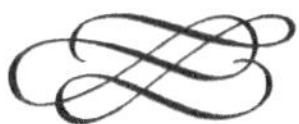

ALTHOUGH Sylvester nodded sagely as Bertram Brightwell waxed lyrical on a sure way to roll the dice in one's favour, he was having a hard time attending. Out of the corner of his eye he was acutely aware of Miss Brightwell's languid form by the refreshments table. She was alone. And as her ghastly aunt was fawning over Lady Umbrage, this was surely his moment to apologise and, he hoped, orchestrate some future tryst.

When he next craned his head around Lady Quamby's elaborate bonnet, Miss Brightwell had gone but a glimpse of white showed her on the path towards the water garden he knew was encapsulated within the copse of trees some distance away.

"Nature calls," he murmured, turning in her direction.

Bertram followed his gaze, gave a knowing look when he too saw Thea, and sighed gustily. "Only four months left to live." He put his finger to his nose and jerked his head in the aunt's direction. "I'll make sure the old termagant is occupied for the next fifteen minutes."

With a grateful nod, Sylvester set off, circumnavigating the gardens to reach the rock-strewn pond by the east side.

As he'd expected, she was waiting for him, sitting on a rock and dipping her now ungloved hand through the water. A frisson of excitement mingled with pride speared him, for after their last less-than-stellar encounter, he'd anticipated far greater resistance.

His letter must have struck just the right note with its suggestion that if she felt she could bring herself to forgive him, she only had to give him some sign. Yes, indeed a secret message or artfully constructed letter was obviously the way to communicate with greater success than trying to speak to Miss Brightwell.

The look they'd exchanged, and the fiery blush that rose to her cheeks just before she'd started across the lawn, could not have been interpreted any other way than as an oblique indication that she'd be just beyond earshot and out of sight. If the next few minutes went well he'd have to send Miss Brightwell another secret letter with regard to the masquerade ball he would be attending the following night.

Sylvester halted a few yards away to savour the vision. There she was, illuminated in a shaft of sunlight, the sweet profile of her rosy cheek angled so that if he looked a little closer he could see the slight swell above her bodice and the point at which her breasts separated. Intriguing and most lust-inducing. Especially when he considered her dampening response to his initial overtures.

Had that been a test? he wondered. Without a doubt Miss Brightwell was a shy innocent. Perhaps something had changed since he'd tried to kiss her. Was she now more cognizant of the fact she must make the most of the few short months she had left? Surely that must be it, otherwise she'd never have ventured across the gardens, alone, having just signalled to him to follow her.

The knowledge that she'd decided, after all, that she liked him enough to allow him the honour to coax her into a greater appreciates of life's pleasures nearly overwhelmed him.

But he'd be discreet. He'd pretend he'd simply come upon her by accident. That would be far kinder and more likely to elicit the outcome he desired. Of course, if the young lady knew she were dying and looking for some small measure of brightness in a dull and dreary world that otherwise revolved around that gorgon of an aunt, she'd also not want him making any sign that he knew of her impending mortality.

As he was on the point of declaring himself, a bird's call coincided with a splash and the young woman's dismayed cry.

He saw her lean over the water, put out her hand to reach for something, and in a few strides he was behind her, gripping her shoulders and pulling her back. Good Lord, what was she doing? She was about to surely tumble into the murky depths if he didn't stop her.

But he over-anticipated her stretch and, to his acute embarrassment, he actually caused her to sprawl backwards onto the gravelled path.

Stunned, she looked up at him, shading her eyes and obviously taking a moment to gather her surprise in registering that he'd made it so quickly to her side after leaving the others.

"Miss Brightwell, a thousand apologies for my clumsiness!" He knelt at her side, then finding her somehow across his lap and registering her shock, he realised he was again taking matters too far.

He quickly set her neatly and safely back on the flat rock where she'd been before and took a seat beside her. They'd get back to a position of intimacy in good time though with only fifteen minutes he needed to act fast.

"Oh, Mr Grayling, my aunt's locket has fallen into the pond." That seemed to be her primary concern and he was glad to be given the excuse to lean forward so he could put his hand on her shoulder in order to follow the direction in which she was pointing.

He could just see the shiny object lying on the dark, slimy bottom.

"Aunt Minerva will never forgive me if I go back without it." She drew in a shuddering breath. "It's too deep for me to reach it." Giving him a look as if to size him up, she added, ingenuously, "In fact, I think it's decidedly too deep for your arm to reach it, too."

She began to cry. Sylvester stared at her. Were those tears genuine tears of fear for that awful aunt's rage, or cleverly orchestrated so that Sylvester would be induced to play the gentleman?

Which of course would require him to remove his boots and breeches, even if he might possibly reach it without resorting to such drastic measures.

"What are you doing?" she squeaked when he had one boot off and the other about to follow.

Surprised, he halted. But of course, she knew nothing of men. She wasn't a schemer and her words weren't calculated to make him do what a more experienced woman might see as a shortcut to pleasure.

"Er, Miss Brightwell, I cannot bear to see you so distressed." He sounded clumsy to his own ears as he rose and tried to ameliorate the situation with a courtly bow. She was clearly not used to demonstrations of a man's willingness to please. But of course, she wasn't used to men at all. He needed to go very slowly with this one. Barefoot, he stood upon the rock a little above her. "Please allow me to render assistance in the only way I know, though it will require me to undress in order to swim down and reach it. I *think* I caught a flash of it in the light but I'm willing to plunge into the depths if it will save you from your aunt's wrath."

"But the others—"

"Bertram knows I'm here. He's keeping your aunt occupied for the time I need to… apologise to you for my deplorable behaviour the last time we met, and now you've provided me with the perfect opportunity." He lent across and reached for her hand and suddenly he really did feel the need to atone. Let him play the gentleman and let her peek as much as she wished.

He had to swallow to get the next words out for the effects of the curdling warmth he felt at the simple touch of her soft palm against his big, strong, calloused one took him completely by surprise. A great wave of tenderness enveloped him and suddenly he wanted only to hunker down, envelop her in his arms and…just hold her for now, she was so very sweet and appealing.

Instead he said, all manliness, "If you would avert your eyes, I'll do what I need to in order to retrieve your aunt's locket. We can emerge at different times to preserve modesty, naturally." Unable to stop himself, he brushed her cheek with the back of his hand.

He was not prepared for the effect this simple act had on him.

Like a charge of lightning, the softness of her skin communicated itself to his core in a great surge of feeling, and as her large, innocent eyes looked fearfully up at him, Sylvester was swept by the overwhelming desire to be her champion. A champion in far more than simply retrieving a lost locket, or indeed showing her what delights life had to offer. That seemed suddenly venal and self serving. No, he wanted to be her real knight in shining armour. "I pledge that I shan't do anything that might embarrass you, Miss Brightwell." He inched his head a little closer and could hear her short, sharp breaths. Either she was distraught about the locket or his closeness was having as intense an effect on her as it was on him.

"Would you? Fetch the locket I mean? I dare not face Aunt Minerva without it." She turned, covering her face with her hands. "Don't worry, Mr Grayling, I won't look."

Sylvester rolled his eyes as he unbuttoned his breeches, staring pointedly at her back and willing her to venture a quick glance over her shoulder as he divested himself of all his clothes. Let her look now and see what she thought so he could gauge how he might proceed.

But she stood up and walked a little distance away, staring doggedly at the shrubbery, tense as if she were terrified they'd be surprised.

"Do hurry, Mr Grayling, though I'm so sorry for the inconvenience. I'd go amongst those trees if it wouldn't expose me to the others," she added, as if she truly were concerned for his modesty. "Just tell me when you're…when it's all right to turn around."

She could turn around anytime, and the fact she obviously meant when he was good and dressed was not helpful for his sense of manliness, or what he intended over the next few weeks.

Perhaps, in view of her extreme fearfulness, icy water was just what he needed right now. Simply perusing the sweep of her neck as it met her shoulders and the anticipation he felt for running his tongue over the small beauty spot which peeped out like an enticement when he looked down her décolletage had made him hard with desire. Desire had, indeed, supplanted the gentler, protective feelings that had risen to the fore, earlier.

Taking a deep breath, he plunged into the water. It was not deep, but retrieving the locket required full immersion. Fortunately it was easy to locate and within a few moments he was back on dry land.

It was not appropriate to reveal himself, he'd decided earlier, yet surely she would want to know what a real man looked like. He knew it was vanity that he wished Miss Brightwell to observe the delineations of his chest; he wanted her to admire him as a well-made man with strengths; one who had no need of the padding some of his sex resorted to in order to be admired in their tight-fitting pantaloons.

So he waited a moment, not covering himself before crying out triumphantly, "I've got it!" as he stepped onto a flat rock just as she swung round in response to his voice.

With a cry, she clapped her hands to her mouth and swung back to look at the trees again. Sylvester grinned at her rigid back though his tone suggested embarrassment. He'd let the error appear to be Miss Brightwell's this time.

"A thousand apologies, Miss Brightwell, I hadn't meant for you to turn around just yet, only to announce that I'd been successful." He shrugged on his shirt as he spoke, wishing he could see her face.

Her voice sounded strangled. "And when you were only trying to help me. I'm mortified, as you must be, sir. I...I don't know what to say except..."

"No, I've shocked you and I understand the discomfort you must be feeling." He spoke softly as he finished dressing, moving to say over her shoulder, his lips close to her ear, "I think we must pretend it never happened."

She turned her face up to his and nodded earnestly.

"Just like the kiss," he added, his lips just brushing her cheek.

She nodded again, staring at him as if mesmerized. A kernel as large and hard as a walnut seemed lodged in his own throat.

Unable to help himself, he moved his face close to hers.

"I behaved in the most shameful manner, Miss Brightwell. I hope you can forgive me. But truly, I was overcome."

"Overcome?" she repeated, her eyes trained on his lips...which suddenly were grazing hers.

And then she was in his arms and he was cradling her for but the briefest moment before he tore himself away, setting her back on her feet as he stepped back, as if shocked.

"I don't know what I was thinking, Miss Brightwell. Please forgive me! I must go!"

Without another word, he took that path that led into the woods and soon was far from the intriguing, confusing—and, he hoped, confused and equally intrigued— Miss Brightwell while his own equilibrium was, surprisingly, more than a little ruffled.

THEA REMAINED ON THE PATH WATCHING HIS retreating back. He didn't hurry away as if he were embarrassed. He didn't scuttle away in that half-cringing manner Dr Horne had when he left a room. Instead, despite having just been observed naked by a lady, he almost sauntered. The loose swinging of his arms and his easy gait were the hallmarks of a man without a care in the world.

Oh, to have no cares would be a wonderful thing. Mr Grayling was handsome and in search of a wife. Her cousins affirmed this was so. He had a comfortable living and he was personable. And, oh my goodness but he looked utterly irresistible without his clothes on.

She nearly squeaked her shame aloud. Had she really thought that?

She tried to steer her mind to the practicalities. What else did she know of him other than that he had a chest that made her want to run her hands up and down it and rest her head against its hardness, rubbing her cheek against its fine hair?

Once again she gasped at her wicked thoughts. When had such thoughts entered her head? And what young woman of delicacy would think in such a manner? She must get her colour back before she returned.

The moment she re-joined the entertainment, Fanny and Antoinette discreetly disengaged themselves and clustered around Thea. To Thea's relief, Aunt Minerva appeared not to have even realised she had gone.

"What was it like this time?" Antoinette demanded, pulling her out of earshot so that they were alone and separated from the other guests by the broad trunk of a large elm.

Thea stared at her. Had they set this up?

"Hush, Antoinette!" Fanny dug her sister in the ribs. She smiled sweetly at Thea. "We saw you wander over to the water garden and then we observed Mr Grayling follow a few minutes later. Did he? Did he apologise for his disgraceful behaviour when I shamefully thrust the two of you together?"

"Surely he kissed you properly this time?" Antoinette interrupted before Thea could respond. "You were gone a full ten minutes and both of you know there's no time to lose."

"What do you mean, 'no time to lose'?" Thea asked faintly.

"Well, Aunt Minerva is so unpredictable you never know when she's going to get it into her head to take offence at something and decide to return to Heskett."

The churning in Thea's breast redoubled.

"So you *would* mind!" Fanny clapped her hands. "Oh Thea, you're blushing. He's made progress, then."

"Made progress?"

Antoinette made a sound of irritation as she put her hands on her hips. "Would you stop repeating everything we say and tell us what happened? Did he kiss you?"

Thea touched her lips, which burned at the memory. The sun was gently filtering through the leaves and she gazed at the lovely pattern it made on the ground at her feet as she said dreamily, "In a manner of speaking."

"Good Lord, he either did or he didn't."

Thea jerked her head up at Antoinette's sharp tone. "It was very brief and then he was apologising and then he was…gone."

Fanny patted her shoulder. "He left you wanting more? Good. You've engaged his interest and that's a very good start. Tomorrow, at Lady Clover's masquerade ball, you must reel him in even more."

Thea shook her head. "What are you saying? I can't pretend and do things I don't feel."

"Of course not!" Fanny assured her hastily while Antoinette was more robust.

"Goodness Thea, do you want to marry Mr Grayling or do you want to lose out to that insipid Miss Amelia Huntingdon, because when we're all at Lady Clover's masquerade he'll find himself obliged to dance with her, and if she's sufficiently encouraging then who knows where it'll end? You'll be left with the dregs and end up as wife to some impecunious curate or penniless clerk when you're on the wrong side of thirty and Aunt Minerva has dropped dead and left you without a penny."

"Now, now, Antoinette, that wasn't nice," her sister admonished.

Thea shook her head sadly as reality weighed her down. She turned back to look at the knots of gathered guests mingling about the gardens. "It's true, though. And Aunt Minerva said under no circumstances will we be attending any masquerades, so I'm afraid that, no, I shan't be attending Lady Clover's ball."

"Oh no, Thea, you can't miss out!" cried Fanny.

Antoinette shook her head and sighed. "That's too bad, Thea, but don't worry; we'll take care of Miss Huntingdon. I'll turn her into a frog, for I'm going as a wood sprite with magical powers. But do let me press my point, which is that it's all very well for you to weigh up the balance and the risks you're prepared to take when you know you have Aunt Minerva you can ultimately depend upon, but what if that changes tomorrow? Who knows how well or otherwise Aunt Minerva has provided for you, or if she has at all? No, Thea, you must take matters into your own hands if you are to have any security and your future is to be less bleak than it is."

Thea noticed Fanny was staring at Antoinette. Her cousin sounded aghast as she burst out, "Good Lord, I had no idea you gave a moment's thought to the consequences of your actions, Antoinette."

Antoinette shrugged. "Well, I didn't when I let my body rule my head and allowed George Bramley into my bed. Or rather, on the floor in a storeroom at Lady Milton's ball; but my body was on fire to know what it felt like. I admit, I wasn't thinking too clearly at the time. Mr Bramley had been plying me with champagne all evening."

Thea thought she was going to faint. She sent a scandalised look across at her aunt who was talking to Lady Umbrage still, then swung back to Antoinette. "Oh, Antoinette. These words are like a foreign language but I know they mean something…wicked," she murmured before she could help herself.

"Wicked? To admit to what we all feel? Even Aunt Minerva thinks such things when she thinks about Mr Granville." Antoinette's eyes danced. "I'm just more honest in describing how overcome by desire I was after Mr Bramley was so single-minded in his attentions. It was very foolish, I admit, but also very lucky and it enabled me to make a wise decision regarding my future—"

Her sister made a rude noise. "Wise decisions have had nothing to do with anything you've ever done and nothing to do with the success you've achieved. You're only too lucky that I rejected Lord Quamby who then realised you were," she put her head closer and whispered accusingly, "carrying his nephew's child. That's right. Admit it to Thea so she knows exactly what dangerous game you played and how it ran in your favour."

Thea's mouth dropped open as she glanced about her to ensure they were alone. *These* were her cousins? Her own flesh and blood?

Fanny took a deep breath and sent Thea a knowing look. "The truth is," she said more calmly now as she plucked a leaf from an overhanging branch, "that Antoinette has always been a feather-brained peagoose and she got herself into trouble with Mr Horrible George Bramley who was out to ruin her because I rejected him the previous summer. Revenge was his game, and Antoinette played right into his hands. My sister, who only outranks me now due to my orchestrating matters to the advantage of *both* of us, might well have found *herself* having to put her bastard child in the basket at the Foundling Hospital. The fact that she wasn't forced to is due simply to Lord Quamby seeing Antoinette's pregnancy with his hated nephew's child as a wonderful opportunity to secure the family line and produce an heir without having to actually bed a woman."

Thea blinked a couple of times. "Can this be true?" She swallowed, her mouth dry as she put out her hand to steady herself against the tree trunk. She stared at Antoinette. "Are you telling me that you and Lord Quamby—?"

"Well, we're not man and wife in the Biblical sense, if that's what you mean," Antoinette interrupted brightly, idly toying with the enormous glittering diamond on her finger. "He's been very generous, so naturally I'm very fond of him, but our marriage is for convenience only." She glanced up and fixed Thea with a meaningful look. "Lord Quamby has some unusual preferences, leaving me to enjoy my...dalliances." She tossed her head on a tinkling laugh. "Oh, Thea! I can't tell you what fun I've had. Men come in all shapes and varieties and some look at me with moon eyes but then are completely selfish in bed, and then others are more shy and it's a surprise that they know how to set a woman's senses on fire!"

Even Fanny looked a little shocked at this. She cleared her throat. "I'd like to point out, Thea, that my only experience is with Lord Fenton and I chose well, but I also knew what I was getting myself into, and I will admit that I had to use a little cunning. I was nothing like Antoinette who threw caution to the wind. I needed to ascertain if I really did want to spend the rest of my life in Fenton's arms and once I *was* sure the skilful part was making him realise the same, and to ensure he overlooked the fact I was just a penniless debutante full of hopes and aspirations."

"You see, Thea," Antoinette went on, not

seeming to care that her sister had been so uncomplimentary, "you could wake up and find yourself in quite a hole. Suddenly you don't have Aunt Minerva's support and the only person knocking on your door is..." She floundered for inspiration. "Dr Horne. He's a widower whom I've no doubt would love a pretty wife. He'll offer you the comfort of his home and make sure you have nice clothes to wear. The trouble is, he'll want a lot in return. He'll be climbing over you every night, pushing his thing into you whether you're ready or not. You'll start having his babies and they'll be ugly, puling creatures with thin sandy hair and lashes and red screwed-up faces. Every year you'll have another one because Dr Horne has twenty years of being a widow to make up for and he'll be so desperate and so proud now of having a young and pretty wife."

"Don't!" Thea put her hands to her ears. "How can you say such things to me?"

Fanny gripped Thea's wrists to force her hands away as she added, almost fiercely, "Because it's the truth, Thea." Glancing at Lady Umbrage's party of guests who were beginning to depart, she said, more softly, "You're a debutante who knows nothing of the true ways of the world, but you *need* to know and understand what we're saying if you're to seize the opportunities presented to you."

"Surely, Thea, you liked it just a little bit when Mt Grayling kissed you?" Antoinette's eyes flashed with challenge and curiosity and Thea again put her hand to her lips. Her body felt weak and needy all of a sudden and that strange, desperate pulling feeling between her legs was happening to her again.

"Oh, you do!" Antoinette cried happily. She put her head closer and said in conspiratorial tones, "Well, just you remember how you feel when Mr Grayling pays you attention, and compare that with how you might feel if Dr Horne would have you do for him those same things, which is exactly what he'd do—and more—if he made you his wife. It's one thing to reel in a man but you want to make sure he's the right one when your future happiness depends upon it."

CHAPTER 13

THE moment Aunt Minerva stepped into Lord Quamby's drawing room she turned a beaming countenance towards Thea who was chatting with her cousins and, with ample bosom heaving, demanded, "And who shall you be masquerading as, my dear? I hope you've given due consideration to the matter for I shall be mightily put out if you're not ready when the carriage is due to leave."

Her three nieces were struck dumb for a moment. Aunt Minerva was positively glowing.

"I...thought we weren't going to any masquerades, Aunt Minerva?" Thea fingered the locket at her neck while her thoughts wildly traversed the possibilities now opened up to her, and which surrounded the saviour of the article at her neck.

"It is true I said that…" Aunt Minerva twirled a lock of squirrel's tail about her finger and looked coquettish as she settled her bulk into an armchair by the small fire, which she'd again demanded despite the warm weather. "However, it appears a certain gentleman wishes for my company."

Thea and her cousins exchanged a look, which Thea immediately hoped had not been observed by her aunt. Fortunately Aunt Minerva was gazing at the intricate plasterwork on the ceiling, which Thea noticed now appeared to be a myriad of entwined cherubic-looking creatures. They reminded her of the wee babe she'd held the previous afternoon and to her utter astonishment her body exploded into longing, not divorced from a desire to be similarly entwined in Mr Grayling's embrace.

Good Lord, where had that come from?

Swallowing, she whispered, "I haven't given a thought to my costume, aunt."

Both Fanny and Antoinette cried out in unison, "Oh, but I have just the thing for you, Thea!"

And within moments the girls were hastening her upstairs, trying to contain themselves before all but bursting their seams upon the large four-poster in Fanny's bedchamber.

"A gentleman wishes for my company," Antoinette mimicked, leaping to her feet and sticking her chin in the air as she paraded about the room with the customary air of self-importance Aunt Minerva adopted.

She swung round to face the girls. "Who do you suppose this gentleman could be? Surely not the gentleman who rejected her a lifetime ago."

"Mr Granville?" Thea frowned. "In fact, I do believe she's got it into her head that he's come to see the error of his ways and is about to throw himself upon her and beg forgiveness."

"Then if that's the case, do you suppose

she wishes to reject him or to graciously hold him to her bosom?" asked Fanny.

"And crush the air out of him."

Fanny and Antoinette looked at Thea who'd spoken, and suddenly burst out laughing. "Why, Thea, I didn't know you had it in you to make a joke like that," cried Fanny.

"Or to be so irreverent about the woman who has granted you such kindness and generosity; a home and everything else you could possibly want to sustain you," added Antoinette.

After some more shared hilarity, Thea who was now half lying on the bed while her cousins lounged in two chairs by the window, said with crinkled brow, "I think Aunt Minerva has reached a time in life where she wants to know that someone— perhaps some man—does feel something for her." She was serious now. "I mean, she's never been a beauty. She was brought up without brothers and sisters and she must have felt it keenly when, despite her fortune, no man offered for her."

"Well, she would have you believe otherwise, though I don't believe it, and that's because she's sharp tongued and selfish and it's immediately apparent she'd want her way in everything," declared Fanny. "She has only herself to blame."

Thea shrugged and Antoinette said roundly, "Oh, Cousin Thea, don't be so tender-hearted or spend a moment thinking about Aunt Minerva when it's yourself you should be looking at how to protect. Now here, I was going to wear it myself but it'll be just the thing for you." She'd jumped up and withdrawn something from her wardrobe. "Isn't it alluring?"

"Lord no, Antoinete!" Fanny squeaked as she stared at the revealing piece of silk and feathers her sister held up. "Do you want Thea to gain a reputation for being fast and loose?"

"No, that's only the way I'm supposed to pretend to act." Thea blushed as she met with defiance her cousins' shocked looks. "Clearly I'm supposed to appear demure but behave in quite an altogether different way."

Fanny nodded admiringly as she also stood up and withdrew something from the trunk at the end of the bed. "That's exactly right, Thea. And now here is what I propose you should wear in order to strike just that well-balanced note."

So Antoinette did wear her daring little ensemble and Thea trembled to think her cousin had thought it suitable for *her*. Beneath Antoinette's dark satin cloak lined in scarlet, she wore…

Thea died a little death inside. What if the breeze was to flap it open causing the whole assembly to see the tiny sparkles that covered Antoinette's nipples? As for the rest of her, only a tiny white swansdown triangle nestled at the juncture of her legs.

Even Fanny had been scandalised.

"You are *not* wearing that!" she'd raged, but Antoinette had been unmoved. "No one shall know except the man who is answered in the affirmative when he asks what everyone asks at a masquerade: 'Do I know you?'"

Now, as the music grew louder as they

proceeded up the steps of the grand venue for that night's entertainment, she touched Thea's arm. "Fanny was right," she conceded. "You make a very lovely milkmaid. Your innocence is like a halo and a lot of men are attracted to that. Not the ones I like, though."

"Indeed, Lord Quamby—" Thea began before realising her mistake.

Antoinette gurgled, "Oh, silly girl. No, I've the loveliest gentleman I met last week with whom I have a secret assignation, so I'm afraid Fanny will have to keep you in check." She levelled a mock-severe look at Thea then giggled as they were ushered through the front door. "Oh, do make sure you have fun, Thea. If you don't, it won't be our fault."

And then suddenly she was gone, swallowed up by the crowd, while Fanny and Thea, flanked by Lord Fenton and Aunt Minerva, made their regal entrance; meanwhile Bertram, who'd arrived having greased himself with more than a thimbleful, stumbled in their wake.

"You will promise me a dance, Cousin

Thea?" Lord Fenton asked. Thea recognised the kindness in his voice, which was in such contrast to the slavering longing Thea saw in his eyes when he beheld his wife.

And Fanny had only just had a baby. They'd been married a year and he still looked at her like that. Thea's legs felt wobbly just thinking about being married to such a handsome man who looked at *her* like that.

The ballroom was already well populated by the time they elbowed their way into the centre of the room. Aunt Minerva, dressed in black with a sweeping white ostrich feather in her white toque, cut quite a dramatic figure. In fact, Thea had never seen her look so imposing. And the glint in her eyes was something she'd never seen before. For once her aunt carried herself like a sashaying coquette, her chin raised and her glance expectant as she scanned the room.

Looking, no doubt, for a handsome elderly gentleman with greying hair and a monocle: Mr Granville, the rejected suitor whose heart she'd supposedly broken.

"How will he know you, Aunt, if you're

wearing a masque?" Thea had asked, but her aunt had told her not to be stupid.

"He said I must give him a sign," she'd said.

"A sign?"

"He wrote another letter. Now please don't be so impertinent as to quiz me further." Dismissing Thea with a wave of her hand, Aunt Minerva scanned the crowd. "I'm sure Fanny needs you more than I do, my dear. I can look after myself perfectly well."

Fanny and Thea exchanged looks at that and Fanny quickly took her wrist and pulled her away. "Now you must make sure you and Aunt Minerva don't cross paths again, for I can tell that the moment your aunt finds herself disappointed she'll need you to bolster her sense of superiority."

Obediently, Thea followed Fanny through the throng, which parted to let them by, many of them, Thea noticed, looking more than interested at the unusual contrast they made, for Fanny was dressed as an exotic creature from the orient, in voluminous orange chiffon pantaloons with matching tunic, her dark hair cascading down her back.

"I believe I'm quite scandalising everyone here but you'll be my foil. Oh look, here's someone who wants to pay their respects. Good evening, Mr Bramley." Fanny nodded and fluttered her eyelashes. "Goodness, how original, you must be the tenth domino I've seen tonight."

"I am here to observe, which is what dominoes do." The young man looked haughty and as if he wished to pass on by, but was compelled to remain. "You cut a daring figure as ever, Lady Fenton."

"I do, don't I, Mr Bramley?" Fanny simpered and Thea was struck by the artificial merriness of her reception. "We haven't seen you in a while. Lord Quamby was saying it just the other day. But I'm very much looking forward to seeing you at the christening of Lord Quamby's heir. Little George is a fine, robust little chap, like my Katherine. I'm sure you're dying to see the babies."

"Simply dying to, yes, Lady Fenton."

Thea stared. Good Lord, were those

beads of sweat that had popped out on his forehead? Remembering what the cousins had told her, she felt Fanny was treading a fine line with her taunting. She tugged at her sleeve to go and Fanny relinquished the fun she was having and nodded in dismissal.

"Have a pleasant evening, Mr Bramley. Miss Huntingdon is here, I noticed. I'm sure she'd be only too happy to be asked to dance.

"Oh, she's already danced two sets with Mr Grayling. I don't think I'll get a look-in." Pushing his chin into the air, he bowed and left while Fanny turned to reassure Thea.

"He said it on purpose." Fanny looked severe.

"What?"

"No doubt he's pretending he knows Mr Grayling thinks you utterly the most charming young lady in Bath. Yes, that's it. Mr Bramley is very stupid in some ways but he's clever when it comes to discovering a person's weak spot. Just remember that. You mightn't know him very well but he's a very dangerous enemy."

The trouble was, when they arrived at

the edge of the dance floor, Mr Grayling was indeed accompanying Miss Huntingdon in a Scottish reel. Thea could tell it was Miss Huntingdon by the colour of her hair and the shape of her face, together with the too-slender frame, despite the fact they were a blur as they galloped by in the midst of the energetic dance.

The fact it was Mr Grayling was only too apparent by the bare chest she saw beneath the snowy sheath of linen, a ripped pirate's shirt with a cutlass at his waist and a pair of tightly moulded black pantaloons that buttoned at the knee and brought back memories of her stolen glimpse of him by the pond. She squeezed her eyes shut and clenched her fists.

"Don't wear your heart on your sleeve," Fanny whispered. "Let him still think you're a challenge."

"I am still a challenge!" Thea responded, affronted that Fanny should think she'd roll over as clearly Antoinette believed she ought. "But he mightn't even know me in masquerade."

"Oh, I think he will."

The words were barely out of Fanny's mouth before Mr Grayling materialized in front of them as the music came to an end. Yet, instead of bowing before her, it appeared he'd not even noticed her for he quickly disappeared into the crowd.

"Don't you let that trouble you when Miss Huntingdon is right here. Besides, he'll want to see you alone," Fanny said, patting her shoulder and leading the way through the large ballroom and into another room, where several tables against the far wall were occupied by revellers deeply occupied by the cards and dice.

A couple was dancing close in each other's arms in a distant corner and Thea stepped back, the scene too louche for her. If Aunt Minerva were to witness such scenes at Lady Clover's masquerade, she'd whisk her niece out as quickly as she'd whisked away the bonbons Dr Horne had surprisingly delivered by proxy the night before.

"Why, there's Mr Granville," Thea said suddenly, pointing to one of the whist players. He was at a table with several other gentlemen and it was clear it was he, despite the fact he wore Oriental robes and a masque that covered half his face.

"He had a box of bonbons sent to Aunt Minerva last night. You'd already gone to bed, Fanny, but she was in transports."

Fanny's look of scepticism did not need to be translated into words.

"Who'd believe that Aunt Minerva has an admirer," Thea persisted. "The last couple of days, I keep catching her in the drawing room as if play-acting the role of some lovelorn romantic heroine, staring through the window as she sweeps her hand across her brow muttering verse. I'd laugh if the sight wasn't so truly tragic."

"You can't mean it!"

"On my honour. Oh! Look, it's Mr Grayling again. Only this time he's looking directly at us."

"At *you*, Thea. Oh my, that's an invitation to ask the question that must be asked. I do love masquerades." Fanny gave her a gentle push. "*Do I know you?*" she whispered. "Those are the magic words. Go over and say them."

"Alone?" Thea squeaked, resisting as she followed her cousin towards the saloon, where most guests were mingling. Beneath the chandeliers of many thousands of beeswax candles the brightly garbed revellers looked like precious jewels amidst the ranks of the mysterious, black-clad dominoes. The thought of entering their ranks was terrifying.

Her cousin sounded impatient. "Shall I find Aunt Minerva, then? If she's really smelling of April and May instead of that ghastly violet scent she drips all over her, you may well find yourself looking for a new home?" Fanny looked severe. "It's time you looked to your future, Thea. Weigh up what's in your heart and what you can do to garner the response you'd like from your charming Mr Grayling. He really is very charming, you know. Why, he helped me rewind a whole ball of yarn the other night when Aunt Minerva had you closeted in her room rubbing her feet. The poor man thought you didn't want to see him, for you went straight to bed and didn't even come down to say goodnight. You're a faithful nurse, I grant you that. And if you can suffer yourself to massage smelly unguents into smelly feet, surely you can push down your aversion to some of the things men like to do when they have a woman to call their own."

"But that's for after marriage," Thea hissed. Tears came suddenly to the fore, swelling her throat and stinging her eyes. "I cannot compromise my reputation for an uncertain future. I will not be like that poor woman who had to give up her baby in the basket."

"Oh Good Lord, have you learned nothing? That only happens when passion completely overtakes one, and that's not going to happen under this roof with all these people around." Fanny reddened suddenly and stopped abruptly. "Well, it *could* happen here," she amended, clearing her throat. "I'll admit it happened to me and Lord Fenton in a pit of cushions during one of Lord Quamby's balls, but that's when we knew we were utterly made for one another, even though others like to infer I was simply a fortune hunter because we Brightwells are not in general blessed with papas who know how to keep their fortunes."

She gave Thea another little push. "Now weave your way through the room, Thea, and pretend you have no idea who he is. Your very rigid sense of propriety reassures me that you'll not be tempted into doing anything that might result in a baby in a basket. Antoinette has already told you in graphic detail how that happens and you were quite revolted, but if you could just let him kiss you, I think you might find matters progress rather nicely from there. He's the ideal catch, Thea, and he clearly has his sights trained on you. Show him that you'll give him the loving kindness his first wife so cruelly denied him, at least. Here." Snatching a coupe of champagne from a passing footman, which she pushed into Thea's hand, Fanny left her.

Reluctantly, but with every attempt at appearing at ease, Thea wove her way through the sparsely populated room and into the antechamber just beyond, where Mr Grayling had disappeared after leveling a very knowing look at Thea.

Its smaller size made it less daunting, while the heavy festooning of gold and black satin and guttering wax candles added to the atmosphere.

Mr Grayling was just inside, near the fireplace, pacing, but he turned immediately when he saw her and, after a sweeping bow, whispered, *"Do I know you?"*

Thea tossed back her glass of champagne in just a few sips, and suddenly found the glass whisked from her fingers as, swaying, she replied, "I am the one."

"You are the one?" He quirked an eyebrow and chuckled.

"I mean, yes, you do know me." What had she said? Mortification made her turn her head away.

"Well, my dear, if we've been safely introduced and you clearly are the one, let us take a stroll through his lordship's long gallery." He pointed upstairs. "We can look down upon the guests tonight. I think you might find it diverting sport, while I'd be most diverted to see your reaction to some of these outrageous costumes."

Thea's fears dropped away. Fanny had all

but suggested he'd drag her into another room and try to kiss her but here he was, suggesting something public he thought might entertain her.

"That's if your aunt won't require you and send out a search party or make a loud announcement."

Thea giggled. "My aunt is occupied with her own amours tonight."

"Good God!"

She clapped her hand over her mouth to see his genuine shock, nearly extending her other hand to clasp his shoulder in a gesture of overt familiarity as she might do to one of her cousins. Putting her state of unusual relaxation in his company to too much champagne, she nodded. A public promenade would be far safer than anything she'd feared. Not that she'd intended doing anything that might get her into trouble.

Caging her hand on his arm, he ascended the stairs with her, his body close. Very close. When she raised her head in inquiry as they rounded a bend in the staircase, his hand suddenly clasped her waist. "I thought you were going to bump against the newel post."

Thea was acutely sensitive to his touch. His hand covering hers, the touch of his thigh, were things no one else could see or remark upon, but to her, such a physical connection was entirely foreign to her.

And she liked it. The strange warmth and feeling of companionship with the man beside her was enveloping her like a cosy glove.

She looked up at him and smiled and he, looking down, caught her expression and seemed surprised by it. Then a small smile tugged at the corners of his mouth.

"What a comely milkmaid you make. The perfect picture of innocence."

She noticed he looked sad all of a sudden, then clasping both her hands in his, he suddenly whisked her up the last two stairs and behind a large roman bust at the back of the gallery, where there was little chance of being observed.

There was no warning, no request or lead-up. Nothing to prepare her for suddenly finding herself enveloped in his arms, the warmth of his embrace pushing up from the tips of her toes to flood her entire body, so that her lips naturally parted to receive his kiss while her whole body responded with a great wash of feeling. Weak and suddenly needy, her knees buckled as he supported her in his arms while his kiss deepened, his tongue seeking hers.

Her responses seemed taken to a new level. The languor was replaced by a deeper awareness, her palms tingled and the back of her neck prickled; her breasts were suddenly sensitive, as if they were crying out to be touched, and Thea pressed herself against him even more as she greedily took everything he was offering.

It was he who broke away, looking down at her with a slight crease between his brows.

"Oh, you didn't like it?" she burst out before she could think of what one should say in such an instance.

"Good Lord, it was the best kiss I've ever enjoyed." Cupping her face, he looked into her eyes. "What a delightful experience, Miss Brightwell. I had so hoped you'd come tonight, for it had come to my ears recently that masquerades were not something your aunt thought proper."

"Oh, now that my aunt has suddenly found herself an admirer she's not keeping an eye out for me at all."

She realised how much like a schoolroom miss she sounded.

But he seemed charmed. "Not keeping an eye out for you, eh?" He rubbed his chin. "I was going to take you downstairs now, but perhaps..." With a nod, he indicated a decoupage screen in the corner. "We're a trifle exposed here and I rather fancy trying another variation on our ...delightful kiss. Would you care to risk it? Remember, I am a conscienceless pirate and you are a young lady with your reputation to uphold. It would be very dangerous, which is perhaps why I ought to take you downstairs now."

"Oh, do let's try it again." Impulsively, Thea took his hand and pulled him towards the screen. "Just another quick kiss. We've already done it once so doing it again can't make me any worse."

He looked amused. "That's one way of

looking at it, though repeating something does of course increase the risk of being caught."

"There's no one nearby and we'd hear if they approached for there are three very squeaky treads on the stairs."

"What a clever girl you are to notice that."

"That's because I'm always creeping around at home, hoping Aunt Minerva won't hear me because then she'll immediately get it into her head that she wants me to do something."

"That must be very tiresome."

"I'm used to it. The doctor says—" She broke off suddenly. She didn't want to talk about Dr Horne and his long lectures about what she must do to facilitate her aunt's ease in order to extend her life.

Mr Grayling gripped her hand. "You mustn't think about what the doctor says. Life is too short as it is. Let's make the most of what's left, shall we, for I'm quite simply dying to kiss you again."

And Thea was quite dying for him to run his hands over her body, which she discovered was a riot of sensation craving attention. She arched against him and although he'd begun in the most gentlemanly manner, holding her waist and her hand, no gentleman could have mistaken her ardour. She didn't care. The champagne had gone to her head and the night was just perfect for romance. Let her dalliance in Bath be something to remember her whole life. She didn't want to be like Aunt Minerva, who had only bitter memories of what might have been. Thea doubted Aunt Minerva had ever been kissed in her life.

But this was wonderful. She drew in a shaking breath as his hands strayed to her bodice; and her mind, which she'd imagined would revolt at the prospect, now screamed silently for his touch and the caress of her naked skin.

Sprawled in a chair at one of the card tables, Bertram watched Thea disappear up the stairs with Mr Grayling and gave a great sigh of satisfaction.

Oh, but if there ever was a man to effect a triumphant outcome when all other avenues were set to fail, I am he, he thought as he toyed with the buttons of his checked waistcoat and considered his cards.

His companion, the odious George Bramley, picked up from the pile while Bertram grinned at his own modest hand. No matter, he had a rare ability to turn the tables and Mr Bramley was in his cups—unlike Bertram who was keeping a very cool head, if he said so himself.

"You're looking mighty smug," his companion remarked with a sniff.

Bertram glanced at George. "And come to think of it, you've been mighty long in the mouth all evening."

George harrumphed. "Your sister reminded me that my attendance is required at the christening of my so-called nephew." His lip twitched and he glowered at Bertram as he muttered, "My uncle's bastard, that is—and as you well know."

"Come, come, all's fair in love and war. You were hell-bent on ruining my sister. Ruining all of us Brightwells, if the truth be told," Bertram said equably. "I don't know why you're here playing cards with me, come to think of it."

"I always win, that's why," George muttered, leaning back. "At cards, that is. And you always think this time it'll be different. But don't you worry, I'll not only win this game, I'll wreak my revenge on you and your upstart clan. Now, match that."

Bertram groaned as he conceded the point, placing face upwards his inferior five. To make himself feel better he sniffed and added, "My sisters have already run rings around you, and I'm not so silly either." George Bramley was insufferable with his misplaced sense of superiority. The man had never got over being rejected by Bertram's sister, Fanny, and then cuckolded —if that was the right term—by Antoinette.

So Bertram puffed up his chest and tried to keep his mouth shut but the desire to beat his own drum was too great. Of course he should keep mum. The less George knew, the better. Bertram was astute enough to know that. But all it needed was George to say, with a singularly interested look, "Well, spit it out Mr Bertram Brightwell, who is apparently so clever. I can't imagine you've ever been clever in your life. In fact, I can't imagine how your sisters put up with you, to tell the truth."

No, Bertram just couldn't resist giving just a hint of his cleverness, even though he knew as he spoke the words he should be biting off his tongue instead. "Oh, I'm devilishly appealing in my own appalling way, is what my sisters tell me when they're not berating me or beating me over the head with a slipper. That's exactly what Antoinette did only last night when she learned how clever I've been." He cleared his throat and ordered his features as common sense returned. "Anyway," he added resolutely, "I can't say more because to tell you would not be very clever at all."

"I can't tell if you've been clever unless I know what you've done that may or may not warrant the term 'clever'."

Bertram considered this with a frown. "True, true." But of course he couldn't tell George. Not their arch enemy, though of course George would have no interest in innocent little Thea who wouldn't say boo to a goose, and Bertram knew George reserved his spleen for those who'd directly opposed or bested him.

Inside, Bertram glowed at the way his plan was taking place. The problem with devilishly cunning schemes, though, was that success usually relied on keeping them secret.

But just a hint might be enough to win George's interest and regard; get his brain working and wondering…

"It's just a little matchmaking matter I've orchestrated. Nothing you'd be interested in." Bertram leaned forward and began to shuffle the pack, hoping on the one hand George would persist with his questioning so he could be elusive and thereby irritate his opponent, while on the other hoping he'd not inspire Bertram to any kind of further discovery.

"Arranging the futures of baby George and Katherine already?" George asked sourly. "Or your own? Lord knows, there's not a young lady in the whole of England who'd take on a reprobate without a single redeeming feature, I don't imagine."

"What, me?" Bertram enquired, offended. "Good Lord that's rich, coming from the blackguard who seduced my sister as revenge for the other one rejecting him."

"Is that what they told you!" George straightened in indignation before relaxing again, adding, "I shan't dignify that with a comment." He sighed, knocked back the last of his drink then fixed George with a baleful stare. "You know, Brightwell, you and I are both beyond the pale. Untouchable as far as the fairer sex is concerned."

"Speak for yourself, Bramley."

"I haven't seen you sneak up the back stairs with some tidy little piece to make love to behind some Roman plinth like Grayling, the old wolf." George's sourness had not abated. "Only if you pulled off such a feat would I hold you in any esteem whatsoever. I can't imagine how Grayling managed it, unless he's with one of your sisters. Certainly no one but a Brightwell would be bold enough to risk her reputation like that."

"Or someone who's dying."

George's bulbous eyes grew larger above his thick nose. "You've had too much to drink, old chap. You're not making sense."

Bertram tried to hold his tongue but even focusing on a very luscious redhead who was, he was certain, sending him speaking looks from the doorway couldn't still the words that rose to his lips.

And when the redhead tittered and blew a kiss at a puffed up popinjay who happened to be standing behind Bertram, those words came tumbling out.

"I say that if someone was told a person was dying, or they *believed* they were dying, who knows what risks they'd be prepared to take?" Bertram tried not to look so self-satisfied, fearing the depth of George's inevitable interest. He wanted to be questioned only enough to be admired. After that, he'd close his mouth.

"Grayling is dying? Where have you heard this?"

"No, the young lady Grayling is with is dying."

"Good God, are you plotting murder

now, Brightwell? How will that aid your cause? Why, you're stupider than I'd thought."

"I am not stupid!" Bertram jerked forward angrily, scattering his hand and causing he redhead to jerk her head up in alarm before she took the arm of her padded dandelion and swept from the room. Bertram felt doubly riled. "I told Grayling the young lady in question was dying. I said it would be a kindness to show her what pleasure she'd be missing out on if she was destined for her deathbed in the next six months."

George looked as if he failed to understand Bertram's reasoning. "Good Lord! But if she's a young lady worth her salt, she won't let him near her with a barge pole."

Now it was time for Bertram to appear enigmatic. "She will if she believes he's looking for a wife with a bit more fire than his first and she has not a penny to fly with."

"Grayling's been married before?"

"Lord, now look who's being stupid. I don't know if Grayling's been married before. What's important is that he thinks she's dying and she thinks he's after a wife—one who's prepared to go the distance." Bertram pointed up at the long gallery above them where a distinct gasp was borne to their listening ears in a sudden moment of quiet from the orchestra.

He looked challengingly at George. "Why don't you go up and disturb them? Take an audience with you and then he'll be obliged to marry her."

"Who's the girl?"

"Lord, I'm not telling you that." George leant back, his hands laced over his stomach as he grinned at George, watching the fellow's mobile ugly face and feeling as if he'd scored a great victory. It was good to know that once again that odious villain George Bramley had been bested.

With growing satisfaction Bertram watched the surprise on George's face turn to prurient understanding before George chuckled.

Ha! Bertram felt very clever indeed as he faced his arch enemy over the ruins of the card table but it was he who was going to have the last laugh as another Brightwell scored a magnificent marital coup.

And to think that George Bramley believed he was so much cleverer than all of them put together.

CHAPTER 14

PERHAPS I'll wear the pink and grey waistcoat after all, Nesbitt." Sylvester stared critically in the looking glass before turning to gaze out of the window while his valet fetched the garment. The grey cobbled street below was wet with rain while a tenacious sun tried to penetrate the thick cloud.

Like Sylvester's mood, the day had switched between dismal and full of expectation. The sweet kisses the adorable Miss Brightwell had showered upon him during their several stolen moments in the Long Gallery had been deeply addictive; their time together too short.

"And, I think, my diamond cufflinks. Ah, thank you." He took the neck cloth held out to him then deftly executed a Mathematical Tie which he'd recently adopted in preference to the more severe Oriental.

The last thing Miss Brightwell needed was severity. He wanted her to regard him in a gentle, welcoming light.

He also wished to be immaculately turned out today, and not just for the benefit of the ladies Quamby and Fenton, the christening of whose delightful little cherubs he was attending.

He paused a moment as he contemplated the past couple of days. It was rare he'd kissed a woman and come back wanting more to such a degree. The contact had been brief, chaste even, but the memory of the smooth, soft cheek he'd cupped and the brush of her chestnut curls across his own jawline was incendiary.

He wanted her with an intensity he found hard to fathom. She was enchanting.

But she was also dying.

The thought gave him a jolt of real dismay.

Dying. He shuddered. He didn't want her to die. Nor did he want to feel pity for her. No, he wanted her like a real woman, to share his life and his bed.

As he fastened on his cufflinks he paused. Had he really thought that? He wanted her as his wife?

Why, that was impossible. Miss Brightwell was dying and Sylvester was required to focus his attention on the living; on choosing a suitable bride of impeccable lineage with at least an adequate dowry.

Unlike the very suitable and clearly enthusiastic Miss Huntingdon, Miss Brightwell had neither.

"Thank you, Nesbitt. How do I look?"

"Like a man on outfitted for success."

Sylvester grinned at the ironic smile his loyal retainer had flashed at him as he rose from his bow, then turned towards the door with a final glance outside.

The sun had succeeded in burning a hole through the cloud and he was struck by the parallel with Miss Brightwell's bold attempts to seize life and love. To be so full of both at this moment but to know death was imminent. Lord but she was brave. And he deserved to make her final months or weeks of good health ones she'd remember until the very end.

The chapel on the Earl of Quamby's estate was full when he arrived, and he took a seat in a pew near the back, his attention fully on alert when he saw Miss Brightwell enter in the wake of her cousins and take up position as godmother to the baby George. Lord Quamby looked smug and patted his wife's arm a number of times as he appeared to congratulate her, though he noticed the earl's cousin, Mr George Bramley, who was godfather, seemed particularly out of sorts today as he glowered in the background.

A surprising choice of godmother, he reflected, considering Lady Quamby must know of the girl's imminent demise. Though perhaps it was her final kindness.

Across the sea of heads he caught Miss Brightwell's eye and smiled. Yes, the kisses that had fired him up in the long gallery had made him desperate to take matters to the next level.

The problem of course was the lack of freedom Miss Brightwell was granted by her aunt. If he could only find some means of dealing with the old termagant.

After the service, parents and godparents moved outside with their offspring while members of the congregation milled around, offering their congratulations.

Sylvester seized his chance when Miss Brightwell was beside Lady Quamby whose placid baby was garnering such attention. He was about to address the countess when Lady Quamby handed over her child, and now the recipient of everyone's good wishes was in the arms of the very woman he wished to speak to. He'd be able to get close without causing undue interest, for he certainly had no wish to be seen dangling after the girl he knew desired—so sweetly and innocently—to know the pleasures of seduction before her world ended.

And with mixed feelings, he was ready to cater to her desires. Her family sanctioned such intimacies; indeed, Bertram Brightwell had made this very clear in a brief and subtle conversation they'd shared not two minutes' before, out on the path by the rose garden.

And subtlety was what was required. For the sake of Miss Brightwell's reputation, Sylvester would let the world think his sights were set on Miss Huntingdon.

Sadly, he felt it inevitable that he was set on a path to marrying Miss Huntingdon. The fact was, however, that his heart was wholly engaged by Miss Brightwell.

Sylvester gazed at the dark-haired little mite who was squirming in Miss Brightwell's arms. Its cross little mouth was pursed until it seemed almost to split open, suddenly ejecting a spatter of regurgitated milk upon Miss Brightwell's shoulder. To his surprise, the girl laughed while her cousin, the child's mother, simply screwed her face up in disgust and turned to speak to a red-haired young man.

Sylvester was about to make some trite remark about infants and to sympathise, but Miss Brightwell's expression stayed him. Miss Brightwell had put her cheek to that of the cherubic child, closing her eyes and smiling to soothe it, and in that instant a strange thing happened to Sylvester's heart. He could almost picture himself in a situation of domestic bliss with the mother of his child gazing upon their joint creation with similar adoration.

Sylvester had had little to do with children but his own upbringing had been devoid of parental affection. The pater and mater were both fond enough of him in their own way, but a succession of nurses and nannies had supplied all his needs and his parents were somewhat superfluous and distant personages who made polite enquiries over matters that were of mutual interest, like horse racing and hounds in his father's case, and town gossip in his mother's.

To see Miss Brightwell so obviously enamoured with another woman's child was extraordinary; to witness such genuine maternal sentiment, yet to know, also, she would never experience the joy of her own children was suddenly extraordinarily poignant.

"What a picture of bliss, Miss Brightwell," he murmured. "I suspect this won't be the last time you'll be offering your services to hold Lady Quamby's beautiful baby."

Miss Brightwell blushed delightfully and his gaze was drawn to her pretty pink lips, whose softness he remembered so well. In contrast came the memory of the thrilling tautness of her nipples when his hands strayed beneath her bodice. Perhaps she remembered it too, for she reddened even further as a look of acute shyness crossed her face.

"I do adore babies," she confessed.

"Of course I know it. I remember well your distress when you observed the unfortunate incident of the child near the foundling hospital."

"And then the poor gypsy child who had my Aunt Minerva's name bestowed upon her. Oh, but I hope it's not a curse." She put her hand to her mouth and glanced around, clearly fearful her aunt may have overheard. "You won't tell anyone I said that, will you?" She looked guilty but also conspiratorial, and Mr Grayling surreptitiously put his hand on her wrist. "Only if you don't tell anyone about the long gallery."

Even her ears went pink at this. She cleared her throat and checked to see if anyone was in earshot but it seemed baby George's puking had put everyone off for they were now alone. "Mr Grayling, I was deeply wrong to…to…"

He raised one eyebrow and looked enquiring. "To what, Miss Brightwell?"

She shook her head. "You know very well what I mean."

"I think perhaps you'd better meet me at the Oriental Pavilion, where you can be more explicit, Miss Brightwell." He raised his head, contemplating the sky before adding, "Let's say in ten minutes? There's not much we can do when you are so closely chaperoned but if you can somehow be granted twenty minutes' freedom, then we can arrange somewhere later on that's a little more…private?"

He laughed as her mouth dropped open, though he pretended he was about to address Lady Fenton on Miss Brightwell's other side when he added, furtively, "Lord, but you are adorable when you look so shocked. I do love an innocent. One who

has fire inside—and who can set *m*
fire."

"Mr Grayling!" Her bosom heaved
her expression was a mixture of ou
mixed with reluctant collusion and,
very obvious intrigue and desire. She
in a shaky breath. "The Oriental Pavili
ten minutes? Alone? What can yo
thinking?"

He slid his gaze from her moist, p
lips to ensure there were no sudden i
ruptions from the guests gathered
Lord and Lady Quamby, for Lady Fe
had moved away now.

"That I want to kiss you again,
Brightwell," he murmured, dipping his
slightly, as if he were cooing to the chil
swallowed, feeling himself harden, his
gruff as he admitted, "I feel enslaved b
need to know how you would re
me if…"

"If what, Mr Grayling?" Her voice
also strained with desire; for he could
ognize desire in a woman's voice and
wondering, wanting expression in her l
nous eyes confirmed this.

"If you were completely alone with me. If you would trust me to—"

The impromptu arrival of Mr George Bramley cut short her rejoinder but Sylvester was relieved to note that shortly afterwards she whispered something in Lady Fenton's ear and was rewarded with a quick nod.

Arranging an assignation? Lord, he hoped he was going about this the right way.

The christening party was a large affair and this enabled less scrutiny. The fine weather had held, and like Lady Umbrage's name-giving ceremony, the event was being held outdoors.

Several dozen guests were now con-verged about the trestle tables between the river and Quamby Park further up the hill which was reached by a series of rambling terraced walkways. It was a brisk, five minute walk along the river's edge before the path skirted sharp left, twisting a little up the hillside to where the Oriental Pavilion nestled amidst a copse of trees with

its magnificent view of the surrounding countryside.

Few guests would know of its existence and besides, they were more interested in the jellies, pies and tarts laid on in abundance, so Sylvester had no difficult in slipping away at the appointed time. He'd not be noticed.

When he looked over his shoulder, he saw Lady Fenton and Miss Brightwell walking companionably along the wooded path in the direction of the Oriental Pleasure Pavilion, and a little spurt of excitement spurred him on. Lady Fenton would abandon her charge, ensuring she was not seen to be alone at any point. She was cunning, that one.

Sylvester hastened his steps, arriving breathless at the pagoda-like structure which was fully enclosed, and immensely private, despite its magnificent view.

He pushed open the door and gazed about him. Bertram Brightwell had not lied when he'd informed Sylvester that its layout and location were ideal for what was required.

And what *was* required?

With a jolt of surprise, he saw that a very commodious bed covered by a Chinese-inspired counterpane and an abundance of cushions took up much of the space. Window seats lined the walls however it was clear that the Oriental Pavilion was used as a secret trysting place for Lord Quamby and his countess—no doubt with their respective amours.

His skin felt suddenly highly sensitive and his breathing came with difficulty as desire slammed through him. Bertram knew exactly what he was talking about when he suggested to Sylvester that this would be the ideal place to lure his cousin.

Not that Miss Brightwell needed much luring. Every glance and uttering confirmed the fact that she would be relishing just as much as he, what lay ahead.

Otherwise, why would she be colluding with all three of her cousins to escape her smothering chaperonage to be with him —alone?

And sure enough, a few minutes later, there was Miss Brightwell, with no one else in attendance, hurrying the last few yards towards him as he opened the door of the pavilion to welcome her.

Instantly she was in his arms, clinging to him and offering her mouth while he responded with equal ardour. Two small stained glass windows illuminated the bed, bathing the room in a soft, intimate light.

Still kissing her, he circled her waist with his hands, picked her up and settled her on the edge of the bed, his hand travelling up her skirts in one fluid movement. For a moment he was confronted by her utter shock but as his probing fingers skimmed her heated inner thigh, she arched into him with a soft moan.

What an extraordinarily erotic sensation it was to find an untutored virgin suddenly so very willing. Willing to throw herself into lust with him while throwing caution to the wind.

"Perhaps we shouldn't… Oh…goodness," she gasped as he skimmed the slickness between her legs before intensifying the pressure.

Her eyes widened even more and for a

moment she looked on the point of objecting, but as he redoubled his efforts to pleasure her, she sagged upon his shoulder, her breath hot against his ear.

Meanwhile he was all but bursting his breeches, but for now, this was all for her. As if it had been a sacred duty, he'd taken upon himself the duty of showing her what pleasure was, and he'd do it without compromise. Later, he could show her how it might be beautifully mutual.

Her arms tightened around him but he prized open her grip so she could lay her back down upon the bed and curl her against his side.

Nothing would have given him greater pleasure than to cage her beneath him and to release himself from his breeches and plunge inside her when the time was right.

Except the time wasn't right. This was for her.

She hadn't closed her eyes but stared at him, as if unable to either object or voice her excitement for excitement was clearly what she was experiencing. He saw it in the flare of her large, dark pupils, through her labored breathing, her barely audible moans of pleasure and the sheen of sweat on her forehead. Her jaw was clenched and the concentration in her eyes was intense.

So was his own need and desire but for now he was orchestrating all this for her, for soon she'd be dead. A wave of the greatest sadness settled upon his shoulders which he tried to banish with the knowledge that at least Miss Brightwell would go to her grave knowing she'd been worshipped as a desirable woman; and that she'd experienced the greatest bodily pleasures.

But the sadness persisted, lodging in the core of his being as a terrible grief. Yes, the emotion was, indeed grief as he realised that Miss Brightwell was the very woman he'd been searching for his entire life. Not only was she beautiful, but she was genuinely kind, maternal, nurturing, and, he truly believed, deeply in love with him.

"Oh…oh…" She was panting softly now, her hands clenched into fists, her hips moving gently in rhythm to his ministrations.

"Come, my darling," he whispered as she shattered into his arms, gasping her astonishment and then her shock, too, for in taking such pleasure she knew that she had sinned.

He kissed her lips, helping her to sit up, to climb off the bed—for he knew they had so little time—smiling as he murmured, "Did you enjoy that?"

"I had no idea." Shaking her head in wonder, she looked down at her skirt, now demurely at her ankles. "But is that...oh, what have we done?" The dim light of the room and the muffled silence, punctuated by birdsong, lent an air of unreality to the situation.

"You're still a virgin, if that's what you mean?" he reassured her, holding her against him before quirking his eyebrow. "However, there's plenty of variation on that theme if you want to explore more of such territory with me."

Her obvious inner turmoil tugged at Sylvester's heart. She'd be calculating how much time the doctor had given her before her decline became debilitating. Right now, the glow from her recent experience imbued her features with a softness that was almost mystical. Various renditions of Madonna without her child raced through his mind and the residual sadness that had lodged within him roared back to life as something so much more.

How cruel it was that Miss Brightwell, so full of life now, would soon decline so rapidly. She deserved better. She certainly deserved to be a mother for she'd love her offspring in a way Sylvester's distant mother never could.

The idea of a wife who'd love their children, shower them with affection, and also adore her own husband had never seemed more important than right now.

And Miss Brightwell was that woman.

As he stared at her, connecting the images of Miss Brightwell's concern for the foundling babe, her maternal softness holding the Quamby heir and her enthusiasm for his ministrations just now, he imagined what it would be like to combine all that and package it up in his own life.

The only way he could even start by

quelling the consequent dismay that Miss Brightwell's impending death made this impossible was by reminding himself that he could not, of course, marry someone without a penny, no matter how charming he found her. He simply could not afford it. Not only would the privations make them both miserable, but the rambling estate he was more than likely to inherit from a great uncle needed a great deal of money poured into it if it were to be restored to its previous grandeur and family honour restored. A wife with a more than respectable dowry was absolutely essential.

Besides, not only did Miss Brightwell deserve better than he, the truth was that even if she were in robust health, she'd be lucky to win the hand of a poor clergyman, having no portion whatever.

He gazed at her sadly then reordered his features. He could not let her see his pity.

"A virgin still? Oh, thank the Lord," she whispered, putting her hands up to her face. "I completely forgot myself. What was I thinking? What have I done?"

"You've had a taste of what pleasures are

to be had between a man and a woman who share a deep attraction for one another."

Her radiant smile sent a completely different wave of sensation through his veins as she asked, "You have been disappointed by women before? By their reactions, I mean?"

"I…have always tried to ensure their pleasure." Her words took him by surprise. "Good Lord, Miss Brightwell, this is not something I wish to discuss with you." *Had* he disappointed women in the past? The idea that he had even been a less than ideal lover was highly uncomfortable. He certainly would not be guilty of *that* when he next held Miss Brightwell in his arms.

"Of course not," she said, immediately pressing her lips together. She put her hand on his shoulder, her smile full of sympathy as she raised her wondering gaze to his. "I think you were wonderful. What you did…" She shook her head. "I should feel ashamed but I don't. It was the most wonderful sensation I've ever felt. I thought I was on a star that was taking me though the heavens and then I thought I would die of pleasure. You were masterful, Mr Grayling, though what must you think of me?"

He bent down to kiss the crease between her brows. "What do I think of you? Why, that I would spend every minute if I could, making you happy."

He caught himself up. This sounded like the prelude to a proposal and he couldn't have that, though she'd know her health would not permit the rigours of matrimony. Still, he *could* let in a chink of hope before changing the subject and he was about to speak when Miss Brightwell stiffened in his arms at the sound of footsteps before she relaxed in relief. "It's Cousin Fanny calling me. She said she'd return to collect me and take me back to the others." Pulling out of his arms she hurried to the door, turning and putting her hands to her rosy cheeks. "Will they know?"

"That you've experienced a small sum of what any happily married matron has experienced every morning she wakes up?" He grinned.

"Would you like to do it again, Mr Grayling?"

"I say, that's bold." He was impressed.

Breathlessly, she said in a rush, "Perhaps we could meet when there's more time so we could—"

"Could what, Miss Brightwell?" he asked when she stopped abruptly, reddening.

"No, I don't know what came over me. Please, forgive me?"

"Forgive you?" He reached out his hand and whisked her back into his arms. Gently he put his lips to hers, drawing back slightly to murmur, "I would forgive you anything, for you are irresistible."

Her look of coy innocence, even after what they'd just done, was charming.

"Yes, let's meet here again."

Lady Fenton's called echoed once more through the trees as he calculated quickly. Hastily he murmured, "I'll send you a note. We'll have to be careful, though. This is your cousin's estate and I doubt she'd approve."

"Oh, Cousin Antoinette thinks you are marvellous," Miss Brightwell said happily as she opened the door, turning to add over her shoulder, "She'll help us, I know it."

"Then wait for a sign from me. It may be cryptic for the sake of security. But know this, Miss Brightwell..." He swallowed painfully. In fact, he felt in the greatest physical pain simply at the thought of what pleasures were in store the next time they did meet, "I am your slave. You have set me on fire."

"OH, MR GRAYLING!" HIS WORDS RELEASED A flood of feeling Thea was unable to resist. Rushing back into his arms she surrendered to the exquisite feelings his touch engendered as he brought his mouth hard upon hers.

As he supported the back of her head with one hand, the other kneaded the bud of her right nipple. The wicked warmth between her legs made her lightheaded with desire and she couldn't help herself from escalating the contact, pressing herself against him, taken aback by the enormous bulge she felt in the area of his groin. So this was what Antoinette and Fanny had tried to explain to her.

To think that she'd trembled with revulsion at the thought of such a thing being pushed into her for the sake of a baby. When she'd unexpectedly glimpsed him, naked, after he'd emerged from the pond she'd thought his physique as fine as Michaelangelo's statue, *David*. Back then, though she'd torn her gaze away quickly, she'd noticed nothing frightening, rod-like or rigid, as Antoinette had suggested. Now she was beginning to understand how a man's body worked.

And the dismaying fact was she felt the very opposite of repulsed.

In fact, her insides felt quivery and wanting, and there was nothing more she could have desired in that moment than to feel his weight and width pressed against her.

Into her.

Yes, it was madness, but she truly felt emboldened and if he wanted final proof that she was the wife for him, she'd gladly give it to him.

"Thea!" Fanny's voice came again, this time more insistent. "Aunt Minerva is asking for you."

Thea pulled herself away.

"Goodbye, Mr Grayling." In the doorway she hesitated, though she knew she was compelled to do Aunt Minerva's bidding.

"Goodbye, Miss Brightwell." He cleared his throat and seemed suddenly slightly awkward. "I shall need a little while to gather myself before I return."

She nodded.

"But we shall meet again in the Oriental Pavilion Room. You are not afraid to come?"

"Oh no, Mr Grayling," she whispered. "I can't wait."

CHAPTER 15

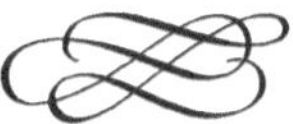

"TELL me what happened? I hope he did more than just whisper sweet nothings in your ear. Is he as charming as you believed?" Fanny fired off the questions like a volley of cannon fire, for they were fast approaching the gathered throng.

Thea's flesh heated to combustible levels it seemed for the second time that day. "Oh, he was…amazing. He was so sweet and clearly wanted to show me that matters between the sexes are not at all the dreadful, labouring affairs Antoinette made them out to be."

"Antoinette did not say that! She explained it just as it is."

"No, she did not! She made it sound a lot of panting and awful parts going into places we…don't talk about. And—" Thea turned her head away, realising she'd said far too much.

"Oh my Lord, you didn't!"

"Of course we didn't. I'm still…pure, if that's what you mean," she reassured Fanny in a hasty whisper. She could not believe she was having this conversation with her cousin yet at the same time it was catharsis to speak plainly about matters that were normally shrouded in such obscurity. Matters never spoken about. Well, not by anyone other than Cousins Fanny and Antoinette. Just to ensure Cousin Fanny had no doubts, she added, "At least, Mr Grayling assures me I am still a…a virgin." She dropped her voice to a hush as the vista of the river, and the mingling throng, came fully into view. "He seemed mighty pleased with how much I enjoyed it. I think…" Embarrassment made her squirm but if there was anyone with whom she could speak about this, it was Cousin Fanny.

"You think what? That he ought to be

suitably satisfied that you'd make a wife who'd enjoy to the limit the debauches that are what drive most men? Unlike his first wife?"

"No! You make it sound…so crude. It wasn't like that. It was…" Thea halted and stared at the trees ahead as memories of the warmth and companionship she and Mr Grayling had shared seeped through her. "It was just lovely."

"Just lovely is exactly how I'd describe it, too. Why, Lord Fenton and I couldn't get enough of each other when we first met. We still can't."

Thea looked at her wistfully. "I'd so love to have what you and Lord Fenton have."

"And you shall." Fanny spoke decisively, taking her arm and leading her on, for there in the distance was Aunt Minerva, a monstrous figure in purple, clearly on the lookout for Thea if the waving ostrich plume in her matching purple velvet toque was anything to go by. "You and he are made for each other; that's quite clear. And you have all the credentials for a discerning fellow like that."

"Except a dowry." Thea felt the weight of the truth on her shoulders like lead. Tears welled up in her eyes but Fanny patted her decisively on the shoulder, saying, "Nonsense, not every man is motivated by pecuniary interest. Love is just as important as a portion."

"You really think Mr Grayling would consider his feelings for me more important than what I could bring to any union?"

"Of course! I can see it in his eyes." Fanny's own twinkled as she led her cousin towards where Cousin Antoinette was pressing baby George into his godfather's arms.

"Really, Antoinette," protested Cousin Fanny, "surely you can see Mr Bramley doesn't like babies. Give him to Thea."

Thea held out her hands, a wash of affection warming her as the baby snuggled against her chest. She cooed and murmured to it and the sweet thing rewarded her with a gummy smile.

Glancing up, she was surprised to see a few minutes later that Mr Grayling had arrived. Not only that, but the look in his eyes was one that any new mother would be glad to observe in a proud father gazing upon wife and infant.

She pushed the thought away quickly but the hope remained. Perhaps Mr Grayling truly did have intentions towards her that would see him making her an offer. She'd felt the attraction between them from the start and barely moments before they'd crossed a very serious line. She'd demonstrated that the strength of her feelings equalled his and that she was not repulsed by what went on in private.

"Such a picture of domestic bliss and harmony."

Unfortunately it was George Bramley, and not Mr Grayling, who spoke. Thea tried to smile but the distrust she felt made it difficult.

Antoinette stroked her baby's head and pressed her cheek against it for a moment. "He is a darling, isn't he, but Thea is so much better with babies than I am. She's just made to be a mother."

"While you're made for...?" Mr Bramley's half-posed question made Thea squirm with sudden horror. She glanced between Mr Grayling, Antoinette and Mr Bramley and saw the combative gleam in Mr Bramley's eye, which Antoinette met with a giggle.

"Oh, you are too terrible, Mr Bramley. Just because Lord Quamby and I are the perfect match for each other and, I will admit, enjoy society's revels, doesn't mean we don't dote on young George, and that I'm not a good mother when I need to be. You're a very special uncle, and now you're George's godfather and can see as much of him as you wish."

"Not exactly what I meant," muttered Mr Bramley.

Still feeling uncomfortable, Thea tried to turn the subject. "Shall we seat ourselves over there? Bertram is waving us over."

By a pond, a cluster of seating had been arranged for the guests and the scene was charming and inviting. The Quamby Estate was magnificent, Thea thought, casting her eye over the gently rolling hills of the gardens, which contained many opportunities for rambles and gatherings like this.

"I've just persuaded Fenton to build me a folly," Fanny declared as she sank onto a plush crimson tasseled cushion. "Just like that one over there." She pointed to further up the river's edge where part of the mosaic roof of the Oriental Pavilion glittered in the sun.

"Sisterly rivalry," Mr Bramley remarked, pretending to be jocular, Thea noticed. She wished she'd not been so inclusive in her invitation, for she'd expected Mr Bramley to move to other company when the rest of them went over to join Bertram.

"Not rivalry, exactly, for I did much better when I married dear Quamby, who is an earl, to Fanny's chagrin, for she had always enjoyed outranking me." Antoinette simpered playfully across at her sister. "Now of course I get precedence. I'm sure that's why Fanny always has to have the most a la mode bonnets trimmed with the biggest blooms."

"It's my life's mission," Fanny responded drily, with a smile at her husband. "Poor me, having to satisfy myself with a mere viscount."

"I might see myself elevated yet, my dear, thanks to the shaky family line. One never knows who's going to drop off the perch without the expected heir." He raised an eyebrow and looked directly at Mr Grayling. Thea noticed that when Lord Fenton spoke, everyone listened. There was a commanding quality to his discourse despite the fact he had also been an acknowledged rake. Now it seemed he was directing his energies towards the more noble pursuits of public office. She'd heard his name mentioned with regard to an important government sinecure.

Perhaps, Thea thought wistfully, she, too, might have the same happy influence on Mr Grayling after he'd asked her to be his—

She drew herself up at the thought. Matters between them were far from settled. Yet when she glanced at Mr Grayling she found that his own gaze was resting with considerable fondness upon her and her heart lurched.

"There were many who questioned my choice of wife when I could have chosen an heiress." She realised Lord Fenton was speaking and that everyone was listening, so, dutifully, she turned her attention towards her cousin's handsome husband. "But as we are allotted such a few short years on this planet, they may as well be happy ones."

"I heard a story," said Mr Bramley loudly, clearing his throat, "along those lines."

"Pray tell, Mr Bramley," Fenton invited, leaning back in his chair, seeming very relaxed. "Of harmony versus pecuniary desire? There are so many of them, but I'd choose marital felicity any day."

Thea inclined her head, politeness forcing her now to look at Mr Bramley, a man she found personally repugnant and who she knew her cousins regarded as their greatest foe. Yet here he was, in their midst by virtue of being, of course, baby George's godfather. She nearly choked on the knowledge that, in fact, he was so much more, and wondered how many others knew it.

"It was a friend who told me, actually, of someone he knew, and his pecuniary considerations were decidedly at the fore." Mr

Bramley leaned forward and tapped his fingers upon the table as he gazed about the company, one brow raised as if to ensure he had everyone's attention. There seemed a coiled tenseness about him that, Thea was sure, made not just her feel uncomfortable, and she wondered how Cousin Antoinette had ever found him attractive.

"Nevertheless," Mr Bramley went on, "to make his plan work, he dressed his intentions up as good works in the guise of marital felicity being the intended outcome."

"Anyone for champagne?"

Thea was surprised at the haste with which Bertram stood up. He brushed back his errant hair and fiddled with his stock, clearly agitated, but Antoinette said mildly, "No need, brother dear. We have servants for that, and here is one now. I say, what a lovely day it is. Mr Grayling, do you not think so?"

"It has been a very lovely day."

Thea felt something akin to warm treacle flood her, inside and out, seemingly, as Mr Grayling smiled across the table at her. It was as if he were secretly communicating with her that not only had matters just now gone very much to his satisfaction, he certainly intended continuing in this direction.

Thea shivered with anticipation while Mr Bramley cleared his throat and raised his voice. "Yes, this friend of mine," he persisted, "was most anxious that his lively and attractive cousin should not be overlooked purely on account of her parlous pecuniary situation. In other words, she had not a feather to fly with, poor girl, and was reduced to living on the handouts of a wealthy relative."

Poor young woman, thought Thea. *She sounds exactly like me*. She hoped the story had a happy ending.

"So this friend hit upon an ingenious plan in order to snare a particular gentleman who *would* have been interested in making the young lady an offer — but only if she had money."

"I say, Mr Grayling," Fanny interrupted, waving a languid hand in Thea's direction, "perhaps you'd like to take Cousin Thea for a walk to the refreshments table while Mr

Bramley finishes his story. She's been eyeing the strawberries longingly since she sat down."

Mr Grayling looked both surprised and pleased as he rose obediently and offered Thea his arm which she took with alacrity, though she hesitated because she did want to hear the end of Mr Bramley's story.

Indulgently, Mr Grayling waited, caging her hand on his arm as Mr Bramley went on, eyes bright and roving, voice fraught as if he were about to deliver the *coup de grace,* "And would you believe that the success of this ingenious plan revolved around telling this erstwhile suitor that the young lady in question had only six months to live! Can you believe it?"

Mr Bramley raised his voice to finish his story while Lord Quamby, scratching his scalp, appeared perplexed. However, Lord Quamby often looked perplexed. "But what purpose would that serve?"

"Why indeed?" Thea nodded in agreement, disappointed by the ending before nearly losing her step as Mr Grayling, who had already started to move away from the table, swung round and dropped his arm and thus Thea's means of support."

Determined not to apportion blame, Thea regained her composure, murmuring as she navigated the chairs about the table, "Shall we go, Mr Grayling?"

When he didn't answer she glanced up to find his expression dark with no trace of the affection she was expecting. Discomposed, she transferred her gaze to Antoinette where she observed with surprise a flare of what could only be considered horror while her cousin looked directly at Bertram who was running his finger round the inside of his stock and looking distinctly green around the gills.

"You ask why, Miss Brightwell?" Mr Bramley seemed the only one entirely at his ease as he looked directly at her. "Why would he do such a thing? Why would he tell such a lie?" he repeated, before answering his own questions. "Why, to encourage a suitor who'd never make an offer for a penniless girl. Well, not unless she had only a few months of good health left to her. And then, what do you suppose would happen? The interfering cousin would orchestrate a moment where the gallant gentleman would be caught in the act of making love to the lady, and *voila*, a marriage proposal becomes the only recourse for the poor trapped, would-be suitor. Except that of course the gentleman in question was never a suitor." He spread his palms outward. "And the girl was never dying." Shaking his head, he sighed. "Can you believe this story, and yet it is true as I live and breathe."

Thea frowned. It was a silly story which Mr Bramley had surely made up. And if it were true, it was hardly a very edifying example of the kind of husband-hunting scheming that no doubt went on in more ambitious and calculated circles than those to which Thea belonged. Nevertheless, she was surprised at the tense silence that greeted Mr Bramley's anecdote.

"Yes, clever indeed!" Mr Bramley chuckled. "The penniless orphan has snared the husband she set her sights on by ensuring she has witnesses to the impropriety orchestrated by her cunning cousin." With a flourish, Mr Bramley snapped both fingers, his grin almost parodying amusement.

And while Thea disliked the smug look on his face, she was more concerned by the change in Mr Grayling's demeanour. The light had gone from his eye and the expression he levelled upon her for just a moment was very bleak as he gently disengaged her hand from his arm.

"Mr Grayling?" Uncertainty made her voice waver.

"Excuse me, Miss Brightwell." He nodded abruptly to the assembled company. "I'm suddenly not feeling at all the thing." And indeed, his complexion was distinctly pallid. Thea had the sudden panicked feeling she was responsible, though she had no idea how. Could it somehow be that as she'd been the one to experience all the pleasure he had suffered through being denied release? That was the word Antoinette had used, she seemed to remember.

"I'm so sorry to hear it, Mr Grayling," she murmured, but he did not heed her. Certainly he did not acknowledge her as he rose from his bow then turned and navigated his way through the knots of guests towards the front of the house where the carriages were lined up.

She watched in an agony of indecision as to whether or not to follow him while he nodded to various personages on his journey towards his phaeton.

Self consciously Thea reseated herself at the table. All eyes seemed to be on her, as if they could read her thoughts. What a little innocent she must seem, wearing her heart on her sleeve. "I do hope Mr Grayling is not coming down with something." Her voice sounded small and insubstantial to her own ears.

"No, no, I'm sure it's just a touch of the sun on top of last night's excesses." Mr Bramley spoke robustly, his green eyes seeming to size her up. No, he was not a nice man, she decided.

Fanny reached across the table in a gesture of support and touched her fingertips. "I'm sure he'll come round soon enough, you'll see. He'll be at the Assembly Rooms ready to dance a jig by tonight, I'm sure of it."

"Yes, yes, quite sure of it." Cousin Bertram cleared his throat and Thea thought suddenly that he looked even worse than Mr Grayling had.

Sylvester felt lightheaded as he climbed atop the box of his handsome equipage, picked up the reins and set off at a brisk trot. He and Miss Brightwell had covered quite a distance this morning, in more ways than one. He'd felt like the chosen, initiating the poor innocent young woman…dying young woman…into the realms of pleasure.

Dying?

"Dr Horne! A word, if I may!" He dropped the reins as he drew to a halt, leaning down and address the man. How fortuitous it was to see the doctor leaving the gathering, walking briskly down the elm-lined drive, his ginger hair bright in the morning sun as he scratched his thinning pate before replacing his hat. He glanced up at Sylvester in enquiry.

"Perhaps I could offer you a lift."

The doctor's eyes flared with surprise before he inclined his head, climbing with surprising nimbleness onto the box beside Sylvester.

Sylvester picked up the reins again and gave the horses their heads while his own was reeling with the new knowledge he'd recently acquired courtesy of Mr George Bramley. Well, here was the doctor himself, captive and about to explain matters to Sylvester's satisfaction.

They galloped down the avenue and Sylvester allowed the doctor to wax lyrical on Sylvester's prime horseflesh before Sylvester finally turned the conversation to the only matter of importance right now: Miss Brightwell's health.

Health? Ha! He'd never seen a young woman in more robust health. He wondered if the doctor was in collusion. Well, now was the time he'd find out. He'd just have to rein in his anger sufficiently to get out the questions that needed to be asked.

"Indeed, I'm concerned that the young lady's cousins seem to hold such grave fears for her health," he said after he'd raised the matter. "When I left them just now they were in a flutter, no doubt afraid she'd catch a chill, which of course corroborates the fears of others—" he said this with a pointed look at the doctor— "that she's in the grip of some fatal malady."

Though Sylvester had to keep his eye on the road, he was also careful to gauge Dr Horne's expression.

The doctor suddenly appeared tongue-tied, as well he might. No doubt under the orders of Bertram Brightwell he'd confirmed in Sylvester's mind the lie that Miss Brightwell was all but on her deathbed. No doubt Dr Horne would be wondering what Sylvester truly knew and was being cagey in his answers.

Sylvester tried to keep the acid out of his voice as he went on, "With the few months remaining to her, they are keen to ensure she enjoy all the entertainments available this summer before her declining health prevents her from even venturing outdoors."

"Good Lord, is she *so* ill?"

The suspicion manifesting itself in

Sylvester's breast hardened to anger. "You certainly made clear your concerns to *me*, doctor?"

Dr Horne looked confused but another sharp turn had him clinging to the seat before he replied, querulously, "You say that her *cousins* endorse the poor woman's precarious health?"

"They, too, were most insistent that Miss Brightwell had but months, Dr Horne." Sylvester slanted him another glance, his suspicion hardening that the doctor was trying to detract blame from his own conduct. All of a sudden Dr Horne seemed very eager to put a different slant on matters. As if he hadn't enthusiastically endorsed Miss Brightwell's impending mortality! "What do you say to that, Dr Horne?"

"Eh, what?" Dr Horne seemed suddenly rather agitated; though of course Sylvester was driving very fast. "Oh, well, I think the young lady is bearing up very well, all things considered, wouldn't you say?"

Bearing up very well. Sylvester nearly choked. Oh, she'd borne up remarkably well in their bower of love. No sign of the wilting virgin—though she was one, he was sure—or violet there. No doubt she'd meant to entice him to go all the way with her, whereupon she'd make some sign that would bring everyone running. Thus discovered, his honour would be called to account and he'd be forced there and then to make her a marriage offer.

"To my mind, there appears nothing wrong with her," Sylvester said, challengingly as he narrowed his eyes at the doctor. His lip curled as he added under his breath but loud enough for the doctor to hear, "Though that is not what I was led to believe. In fact, I believe she may be for this world a lot longer than anyone could have hoped for."

He brought himself up short. Had he really hoped she was only destined to live a few months, during which he could enjoy the pleasure of her, supposedly to further hers? Shocked at himself, he tried to justify such thoughts.

He'd nearly been tricked by the basest of lies. Of course he would be angry...though not to the extent of wishing harm to Miss Brightwell.

Perhaps Miss Brightwell had initially resisted being used to further the pecuniary ambitions of the Brightwells. Lady Quamby and Lady Fenton had been avaricious social climbers. Sylvester might not fully concur with George Bramley's scathing assessment, but the facts spoke for themselves. Though it was true that a year later each young lady appeared to have retained the regard of her respective consort and to enjoy a situation of great mutual felicity, the fact was that they were avaricious and ambitious and they had used him.

Well, Sylvester couldn't afford to marry a penniless chit, no matter how charming he found her.

And indeed, he'd never come across anyone as charming as Miss Thea Brightwell.

A surge of frustrated desire and pained fury at being the object of their collective trick found their outlet in a burst of energy as he managed the horses, and Dr Horne cried out, "Dear me, sir, they are frisky beasts, indeed!" as he once again grabbed the edge of his seat in the midst of another of Sylvester's sharp but skilful turns. "You can put me down here, sir! Please!"

They were now in the town and the traffic brought Sylvester to a halt. He'd not nearly finished quizzing the doctor but he was satisfied that Dr Horne's agitation was sufficient proof that he was in on the subterfuge.

Obligingly Sylvester set him down, with little indication of the fury within his breast, then continued to where his beasts were stabled a short walk from his own townhouse. But his painful thoughts were far away, centred on images of the tumble he'd enjoyed earlier that afternoon with a sweet and willing young miss of good breeding who had not a penny to her name and who was willing to trade everything on the hope that she could trick him into matrimony.

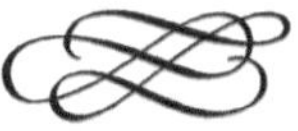

"THE moment George Bramley had left their gathering, Fanny rose and, extending her arm, suggested Antoinette might accompany her for a short stroll to the lake.

"A fine idea," said Fenton, rising to take her hand, but she shook her head.

"No, Fenton, you must stay with Cousin Thea. I'm afraid I require only Antoinette and Bertram's company. When I'm back you and I can take a short turn about the rose bushes."

She gave him an ameliorating smile before he murmured, putting his head close to hers. "A Brightwell family meeting, eh? And what wickedness are you cooking up?" He chuckled, adding in an undertone, "I take it there are matters to arrange concerning Cousin Thea's and your matchmaking efforts. Not all going to plan, either—not that I'm surprised. Mr Grayling is not as plump in the pocket as either Quamby or me. Nor, perhaps, as easy to manage."

"You were not at all easy to manage, my Lord," Fanny reminded him, archly. "And might I add that it was only when your pride was piqued after I secured a marriage offer from an earl—" she smiled meaningfully at Lord Quamby—"that you chose to act."

"And I shall be forever reminded of the fact." Fenton shook his head and sighed theatrically. "Ah, but how well you managed me, and how well you know me, dearest wife." He turned back to Thea who was staring vacantly towards the Oriental Pavilion. She jerked into awareness as he addressed her, to find his expression both earnest and also sympathetic as he leant across the table. "I know you harbor hopes, Cousin Thea, but it would be wrong of me not to remind you that Miss Huntingdon is by far the strongest contender for Mr Grayling's attentions—his honourable ones, that is. Indeed, it would be wrong of me not to tell you that I've heard rumours he intends to offer for her before she leaves Bath at the end of next week."

This was so contrary to what Thea had been imagining was her likely future until barely seconds ago that she could not speak for the dismay and horror that swept through her.

"But he can't!" Antoinette, who'd already risen in anticipation of their turn about the gardens, gripped Bertram by the shoulder. "How could such a thing even be in the wind after—?" She stopped abruptly. "Come, Bertram! Fanny!" Her expression was full of steely resolve as she tightened her grip, causing her brother to protest mildly as he did her bidding.

Fenton rose and offered the siblings an ironic bow while Thea looked on, mute with confusion as her brother-in-law went on, "What a fearsome trio you make. Poor Mr Grayling ought to be quaking in his boots, and I wish you good luck, but the truth is that I don't hold high hopes, though I'm sorry to say it, Cousin Thea." He turned and shook his head. "I don't know how much he has led you on to believe otherwise, but Mr Grayling has no conveniently rich and elderly relatives languishing in the wings from whom a sudden fortune will shower him with the freedom to choose a penniless wife."

This earned him nothing more than a baleful glare from both Fanny and Antoinette while Thea gave a little sob.

She wanted to refute this with a proud exhortation of what had happened in the Oriental Pavilion but the experience seemed cheapened by Fenton's suggestion that Mr Grayling was merely toying with her affections.

How could that be true, after what he'd said? What he'd led her to believe?

She dropped her head and stared at her interlaced fingers as Lord Fenton gallantly offered to escort her to the refreshments table.

Mr Grayling loved her! He'd all but said it.

And then he'd turned suddenly cold though she'd thought at the time she'd only imagined it. Now Fenton was doing his best to persuade her there was no hope in that quarter. It didn't make sense. Not after what Fanny and Antoinette had said regarding Mr Grayling's desire for a wife who could show him the warmth and passion which had been so lacking in his first wife.

"I think I'd like to go back to my room and rest awhile," Thea said with an apologetic smile as she shook her head at the idea of more refreshments. "I think the events of this afternoon have proved more exacting than I had realised until now for I am very tired and would like to be on my own."

WHEN THEY WERE OUT OF EARSHOT AND standing on the river bank protected from view by a gnarled willow, Fanny put her hands on her hips and announced, "Well, we're undone. You saw the way Mr

Grayling looked at us and then Thea after George Bramley uttered that instructional tale. Fenton's right. Aside from the fact that Mr Grayling realizes he's been tricked, I'm come to believe that the sad truth is he's not a suitable contender, mutual attraction notwithstanding. If Mr Grayling isn't mad for Thea and willing to take her with nothing, I'm the first to admit that love can die very quickly for lack of funds."

Antoinette looked thoughtful as she tore a willow switch from the branch and began stripping the leaves. "I thought our plan couldn't fail when it was clear they were both so enamoured of one another," she muttered. She dropped the mutilated branch and looked from Fanny to Bertram. "I can only imagine the things he's thinking after what our odious arch enemy said at the table. Oh, but I hate Mr Bramley so much! I just hope my little George doesn't inherit anything of his ghastly character." She stopped, bit her lip, then declared with great vehemence, "We can't admit defeat just yet! What if suddenly there was someone ridiculously wealthy making

Cousin Thea an offer? Wouldn't that make Mr Grayling reconsider? After all, Fanny, that's exactly how you snared Fenton."

Fanny grunted, dismissing her sister's words with a wave of her hand as she gazed at the gently flowing river. "You are not taking account of the fact, Antoinette, that Mr Grayling isn't as plump in the pocket as Fenton."

"Then maybe we can arrange someone who is. Someone like darling Quamby who will allow her all the freedom my dearest allows me."

Fanny raised her eyes heavenward. "Cousin Thea is not like you, Antoinette. Such a situation would be unutterably distressing to her."

"What about someone much older who is in the market for a young and pretty wife. Someone who has already sired his heir?" suggested Bertram which brought his sisters' scorn raining down upon his shoulders.

"You've missed the whole point if you think Thea just wants a wealthy husband. The truth is, all that will satisfy her now is

Mr Grayling—and that's entirely your fault!"

"Besides," Fanny added, "it's as Fenton says...the two of them will never have enough to live on and be happy. I think perhaps our matchmaking was doomed from the beginning, or rather we made a poor choice, for we should have selected a potential suitor Thea could have been induced to like, rather than encouraged her to lose her heart to Mr Grayling." She uttered a despairing sigh. "Well, none of it matters now. Mr Grayling knows he's been duped."

"All very vexing," muttered Bertram. "I'm a dab hand with the cards and I thought I was a dab hand at the old matchmaking when I came up with that grand plan to make Mr Grayling believe Cousin Thea was dying."

"Yes, but it wasn't such a grand plan after all in view of the fact that Mr Grayling simply can't afford a poor wife. Or, at least, not unless he were prepared to give up so many of the pleasures he takes for granted and there are few men I know who would, I'm sorry to say." Fanny dampened her irritation both with herself and her brother. It was not a plan she'd have chosen but having seen how love had blossomed and how easily Mr Grayling had bought the story of Thea's tragic illness, she'd been buoyed by its possibilities. "Come, I think we should go back to the others."

She turned, just as Bertram slapped his thigh. "That's it! Time to transfer my skill from matchmaking to card fixing. I shall *make* Mr Grayling a man of fortune and he won't even know it. Oh my Lord, some of these nights, after I come back as dawn is breaking, I've seen fortunes won and lost in minutes."

"Indeed, you've lost the collective Brightwell fortune a dozen times over, Bertram, so I don't really think you can hope to be successful in such a venture on Mr Grayling's behalf," Fanny said drily.

Antoinette sent him a sympathetic glance. "I think you should try to keep anything there is to be won for yourself, Bertram. I did notice darling Quamby seemed just the teeniest bit annoyed when I asked him to bail you out again last week."

Bertram gave a dismissive snort. "I have a plan, sister dear, that will more than repay Quamby for every time he ever *has* bailed me out. And after I'm done, I'll be back in old Grayling's good books and he'll be forever grateful to me for lining his pockets with gold and supplying him with a pretty wife to spend it on."

***

It was not often Dr Zebediah Horne stared with such critical fascination at his mottled reflection before making a house call, and it was not as if calling on Miss Minerva Brightwell were a rare occurrence either.

He wiped the beads of moisture from his pale brow with his handkerchief and practised his most winning smile. The day was warm though it did not warrant the moisture gathered between his neck and the limp linen of his stock.

He'd thought to walk the distance between his abode and hers, but as he wanted no flecks of dirt to mar his finest pantaloons, Dr Horne took a conveyance Lord to Quamby's grand estate.

In the grand entrance hall he greeted Lady Quamby with all the deference she was due, though he could never reconcile the chit with being a countess. Indeed, disapproval almost to the point of abhorrence warred with reluctant appreciation as he rose from his bow. The young woman—and a mother to boot—was undeniably a lovely creature but her reputation was scandalous, as was her sister's.

Poor Miss Thea was tainted by association. Throughout the years Zebediah had attended Miss Minerva Brightwell he'd heard the gossip surrounding the conduct of her nieces and wondered how there could be a blood relationship. More than one wager had centred around who would snatch the virtue of the young ladies.

Zebediah was of course barred by funds and his station in life from being a member of the clubs so enjoyed by his wealthy clientele, but he'd been summoned to various clubs and the residences of the top ten thousand on many an occasion to attend to various maimed or incapacitated young pups.

No, Zebediah had not one ounce of respect for the idle and dissolute rakes who squandered the family wealth of generations and made such thoughtless wagers.

Indeed, the previous evening he'd been summoned to the saloon of the heir to the Earl of Gillingham where he'd found a Corinthian placed on the billiards table with an arrow piercing his right shoulder.

"An inch to the left and this young man would have breathed his last," Zebediah had told the gathering severely, and been met with the defence that "it was he who bet Lord Mentone two hundred pounds he could not pierce the apple balanced on his head with an arrow shot from 200 yards, and indeed Mentone could not."

Grimly, Horne had proceeded with the grisly task of removing the arrow, only half attending to the banter of the young men who lounged in armchairs about the room. That is, until he heard the wager Harry Gotts proposed: five hundred pounds that a certain Corinthian would propose to a certain chestnut-haired miss in a hot-air balloon at a hundred feet.

Such ridiculous chatter and such outrageous sums. It was as much as Zebediah had to spend on himself and a wife in a year.

But the truth was, Zebediah Horne did have enough to live modestly with a meek and obedient wife who did not demand what he could not provide. A wife who'd be grateful for any kind of life that was better than playing handmaiden to an impossible-to-please old woman.

Bolstered by the irrefutable knowledge that there were few women as demanding, if not downright unpleasant as Minerva Brightwell—and by contrast, few women as meek, pliable, undemanding and potentially grateful as Miss Thea Brightwell—Zebediah reached the top of the stairs as the young Lady Quamby turned from the bottom to call out, "Perhaps you've brought some temper-restoring draught for dear Aunt Minerva, who is venting her spleen yet again upon poor Cousin Thea. I do hope you are as successful at restoring calm as you are in relieving Aunt Minerva's bunions."

The maidservant who let him into the invalid's drawing room a little further down the passage looked uncertain as she told him to wait while she advised her mistress of his arrival; and indeed Minerva Brightwell's glowering presence in the doorway moments later brought immediately to mind Lady Quamby's words.

"What brings you here, Dr Horne?" she demanded, taking a couple of steps into the centre of the Aubusson carpet and looking as if she were about to throw him out. "I did not summon you."

"The fact is, I have come to speak to your niece, Miss Brightwell," he stammered.

The crease between her brows deepened and she cocked her head. "Thea? Thea is perfectly robust, thank you. A little too robust for her own good, I'd venture to add."

"Delighted to hear it." He cleared his throat nervously. "She was looking a little pale when I observed her at the christening the other day."

Miss Brightwell's face darkened. "Pale? I'd say she was looking a little flushed, if anything. Not a day that was a success, by anyone's standards. So tell me, doctor, what do you wish to speak to Thea about?"

Zebediah felt himself flush to the roots of his hair. "The fact is, Miss Brightwell, before I speak to Miss Thea, I must speak to you first. You are the one into whose gentle care the girl has been placed and you have the authority, nay, the power, to make me a very happy man—or otherwise."

Minerva Brightwell moved her regal, Pomona-green-upholstered bulk a few threatening steps towards him. "What are you talking about, Dr Horne?"

Zebediah mopped his sweating brow and glanced from the fire in the grate to his erstwhile patient. "I have not made myself very plain, I see that. The fact is, I had hoped I might make…that is, I might prevail upon…" He took a deep breath before saying in a rush, "I should very much like to make your niece an offer of marriage."

Miss Brightwell looked first horrified, and then offended, and then, to his surprise, she burst out laughing. "Good lord, Dr Horne. *You*? You of all people wish to make my niece an offer?"

He felt the substance in his legs turn to jelly, and the disappointment in his gut poison his marrow. Strange how strong such sensations were when it was not so long ago he'd even conceived the idea. Yet the idea of feeling the warmth of a strong, young female body cleaving to his own had almost obsessed him since he'd come up with it.

"Of course, there must be many who would be contenders for the young lady's affections, I realise that—"

"For her affections, yes, but not for her hand in marriage, Dr Horne. No, do not look so dejected. I assure you I'm not discounting your offer. In fact, the more I regard an idea I'd at first thought preposterous, the more I see merit in it. You see, I have hopes of finding myself in receipt of just such an unexpected proposal. From unexpected quarters, I have been strongly led to believe. Yes, it is true." She simpered, and he watched, fascinated, the mesmerising effect of her triple chin floating into the sea of her ample body. "Thea might then be in need of a home, so perhaps a marriage offer for poor Thea is just the so-lution." She gave a decisive nod. "I appreciate your visit, Dr Horne, but I shall first speak to my niece. She must have some warning of what you are about to offer, for I fear she will hardly believe it is true."

CHAPTER 17

OR did Thea believe it was something her aunt would countenance in a hundred years. "I can't marry Dr Horne! I *won't!*" she gasped, pacing back and forth in front of the fireplace not half an hour after the good doctor had been shown out. "Oh, Aunt Minerva, what have I done that you'd force me to do such a thing?" It was hard to keep the tears from her voice as she turned an imploring look towards the older woman.

"I couldn't force you, Thea, but I could certainly persuade you of the merits. Have you not always wished for the comforts of home and hearth? A husband and children to dote upon?"

Thea brought her apron up to cover her eyes and let out a little sob. Little George's christening was fresh in her mind and it was true, she desperately wanted to be a mother. But...only to Mr Grayling's children!

With difficulty, she stifled the further sobs that accompanied thoughts of the lovely gentleman who'd not made contact since the christening three days previously. He'd initiated her into the secrets of joyful abandon, and then that's exactly what he'd done—abandoned her.

Had she been misled by her cousins? Was her wantonness abhorrent? Or had he merely found her disappointing? Was there something repellent about her body? She simply did not know, and the more she broke her heart over questioning Mr Grayling's feelings, the more uncertain she felt about everything else in life.

Now Aunt Minerva was not only telling her Dr Horne had come to seek her aunt's permission to offer marriage to

Thea, but that Thea would be best to accept it.

"But what about you, Aunt Minerva?" she asked, pausing in the midst of her agitation. "I thought you were not about to countenance my marrying *anyone* because you needed me!"

"It's true, and I may well find that I need you more than Dr Horne needs you, but your cousins have made it clear only a selfish old woman would prevent you from following your heart and discovering the joys of motherhood. If I had my time again, I'd have played *my* cards differently and I'd not be the spinster I am today. I have no wish to see you subjected to the same fate, Thea."

Thea stared at her aunt. "I'd not be following my heart to marry Dr *Horne*, Aunt Minerva," she said. "And I always thought you were infinitely delighted at not having to answer to a husband."

Her aunt looked thoughtful. In fact, a strange wistfulness crossed her features as she settled herself comfortably in her armchair and fingered the corners of her shawl.

"The truth is, the novelty's worn off, Thea." Her look became enigmatic as the corners of her mouth turned up. "And now that a certain gentleman has begun to communicate secretly with me, offering me the chance I brushed off years ago, it is my duty to think of you and your future." She fixed Thea with a level stare. "If you have a better offer than Dr Horne's, my girl, then by all means I'd encourage you to take it." She shrugged and raised her palms outwards. "Otherwise I really don't know *where* you'll live."

"A BETTER OFFER THAN DR HORNE'S," THEA sobbed half an hour later, raising red and swollen eyes from Antoinette's bed and encountering the concerned looks of both her cousins. "I haven't heard from Mr Grayling since…since I…" She couldn't finish, breaking into fresh sobs as Antoinette and Fanny exchanged glances. They knew exactly what Thea was talking about.

"I'm sure there's a good reason," Antoinette offered weakly. "Perhaps he's just gone away unexpectedly."

"He liked you very much, Thea," Fanny said with a forced smiled. "It was quite plain to see, believe me."

"Just not enough to make me an honest offer. Or even to ask me to dance one more time. He saw the beautiful dress you lent me, Cousin Fanny, and he liked my face, but then he learned of my circumstances, my poverty."

"Oh Fanny, what should we do?" Antoinette asked in some discomfort after they'd bathed poor Thea's heated brow and sent her to bed with a sleeping draught. "She's distraught and believes he's forsaken her because she's not good enough. We can't possibly tell her the truth."

"No, we cannot," Fanny affirmed with some force as she lounged in her sister's private drawing room. "It was Bertram's foolish idea to tell him a lie in the first place, and now that Mr Grayling's not done anything that requires him to do the honourable thing, it really does look like Thea is going to have to marry Dr Horne."

"Marry Dr Horne! How can you of all people suggest such a thing?" Antoinette rounded on her, nearly breaking the ostrich feather she'd just attached with a green ribbon to her bonnet. "You did everything you possibly could to avoid marrying Lord Slyther after mama decided that you marrying him was necessary for us all to avoid poverty and disgrace. I do believe you'd have killed him, if you'd had to."

"And risk the gallows? No, he'd have brought on his own early demise through the pleasurable pursuits I'd have devised for him." Fanny winked then added, thoughtfully, "But Thea must play the poor hand she's been dealt. She must take risks just as I had to take a huge risk to make my cards fall my way."

"You know Thea is not a risk-taker, Fanny. Certainly not like you and me." Antoinette sashayed in front of her looking glass admiring the waving feathers in her bonnet. "Poor Thea. She did like Mr Grayling so much and now he's—

"Been wagered to ask a certain fair haired miss to marry him in a hot air balloon," Bertram drawled, entering the door at that very moment. "At least, that's what I propose will happen. Gad, but the wagers that some people do come up with. I've been racking my brains to match 'em but I declare that this one will fire 'em all up, not least Grayling."

Fanny groaned. "And what good will that do? It won't make Mr Grayling any plumper in the pocket if he does propose and as the likelihood is about as good as… you marrying the Princess of Spain… you'll only be asking Quamby to bail you out again!"

She squeezed shut her eyes as she sought forebearance. "No, I fear Mr Grayling is about to offer for Miss Huntingdon and be-sides, five hundred pounds isn't nearly enough compared with Miss Huntingdon's fortune."

Bertram tapped the side of his nose. "I know that my sisters think I'm not so clever sometimes—"

"That's what you said before you devised that ridiculous idea of telling Mr Grayling poor Thea had only six months to live."

Fanny sent him a withering look. "It would have been better never to have raised her hopes, since he clearly isn't the kind of gentleman to put his heart above his pocketbook. Well, I suppose Dr Horne will be kind to her. A poor, impecunious elderly doctor marrying a lovely, beautiful young woman. Life is cruel!"

"But she'll get her offer from Mr Grayling, I told you." Bertram looked offended. "My wager is only the start of something much bigger. Trust me on this, my dear sisters. Everything will go according to plan. In fact, so confident am I that have staked the reputation of the entire Brightwell clan upon the outcome."

And with these encouraging words he gave a flourishing bow before returning up the hill with a decided swagger in his step.

CHAPTER 18

DAMN, but Sylvester could not banish from his mind the images of hope that radiated from Miss Brightwell's shining smile followed by the confusion of her clouded gaze once Bramley had laid it all out on the table, so to speak.

Indeed, such thoughts made him feel like a butterfly pinned to a cork board as he glanced from the looking glass which reflected his clumsy attempts to tie his cravat to the side table upon which lay his mother's no-nonsense missive which made clear that such a union was completely unacceptable.

With a grunt of irritation he tossed the

starched neck linen onto the pile of other failed attempts and picked up a fresh length. It was no surprise that in less than twenty four hours his venerable mater was apprised of how matters stood with her only son. She'd have made a formidable commander in the recent wars with France if she'd been a different gender but as she was the female head of an old and powerful family, she'd made matchmaking her special interest. Her stamp of approval or otherwise carried enormous weight.

Sylvester resumed his task with grim determination though he was not generally so exacting in the matter of his dress. Briefly he closed his eyes. Anything to hold at bay the myriad of uncomfortable, gut-churning thoughts that filled him with desire and remorse—even though he knew he'd been set up and was justified in the self righteous fury he felt.

Of course, a handsome dowry would put things right though of course if a handsome dowry were in the offing there'd have been none of the subterfuge Miss Brightwell's family had gone to such pains to orchestrate and thereby trap him.

And if Miss Brightwell came with a handsome dowry he'd have no compunction in offering for her. She'd have the credentials that would satisfy his exacting family, namely his mama. This knowledge was as uncomfortable as thoughts of Miss Brightwell's distress—and his raging physical desire for her—and he despised himself for it.

So as he finally declared himself satisfied with his fifth attempt at an Oriental tie and prepared to meet headlong the challenges that awaited him at Lady Camperdown's ball, he knew his biggest challenge would be his own conflicted desire.

He simply hadn't the words to tell her that he was no longer a prospective suitor, when of course his ardour in the Oriental Pavilion Room would have told a completely different story.

When he reached his destination and the doors were opened wide to issue him inside he raised his eyes to the shimmering chandelier and prayed silently for fortitude as the warmth of heated bodies hit him.

Of course, the moment he dropped his gaze, fate would have it that the first person he locked eyes with was the charming, damnably irresistible Miss Brightwell.

The intense rush of lust took his breath away but he was ready. All such inconvenient emotions must be tempered by the dampening thought that she—or at least her conniving cousins—had planned to see him in parson's mousetrap; that their machinations were motivated by greed and familial self interest rather than a simple desire to secure the happiness of a beloved cousin.

With a curt nod he turned to survey the rest of the room and found himself being regarded with distinct interest by Miss Huntingdon. She was standing beside her mother and another elderly matron, obviously bored while they nodded their heads together in deep discussion. Three or four days ago, when the situation was very different, Sylvester would have made a beeline for Miss Brightwell, avoiding Miss Huntingdon whom he'd have made a point of acknowledging in a manner that gave her no ideas of anything serious for the meantime, at any rate.

Now Sylvester, racked with guilt, forced himself to adopt a nonchalant attitude as he wandered over towards Miss Huntingdon who, he tried to persuade himself, had eyes every bit as alluring as Miss Brightwell's.

Instantly her mouth curved into a delighted smile, which only reminded him of how damnably kissable Miss Brightwell's mouth was. Clearly Miss Huntingdon was easy prey and quite amenable to a match with him; yet with her handsome dowry she could have snared a man with a title or a far greater fortune than he possessed. Sylvester merely had grand expectations and the weight of five hundred years of family dynastic considerations upon his shoulders.

"Would you care for this next dance?" he asked, hardening his heart to the pain he glimpsed in Miss Brightwell's lustrous eyes.

THEA'S EYES WIDENED WITH HURT AND horror at her aunt's acerbic tones.

"Surely you knew from the outset Mr Grayling was after a fortune, my girl. Stop wearing your heart on your sleeve. You'll only shame yourself further."

Shame herself? Hadn't she done that already? Stifling a sob, Thea swung round, unable to tolerate her aunt's taunts any further, and promptly ran into a gentleman who'd stepped that moment into her path.

"How clumsy of me. I do beg your pardon, Miss Brightwell," came the distinctly recognisable and unpleasantly familiar tones of Mr George Bramley. "Why, I have dislodged the pearl comb in your hair. I shall wait while you adjust it and then let me atone by leading you into this dance. Would you oblige me?"

Others nearby were filing onto the dance floor and Thea, who was quite incapable of the rudeness required to decline, found herself similarly herded into the centre of the room, while the back of her neck prickled and her hands became moist in her neat kid gloves.

"What has occurred to wipe from your pretty face the charming smile I remember from last time we met?" he asked.

Horrified and embarrassed, Thea realised he was alluding to baby George's christening.

"You look shocked, Miss Brightwell. I'm sorry if I've said something to compound my having already found myself in your bad books."

"No, not at all, Mr Bramley." Thea heard her voice as a faint, pathetic thread of sound but it was all she could manage as she recalled just how radiant she must have appeared when he last saw her, having so recently stepped out from the delights she'd revelled in with Mr Grayling in the Oriental Pavilion.

And there, over Mr Bramley's right shoulder, she could see Mr Grayling himself, now conversing with Miss Huntingdon in remarkably animated tones as they awaited their turn to perform their figures down the room.

Could she feign illness and make a hurried departure? The idea was appealing, but at the same time she couldn't rid herself of the thought that possibly, just possibly, Mr Grayling was simply attending dutifully to Miss Huntingdon before he turned the full force of his attention back to herself.

"I'm sorry, Mr Bramley. I'm not feeling myself tonight. I'm sure it'll pass, though."

"I do hope so." He touched her elbow, almost in a caress, and Thea jerked her arm back as she brought her chin up.

His smile was knowing, and with a surge or horror, Thea realised, as the innocent she no longer was, that Mr Bramley was speculating on something. Something unpleasant and pertaining to her.

Staring resolutely over his shoulder, she tried to blank her mind to all but her dance moves, which she realised she now had to perform. Linking elbows with the hateful Mr Bramley, she performed a couple of doh-si-dos, never more relieved than when she could step back and face him with a good couple of feet separating them.

He'd been looking at her with that sly, speculative expression peculiar to him as if he wanted to do with her exactly what Mr

Grayling had already done. Well, something improper. She swallowed down her anguish. Could he know?

No, she couldn't think of it. She wouldn't!

"Miss Brightwell, something really is troubling you. A megrim? Perhaps some fresh air is what's needed."

"I'm quite all right, thank you, Mr Bramley. And I believe this dance is nearly at an end. Please, will you escort me back to my aunt?"

"I'm offended you wish to leave my company so quickly. Let us linger a little, Miss Brightwell. Has anyone told you how delightful your dimples are when you smile? Regrettably they have been absent all evening. I should wish very much to be in a position to restore them."

"You are not able to do that, Mr Bramley." She tried to step past him, for he was forcing her to linger in an area near the French doors where suddenly she felt very alone and vulnerable, his bulk impeding her progress, his unpleasant, sneering face peering with far too much familiarity into her own.

"Unable to? Why so, Miss Brightwell? Because something has made you sad this evening? Surely I should at least be allowed to *try* to rectify that."

"You could never manage that, Mr Bramley. Now please, let me pass. My aunt is only a few feet away. You can leave me now." She knew she was too sharp with him the moment the words were out but she didn't care. She couldn't bear being in his company a moment longer. He was odious. Her cousins were right and she should have heeded them from the beginning and found any excuse not to be in his company. He was playing with her because he could. Because she was fair game and the cousin of the women who'd belittled him in the past.

"Of course, Miss Brightwell. I trust you'll feel better soon." His voice was cold, his eyes full of malice as he bowed in farewell.

"I'm sorry if I offended you, Mr Bramley," she whispered, running a hand across her brow. "You're right; something has upset me this evening."

"I'm sorry to hear it."

He was gone when she looked up once more but Thea was more relieved that she didn't have to pander to his peevishness than concerned at having put his nose out of joint.

"Ah, Thea." Aunt Minerva gave her a distracted pat on the shoulder as she rejoined her. "I'm glad you're back. Mr Granville has been looking in this direction but my eyes aren't good enough to discern the quality of his look, if you will. Of course, his letters suggest he's leading up to something but he's not yet had the courage to act. The fact he hasn't written in a couple of days suggests he is fearful of his reception. Tell me, girl, what exactly is he looking at and how is he looking at it?" She patted one of her chins and gave a little self-conscious toss of her head.

Thea peered in the direction her aunt had indicated and indeed, there was Mr Granville, staring right in their direction. She squinted, widening her eyes with surprise when he smiled broadly at her, nodding in apparent appreciation before offering a well-executed bow.

"Well, what is it, Thea? You look shocked."

"He's just executed a very elegant bow. Surely you saw that, Aunt Minerva?"

"Mr Granville bowing at me?" Her voice was a little breathless. She drew herself up. "Why, when will that man find the courage to do what's been in his heart these long weeks?"

"Not quite two, Aunt Minerva," Thea reminded her, though her mind was on quite another matter. For there was Mr Grayling, staring at her from across the room. And if she weren't mistaken, there was a look of both longing and something else. Anger? No, how could she interpret it as that when, if anyone had a right to be angry, it was she?

Only devastation would be a more apt description. What had Thea done to warrant such a change in attitude? Her body felt both hot and then immediately chilled. *Was there something wrong with her that she didn't know about?*

But then he nodded. Yes, she was sure

that he nodded and indicated the door to outside.

It was an invitation, surely, and Thea's heart was pounding as she hastily made her excuses to her aunt that she'd be back shortly.

Inveigling her way into a large party just leaving, she was soon through the French doors and in the moonlit darkness, hurrying quickly around the side of the building and into the shadows. Never in her life could she have imagined risking her reputation like this, but the alternative—marriage to Dr Horne—meant she'd do whatever she had to in order to find out from the man she truly loved exactly how matters stood.

"Miss Brightwell."

She swung round at the voice that issued behind her from near a large, thick-trunked tree but instead of being filled with joyful excitement, she shrank back. Oh dear Lord, no. How had she stepped into such a trap?

"How delightful to find you here. And all alone? Waiting for me, I suspect. After that convincing little show of coyness, you almost led me to believe you found my company repugnant. Yet here you are, waiting for me."

Thea put her hands up to his chest to push Mr Bramley away, for he'd stepped forward, his arms outstretched as if he truly meant to embrace her. The effrontery was shocking. And yet, she realised she'd put herself in this situation. She had no one but herself to blame and she must call on all her resources to extricate herself.

"I do find your company repugnant, Mr Bramley!" she hissed. "Unhand me this instant!"

"You are very fierce in your desire to be rid of me, Miss Brightwell." Thanks to the slash of light from the brightly illuminated windows above, Thea could see his displeasure was more genuine than merely for show. His eyes were dark with more than just brooding displeasure, his mouth a taut, hard line. In fact his whole attitude was combative; as if he were ready to pummel Thea for every slight he'd sustained, perceived or otherwise. However, he merely gripped her wrists. "Your cousin didn't find me repugnant. In fact, that flirtatious little trollop, Lady Quamby, happened to find my attentions distinctly more appealing than those of her husband, my uncle. She led me a pretty dance and then betrayed me, you know. That's why I'd hoped another Brightwell might show remorse." His voice hardened. "And if not remorse, then atonement."

"Atonement? What kind of atonement?" Thea gasped before she could stop the naïve question. No, she really had no desire to know when she needed to escape from this hateful situation and put as much distance between Mr Bramley and herself as she could.

"What kind of atonement?" he repeated, pulling her closer to him and tucking her head beneath his chin in a parody of affection. "Well, if you came with a fortune I could bear the idea of being saddled with you for a life sentence. You're decorative and I'd enjoy tutoring such a wife in the arts at which your worldly cousin Antoinette excelled." He sighed, unexpectedly releasing her and with a shuddering gasp, Thea staggered back a step and was about to turn tail and run when he went on with simply too much provocation, "Alas, you bring no benefits to any man who needs to consider their long-term future, which clearly is why Mr Grayling has dropped you like a hot potato. I believe he thought your pretty face was accompanied by a portion, no matter how meagre. Perhaps your aunt or your cousins led him to believe such was the case and then he discovered the truth. You'll have to ask him that."

"How dare you!" With a cry, Thea whipped back her hand and dealt him a stinging blow across the face as the tears threatened to flow. "Antoinette and Fanny were right. There is not one single redeeming thing about you, Mr Bramley! Now do not try to stop me from leaving and do not even think to ask me to dance should the occasion arise."

"Oh, I had ideas that were a lot more exciting than dancing. Good lord, Miss Brightwell, what a little termagant you are!" Touching his cheek where she'd struck him, his obvious shock was replaced by amusement. Thea picked up her skirts and ran as fast as she could, back towards the French doors through which she'd come, his mocking laughter and the words, "I have long looked forward to the day a Brightwell begs me for mercy and I believe it is nearly upon me. You have only whetted my appetite, dear Madam!" ringing in her ears.

***

ONCE INSIDE THEA HURRIED TO A LESS populated corner of the ballroom where she stood alone for a moment, unable to stop shaking.

"Whatever's the matter, Thea?"

Immediately Fanny glided over to her side, her calm concern like a balm for Thea, who was then able to take a deep breath and draw back her shoulders and behave with the dignity current circumstances required.

"I...I was such a fool," she whispered, trying not to cry and gratefully taking the dainty muslin handkerchief Fanny offered her. "I saw Mr Grayling look at me like he wanted to tell me something, so I went outside. Only, there was that awful Mr Bramley instead." She hiccupped as another fit of trembling seized her and Fanny marched her out of the view of several interested spectators, tripping over a young man with a florid complexion and bulbous eyes who looked as if he'd never been so entertained. Thea nearly expired on the spot at having spoken so openly of her indiscretions, but as her time in Bath was nearly at an end, as were her hopes for any possibility of a future filled with happiness, or even punctuated with brief patches of it, she told herself fiercely that she didn't care.

"Now sit." Her cousin pushed her down onto a velvet-upholstered banquette and caught the attention of a passing footman, from whom she procured two glasses of champagne at the same time as requesting that her brother, Mr Brightwell, be summoned. "Drink this, Thea dearest," she ordered. "Yes, don't mind the spluttering. A bit of fizz is always guaranteed to ease a dire situation." When Thea had finished her glass, Fanny immediately replaced it with the second, even though Thea protested that she'd be quite dizzy in the head if she drank any more, but as Bertram then appeared and Fanny went into quite a huddle with the young man, Thea was left to stare at the nearly full glass. Deciding that the first had gone down rather easily, she thought that if the second could do an even better job of drowning her sorrows, she might as well do as Cousin Fanny ordered.

But the moment Fanny sat down beside her and focussed a look full of sympathy upon her, Thea promptly dissolved into tears. "I want to go home." She put her head into her hands. "I thought that coming to Bath would be so exciting and that I'd enjoy opportunities I'd never have had if I spent my days attending to Aunt Minerva, but now I see what I should have seen before. That money counts for everything!"

Fanny patted Thea's shoulder. "And so does a great deal of cunning. Now, I've sent my brother on an errand but Cousin Bertram will be back in our midst soon enough and then we shall all return home. I'll arrange for a lovely and calming posset when you're safely tucked up in bed, and hopefully this terrible night won't haunt you beyond the witching hour." Her voice gentled. "Hush Thea, you're so much sweeter and deserving of a kind and loyal husband than I am, but I've always been mindful of the dues I must pay for having secured such unlooked-for happiness. Fenton is a treasure and it's my duty to ensure others—such as you—find similar joy in life." She squeezed Thea's hand and her pert, beautiful face was surprisingly tender. "Trust me, Thea, to do whatever is within my power to see you find it. If there's one thing you can depend upon, it's that I keep my word."

"IF THERE'S ONE THING YOU CAN DEPEND upon, it's that I keep my word," Bertram muttered as he made his way unsteadily down the front steps and around the side. The stables would not be far but he had to be quick if he were to do as Fanny suggested. Each time he encountered Cousin Thea's lovelorn eyes and observed yet another dip in her spirits he felt somehow responsible. Of course, his plan would have been perfectly marvellous had the odious George Bramley not spoiled everything with his malicious public remarks, which had all but made it quite clear to Mr Grayling that he'd been duped and that Thea were as hearty and robust as, well... Miss Huntingdon, with whom Bertram had observed Mr Grayling appeared to be on increasingly familiar terms.

Well, Fanny's little plan had merit too, he was prepared to conceded, if only to further the far more cunning plan he, Bertram, intended to properly put in place.

Once he'd found Mr Grayling's groom, telling him his master had no more need of his services this evening, Bertram headed inside.

His sisters—and Thea, of course—would be delighted with him, he decided as he rubbed shoulders later that night with the other young bucks who were challenging each other to ridiculous wagers in the billiards room.

Lord Milton had just announced he'd bestow five hundred pounds upon Lord

Cardigan if he worked as a footman on his father's estate for one whole day without being recognised.

Bertram raised his voice above the hub-bub. "Who'll propose five hundred that Miss Brightwell won't receive a marriage offer from Mr Grayling in a hot-air balloon?"

The other young men looked at him with scorn and for a moment there was si-lence. "I observed Miss Brightwell slapping the face of our esteemed friend here, Mr George Bramley," interjected Lord Daring-ton, a sandy-haired Corinthian in his cups. "Therefore I'll wager *Mr Bramley* five hun-dred pounds he dare not propose marriage to Miss Brightwell in a hot air balloon."

"Make that seven hundred and I'll accept your wager." George Bramley chuckled. "At least then the chit might be worth the trou-ble. I say," he added, "where'll we get a hot-air balloon?"

"Lord Quamby is arranging for a hot-air balloon at his estate for the celebrations in one week marking the christening of his heir," someone told him.

Bertram tried to speak above the hubbub. "Not George Bramley," he protested. "I wager that *Mr Grayling* be the one to propose."

But the rest of the company ignored Bertram until someone reminded him that, as it was clear Miss Brightwell and Mr Grayling were clearly interested in one another — only Miss Brightwell had not a feather to fly with — such a wager was not worth anything at all.

"I say! I wager that Lady Quamby makes Mr Freddy Rotheringham her next lover before he goes up to Oxford and that she'll give birth to a lovely bouncing, bonny bairn before next Christmas!" cried Lord Darington, at which suggestion Bertram, who'd seen the sheep's eyes each had sent the other, immediately upped the stakes another two hundred, dolefully concluding it was going to be his only means of lining his pockets.

CHAPTER 19

IT was early—not yet midnight—when Sylvester slunk out of the ballroom. For a moment he'd contemplated going to the billiards room, as was his wont, but tonight he felt ill, dispirited and out of sorts. As the doors closed behind him and he breathed in the warm night air, he had to push back his shoulders to counteract the sense that he was indeed slinking away from any sense of nobility.

In terms of what his mind dictated, the night had been a success. The glint in Miss Huntingdon's eye was smug and self-satisfied. Indeed, he'd given her every reason for feeling smug and self-satisfied and he detested himself for it.

For his heart dictated a very different outcome from the course he was navigating.

Miss Brightwell, who exuded an innocence untarnished by his initiation; an innocence belied by the very real suggestion that she was up to her neck in skulduggery —that of tricking him into matrimony—was still far and above the one miss he'd cross crocodile-infested waters in order to whisk into his arms and ride with into the sunset.

But, apart from the fact that devious means had been employed to trick him into losing his heart to the chit, what happiness would they both enjoy when penny-pinching was the order of the day? He had a modest enough income to keep himself in the manner to which he'd become accustomed: an excellent tailor, a fine enough address and sufficient largesse to pay the vails required to gain him admittance to the best country house parties.

But two of them could quickly become three, and then four or more. Miss Brightwell adored children. He was rather partial to them himself. But what of a large family and the inevitable bills? How could he provide dowries to daughters that would ensure they'd not endure the unhappy lot currently facing Miss Brightwell? The irony struck him keenly.

The simple truth was that he did not have the funds to provide for the lovely, sweet Miss Thea Brightwell as she deserved. Love would soon turn to recrimination as the bills mounted.

The night's warm air was no relief as waited in the portico for his carriage, which he'd ordered be brought round early. He was surprised Tom, his coachman, wasn't already there, for he'd sent word ten minutes before and he was leaving well before the departing throng.

A flurry behind him, and excited female voices, made him turn.

"Lord Benton certainly paid you a lot of attention, Thea," he heard as the doors were opened, and as he turned, he found himself locking eyes with lovely Lady Fenton. Her smile was instant and radiant but as he transferred his gaze to the young lady beside her, he felt an unwanted clamping somewhere in the region of his chest. This was accompanied by a decidedly hefty dose of guilt, for he'd not even addressed Miss Brightwell, much less asked her to dance. And this, when three days ago he'd whisked her off to the Oriental Pavilion Room to show her…

He bowed extravagantly, as if that might somehow ameliorate her warranted hurt and confusion but before he could speak he was surprised to see one of the grooms appear at the bottom of the stairs, on foot, a look of great consternation on his face.

"Beg pardon, sir, for the delay but your carriage copped a sideswipe, which has knocked the wheel off. Your coachman is fetching the wheelwright now."

"Oh, too bad, Mr Grayling." Lady Quamby smiled at him past her aunt's waving feather—not her dreadful aunt's, he realised, for she appeared to have already left— while her husband conversed with Lord Fenton. "There's room in ours. Let me oblige you."

Sylvester sized up the party and decided

that, as Miss Brightwell appeared to be travelling with Lord and Lady Fenton, he'd be safe enough. He didn't think he was up to the young woman's warranted reproachful looks.

He was also very aware that after her initial sizing up of him, Miss Brightwell appeared to be studiously avoiding him. It was just as well, he decided, though it only stabbed him with even greater remorse.

However, as Lady Fenton moved towards the carriage with her husband, and Miss Brightwell appeared to be under the illusion she was travelling with them, Lady Fenton turned and waved her away. "Darling Thea, you must go with Antoinette, as Fenton and I have been invited to another party. Didn't I tell you? Antoinette, you've room, have you not?"

And with Lady Quamby's assertion that it was a case of "the more the merrier", Sylvester found himself ushered into the cramped interior of the same carriage in which Miss Brightwell travelled, his knees touching hers, and as she lowered her head to do something with her dancing slipper, her egret feather brushed across the side of his cheek. It was the most sensuous feeling he'd enjoyed in a long while and a shudder of longing racked his body. But he made sure to have his face studiously averted when she straightened though after inadvertently making eye contact once more, she blushed furiously, which Sylvester found curiously discomposing and rather touching. Gad! If he had any choice in the matter he'd divest himself of familial responsibilities and entailed estates and do what was in his heart: make the girl an offer and look forward to a life of rare and exceptional happiness.

Quamby engaged Sylvester in some light banter during the journey home then, to his surprise, announced he was stopping off at some gaming den and did Grayling wish to accompany him?

Sylvester shook his head. He'd stayed away from the cards lately and his pocketbook was healthier as a result. But now he was alone with the two ladies and he felt distinctly uncomfortable under Lady

Quamby's assessing eye, while Miss Brightwell said nothing.

Suddenly the carriage came to another stop outside one of the new addresses, a fine townhouse, and Lady Quamby leant forward. "This is where I get off." She looked both coy and just a touch defiant though she gave no explanation. "Mr Grayling, there's no need to see Thea home, though I do trust to your discretion. It's the only way to get on, don't you think? Goodnight, Thea darling, but I'm expected and I can't possibly break such an important engagement."

"Where are you going?" Miss Brightwell sounded panicked, as well she might, and Sylvester felt another surge of anger. Was this a deliberate ploy to put him in a compromising situation with Miss Brightwell so that he might be forced to do the honourable thing?

To his surprise, it appeared Lady Quamby knew what he was thinking, for she said quite openly, "Please don't worry that it's a trap. I know your interest in my cousin has faded for reasons known only to you, and so I wanted to give you this opportunity to explain why. I promise you I haven't staged anything that will force you to the altar. I merely want you to take the next two minutes en route to your residence to explain matters to Thea, since I think she deserves at least that from you. The coachman will ensure she's delivered home safely once he's deposited you."

Then she was gone, the tense atmosphere such a speech occasioned within the small space in which they were cocooned so thick he could have sliced it with a billiard cue.

With difficulty he tried to articulate some coherent words as the carriage rolled down the bumpy road, Lady Quamby having directed the driver to take a circuitous route around the town. Ten minutes to unburden himself and then Miss Brightwell would be under no illusions as to the cad he was while he would be...free. The thought should have made him relieved, if not altogether happy.

Careful not to come too closely into contact and so compromise his intention of being open and, sadly, brutal, Sylvester cleared his throat. "Miss Brightwell, it does me no credit to say it, but nor could I have been the gentleman to bring you happiness if we were to live on my income alone. Truly, I did not mean to dash your hopes." He hated to see her distress but forced himself to go on. The genuine perplexity and hurt in her expression finally convinced him she had no knowledge of the duplicity which had been orchestrated by the rest of the Brightwell clan in her own interests. As a result, he felt even worse as a flood of feeling washed over him; but he forced himself to go on, as sensitively and earnestly as he could, stiffening against the side of the carriage so he was not distracted by her unsettling nearness. "Your cousins led me to believe you were not long for this world and exhorted me to show you the pleasure you'd not otherwise have experienced. The truth is, my initial feelings for you were tenderness and pity which, I regret, became something deeper at the same time that I realised you were were not in fact dying *and* that I was entirely unable to make you the offer you were no doubt expecting after—" He shrugged helplessly—"I, and possibly you, discovered we were both deceived as to the true state of affairs. Truly, I am…sorry." He watched her dismay turn to horror.

"What are you saying, Mr Grayling? Not long for this world? Why, I am in greater health than anyone I know!"

He almost laughed out loud at her offended expression as she went on to catalogue how very full of health she was, but then she seemed to finally acknowledge what he was saying and burst out, "How could my cousins have misled you like that? *Why* would they?"

She choked on a sob and instinctively he put out his hand and placed it upon her forearm, not minding when she moved it to grip his fingers as if he could provide her the comfort he was in the process of denying her. Now he was the one to choke on his emotion. How desirable she looked with her moist eyes staring at him as if he were documenting someone else's failings and not his own.

He turned slightly and took her other

hand. The horses were moving at a gentle clip now. Inside, they could barely make out one another's features, but the interior was thick with feeling. Sylvester drew in a strained breath. "Your cousins conceived of a cunning plan to entrap me when they saw how much I admired you. They thought they could achieve your happiness by securing me as a husband." His heart hitched and he didn't move away when the carriage rounded a bend and she was thrown upon him, though she moved back quickly. "Yes, they tricked me and they tricked you, too, by saying you were not long for this world, and they've made neither of us the happier for it. I'm sorry you've been deceived."

He cleared his throat and spoke the truth. "Believe me, Miss Brightwell, if I had the funds to provide for both of us in the manner you deserve, I'd be on bended knee this moment." Never had he been more sincere. "The fact is, however, I can only continue my life of relative ease—and indeed, provide a life of comfort to my future wife —if I were to marry someone with..."

"Money," she supplied, which silenced

him a moment as he wished the plain facts of the matter didn't make him sound so mercurial.

He squeezed her hand. "You deserve a life of greater comfort than I can afford to give you, for without money, our love would struggle and die."

She drew in her breath on an audible gasp. "Then you *do* love me?"

She was too close for comfort and her direct question could only be answered with the truth. He'd give it to her, but that would be all. He would not forget himself and make declarations that would give her joyful visions of tripping down the aisle with him having overcome all the arguments he put forward against such a journey.

He wasn't sure how it came to be but suddenly she was in his arms, her soft cheek pressed against his, her little fingers gripping his as she brought their joined hands up to her breast. "You love me but you do not wish to marry me," she clarified softly.

"It's not that I do not *wish* to marry you, I simply am not in a position to *honourably* offer marriage to you." He was very conscious of the swell of her bosom beneath the hand she clasped and had to force himself not to caress it.

One last time, he thought as, despite his very best intentions, he smoothed the silken fabric gently over her bodice, delighted to hear how her breath quickened. He caught himself up and was about to withdraw his hand when she caged it with her own and put her lips to his in the gentlest, briefest of kisses.

The sweetness and tenderness was too much. His body was on fire but her innocence had to be protected. Yet one kiss was surely not too much to ask?

"I'm going to leave you soon, Miss Brightwell," he murmured, eyes closed but reluctant to move his mouth away from the proximity of her lovely face. Her lips were a hairsbreadth away from his own.

"I know," she murmured, her soft breath like a caress.

It was almost more than he could bear; as was the fact that her voice was filled with forgiveness rather than the pain and recrimination he deserved as she went on, "But you have been honest with me, and in fact you've been duped so I can hold no grudges." She drew in a laboured breath. "Of course you must ask Miss Huntingdon to marry you. I would just ask that you kiss me one last time."

It was more than he could have hoped for and he'd meant to do so with chaste gentleness in a farewell tribute. Certainly he had no intention of doing anything that would whip up desires he could not control...but who would have thought that gentle innocence would unleash such a beast within him? She was good to the core of her being and he was a cad who could only cause her hurt and grief.

Yet as their mouths fused, his good intentions fled and indeed he was the beast, uncaged. Only by the greatest exercise of restraint was he able to resist taking full advantage of the invitation she extended towards him as she draped herself over his lap.

Her breasts pressed against his chest, heaved with emotion, while her soft sighs of pleasure only excited him more. Their closeness was infused with raging need yet Sylvester was careful to limit her exposure only to kisses.

They'd done so much more than this, before, but the knowledge this would be their last encounter charged it with an eroticism so staggeringly intense he thought he might lose his senses to the desire to possess her in every sense.

Except he could not; though with her mouth so ripe and yielding and her kisses so inflammatory, it was difficult to remember why he could not.

Money.

A vision flashed before him of his mother; of the estate he would likely inherit. Entailed and needing funds to keep intact the heritage of hundred of years.

If only things had only been different... Lord, how he wished he could make her his while she was so very willing. If not for all the good reasons he'd catalogued preventing such a union, he'd dish out whatever was required for a special licence or whisk her off to Gretna Green. If not for his mother and family expectation, the estate, and the knowledge that he'd soon have to provide for a growing family, he'd do what he wished above all things he was able to do: make her a marriage offer.

It was she who brought their kiss to an end. Drawing back, she looked at him with those unsettling clear eyes of hers that, in the light of the lamp under which they'd drawn to a halt, he saw glistened with un-shed tears. Still breathless, she whispered, "I'm not blaming anyone…except myself for being so naïve."

Though her features were indistinct in the gloom, he could not doubt her sincerity. "My cousins told me your first wife was a… cold woman and that you needed to be per-suaded of my genuine affection for you. I never would have behaved so improperly without their pushing me to be alone with you. I know they did it because they thought that what happened to them could happen to me." She gulped in a breath and straightened. "Mr Grayling, I'm truly sorry I'm not dying for then you'd have pursued your plans of showing me *everything* a woman in love would want to know before she breathed her last."

"You are in love with me?" He'd been about to explosively deny the allegation of him having ever been married but now it was more important to seize the moment and hear those sweet words repeated.

"Of course I'm in love with you!" She sounded indignant as she rested her chin in her hand, leaning into the squabs. The carriage had stopped some minutes ago but they'd given no signal to the coachman who remained obediently in his position on the box above. Perhaps he'd tried to get direction. Perhaps he'd been given instructions to wait quietly until told otherwise. Sylvester didn't care. Miss Brightwell's declaration meant more to him than anything right now.

"I love you more than I can tell you, Mr Grayling, and that's the truth! When you were kissing me, I thought I'd died and gone to heaven. And then I remembered what we did before." She wriggled, as if her body were reliving the experience and he had to exercise every restraint not to move forward and take this as an invitation to slide his hand beneath her skirts in a prelude to the next stage of intimacy. Dear Lord, it was what he wanted more than anything!

Just in time she remembered himself; while she, it seemed was inconveniently remembering just what he was trying to put out of his mind. "Oh, but that was so delicious!" she uttered in tones of rapture, closing her eyes as she moved forward to rest her head on his shoulder. She opened one eye and asked anxiously, "We can have just these few moments together, can't we? I mean, now that you're assured I won't wrongly think it'll lead to offers you're not in a position to make." She closed her eyes and smiled. "Just being with you now is the nicest feeling I can remember." She snuggled closer and murmured, "Until you showed me in the Oriental Pavilion, I didn't know such feelings existed. Now I have something truly memorable to think of when I'm someone else's wife."

The idea of her becoming someone else's wife took on suddenly horrific proportions. To think of someone *else* being in a position to coax such delightful responses from such an adorable, innocent creature was a painful blow to Sylvester's honour, and a sharp dose of reality.

"Someone else's wife?" He straightened and looked down at her while she gazed back, smiling.

"Of course. More than anything I want to be a mother. You've shown me what it's possible to feel here." She touched her heart, adding as she dropped her eyes, which is why I've decided not to accept Dr Horne when once I might have done—"

"Good Lord! What are you saying, Miss Brightwell!" he exclaimed. "Dr *Horne?*"

She looked surprised as she wriggled upright. "Didn't you know? Yes, he's made me an offer which Aunt Minerva is strongly encouraging me to accept since she believes some secret admirer is about to declare for her."

"Your aunt Minerva is about to be married?"

"She believes she is, and that's why she says I need to find somewhere else to live. But however much I try to reconcile myself to what I must do to have any kind of marriage, and knowing that at least marriage to Dr Horne will give me babies that will make my life worthwhile, you've shown me that a whole other side to…feelings I never knew existed, and after this evening I don't think I could ever marry Dr Horne since that'll entail doing with him what I only want to do with you."

"Good Lord!" There! He'd said it again but the idea was preposterous. First that she could even talk about wedding another when she was in his embrace, not to mention making reference to the marriage act, but that she'd actually been considering Dr *Horne.*

She looked so dismayed he held her tightly as he reassured her, "My dearest girl, I had the greatest pleasure showing you how a man and a woman who love one another proceed to show it in the most intimate manner."

"You *love* me! Oh, I do like to hear it!"

She looked so happy about this Sylvester nearly blurted out the idea that had taken root just a moment before and which refused to be dislodged. Yes, tomorrow he would see his uncle's Man of Business. Perhaps, just perhaps, there was some way matters and economies could be arranged to accommodate a marriage that brought in nothing from the bride.

Impulsively he held her tightly, his tone more impassioned than before as he spoke the truth. "I perfectly adore you, Miss Brightwell! And, like you, I cannot stop *thinking* about how well suited we are and wishing we could take this further in the Oriental Pavilion where we had such fun the other day—"

"Before you realized my cousin Bertram's wicked lie had led you up the garden path." She drew back, her look crestfallen as she forestalled the words he would say to indicate his altered intentions. "Do you know," she went on, "I would have taken any risk for you to have shown me *all* the pleasure to be had between a man and a woman." With a tentative glance at his bulging breeches she added, "Cousin Antoinette described what happened to a married woman in the most appalling way. I thought I'd never want to marry except that it's the only way to beget children and I do want a great many children, which is of course another reason why you can't possibly afford to marry me. One's offspring are very expensive, so Aunt Minerva says."

Her sigh was followed by an immediate brightening. "I shall always have wonderful memories of you, though, Mr Grayling. You shall be the benchmark by which I measure all others."

"Good god, how can you say that when I'm about to pass you over for the most mercurial of reasons." Except that perhaps this would not have to come to pass. Perhaps, when he had a proper consultation with his man, Hookes, over his financial affairs, he could find a way forward. He shook his head vehemently, realizing their time together was nearly at an end. At least for tonight. Gripping her hands, he said urgently, "I shall send you a note, Miss Brightwell. Give me a couple of days but if I can effect the means of offering you what you deserve, I shall send you a note requesting that you meet me at the Oriental Pavilion. If

I do that, you can be assured that not only do you have my heart—which you know already you have—but my assurance that I can follow it up with a marriage that indeed can offer you—and our children—the comfort and security we would want."

"Really, Mr Grayling?" She gasped, biting her lip while her eyes danced with excitement. Then she sobered, saying in resigned tones, "And if it cannot be, you will *not* send me a note and will instead offer for Miss Huntingdon."

But already Sylvester had discounted that option. By the time he'd seen her safely whisked indoors by her Cousin Fanny who was clearly keeping a sharp lookout and was waiting near the front door, he knew that by hook or by crook, he intended to find a means of offering Miss Brightwell not just his love but his hand in marriage.

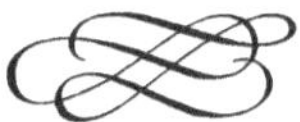

SEVEN hundred pounds simply to persuade Miss Brightwell into a hot air balloon? Another seven hundred to have his proposal accepted? Oh, he could manage that when the girl realised she had little choice in the matter.

And a further seven hundred pounds for the birth of a bonny bairn nine months later.

The more George Bramley pondered such a scenario the more he felt satisfied. Of course, a man like himself ought to be able to snare a debutante with a dowry that was handsomer than this trio of wagers, should he win them, but there was a certain satisfaction to the whole idea of marrying a Brightwell *and* being paid handsomely to do so. Hadn't the Misses Fanny and Antoinette led him a merry dance — but their brother was a fool. Which begged the question of why George had not sought earlier to capitalize on what was common knowledge: that Bertram Brightwell could be made to fall for any trick in the book with a little massaging of the ego.

As he walked the path that led into the woods, he touched his left cheek where the enchanting termagant had struck him the other night, and grinned. There was more spirit to Miss Brightwell than he'd expected. The thought gave him a little thrill. He'd enjoy taming her. So many of his daydreams involved taming her eldest cousin, the haughty, alluring, irresistible Lady Fenton, as she now was, but it seemed whatever he did, the common Brightwell sisters had always been just out of reach. Having witnessed their fondness for their quiet, pliable cousin, Bramley could easily imagine their dismay at his snatching Miss Thea Brightwell from under their noses and whisking her down the aisle.

The pine needles crunched softly underfoot as he anticipated what lay ahead. He was under no illusions she'd go willingly, but this afternoon's visit to a woodsman, the nephew of a man who once owed George a favour and who had since proved his worth, was to shore up what he saw as only a minor difficulty. At least George had the reassurance that someone would be on hand to use a little force if George failed to gently persuade Miss Brightwell into the hot-air balloon that would be waiting to take to the skies as part of the celebrations surrounding the birth of Quamby's heir. He nearly choked on his bile as he thought of the infant—his own son—who had usurped his position as the next Earl of Quamby. But short of murdering baby George, his hands were tied.

Marrying Miss Thea Brightwell was the next best thing. Aside from the fact that the last few days he'd nearly split his breeches in anticipation of possessing such a delectable personification of beauty and innocence and being paid for an outcome whereby she'd find herself in no position to refuse him, he could not wait to see the expressions on the faces of those wretched Brightwells when they had to acknowledge that George Bramley was not only cleverer than they'd given him credit, but in fact cleverer than all three of them put together.

The hovel where George was headed was located deep in the forest about two miles from the Earl of Quamby's estate. George knew exactly where he was going, for he'd called upon Splice on several previous occasions when he needed something doing of a dubious nature. He doubted many would trust the barrel-headed rustic who'd finally answered his summons, but George knew Splice was discreet.

As long as he was paid as agreed.

The light was fading when George stepped over the threshold, so the room in which he was invited to put his proposition was dark and gloomy. Hessian bags covered the windows and the dirt floor exuded a pungent odour that suggested Splice shared his abode with his pig and his goat.

It didn't take long to explain exactly what he needed doing. Nor was there any indication as to how Splice felt about performing what might be deemed an illegal act, were he to have to use brute force rather than enticement.

"One final thing." George turned back after he'd taken a couple of steps. "Bathe in the stream before you meet Miss Brightwell, otherwise she'll smell more than a rat. Those clothes you'll be wearing were borrowed from a gentleman and cost a pretty penny. I'd rather not have to burn them when you're done."

A HEAVY MELANCHOLY WEIGHED ON THEA'S shoulders as she sat at her aunt's feet, holding a skein of thread, dreaming of her last encounter with Mr Grayling.

Her euphoria had drained away once she contemplated the truth of the situation. A gentleman couldn't conjure up a fortune out of nowhere. Mr Grayling could not suddenly be in a position to ask her to marry him tomorrow when the previous day he'd declared himself just as in love but lacking sufficient fortune in view of his multiple familial obligations.

Of course, it was more than just having a carriage and the funds to enjoy the season once a year which might be major considerations for minor gentry. It was how to make the funds available do what they had to do —and Mr Bramley had more than just himself to consider. It wasn't simply an ambitious mama he had to satisfy, but rather an estate he was likely to inherit, which required enormous upkeep. Hundreds of tenant farmers and servants would depend upon Mr Grayling being in a secure financial situation and Thea now realised how important it was to so many for Mr Grayling to make an illustrious marriage.

Yet...and this was where a small ray of hope shone through the rest of the gloom and doom. Mr Grayling had said it had been too long since he'd discussed matters with his man of business. He'd given her distinct reason to hope. And why? He'd discovered himself genuinely in love with her. Yes, he'd been duped and he'd been angry, but that anger was not directed at Thea and it had given way to relief that Thea in fact was not at death's door; that she was a vibrant, healthy young woman who made him realize life's possibilities. Those had been his very words, in fact!

A knock on the door provided instant relief to the boredom of listening to her aunt's heavy nasal breathing, and the rustling and odd muffled explosion muted by Aunt Minerva's skirts.

Immediately Thea's heart began to pound and she put her hand to her burning cheeks. Oh dear Lord, he'd come through like the hero he was! Mr Grayling had sent her a note!

"This was just delivered for you, Ma'am." The little maid held out a silver salver, on which a neatly folded piece of parchment bore an elegant line of script.

Aunt Minerva was quick to pounce on it, slicing off the wax seal like a greedy child before scanning the contents, her hand cupping her breast as she turned it over and read it again. At this, she began to breathe even more heavily, fanning herself with the paper and shifting in her seat before bursting out, "Well, Thea, don't you have some curiosity as to what might be contained in this missive?"

Thea lowered her eyes. "I was afraid you'd consider my curiosity impertinent but of course I wish nothing more than to know what has caused such agitation, Aunt Minerva." She felt dead inside. So the note was for her aunt. Soon it would be bedtime and still Mr Grayling had not contacted her.

"I am not agitated, Thea, I am excited." Aunt Minerva sighed loudly. "Aren't you a girl forever misreading other people's moods and intentions? There you were, thinking Mr Grayling was entranced enough with your pretty face to offer marriage even after I warned you a dozen times or more that a gentleman such as he needs a dowry. Well, he's to marry Miss Huntingdon, if the gossips have their story right, and I'm sorry for it, Thea; that's the truth, for I don't know what's to be done with you when you're no longer living with me."

Thea's dismay at her aunt's blithe comments regarding Mr Grayling's marital intentions was superseded—though not eclipsed—by Aunt Minerva's suggestion that there was a timeline in her offering Thea a roof over her head.

"What are you saying?" she gasped. "I'm no trouble, surely?" She'd not countenanced Aunt Minerva *truly* receiving a marriage offer. "You said I was the best nurse you'd had. You need me." It was a bad tactic but Thea's devastation at her own marital outlook was suddenly grievously exacerbated by the practicalities of where she might live if Aunt Minerva no longer offered her a roof. A whole day had passed since she'd seen Mr Grayling. Until this very minute, in fact, she'd held high hopes of a glorious outcome but now it appeared that not only was *he* was not offering her a home after all, Aunt Minerva was threatening to withdraw her support. She tried to breathe deeply as her aunt continued, placidly, "I like you well enough, my girl, but I don't need you."

Something died inside Thea. If her aunt no longer needed her, who did? What value was she to *anyone*? She might be hard working and pliable and, at the moment in her youthful prime, but without a penny to her name, she was not only worthless, but a complete encumbrance.

Her aunt read her message again and a broad grin lit up her face. She turned to Thea, lips pursed as if weighing up whether to divulge a great secret. Finally she leaned back in her chair and gave a great sigh. "So here is how matters stand. Mr Grayling is marrying Miss Huntingdon and you've received an offer from Dr Horne which you'll be obliged to accept since I really can't see that Mr Granville will wish to start married life with the responsibility of a flighty chit like you under our roof."

"Mr Granville's asked you to marry him?!"

Her aunt sent Thea a warning look. "No need to sound so shocked. And no, the offer has not been put in so many words, however he has intimated as much. First there was his enigmatic presence at the masquerade, designed to whip up my pique, and now this, his suggestion of an assignation." She tapped the piece of parchment and looked smug. "When shall we invite Dr Horne to tea so you may put an end to his waiting? Really, the poor man is getting quite impatient. He was attending to me earlier when you were out and was quite plaintive about his concerns. I told him you were selecting your trousseau, for really, he was quite upset there was a chance you might refuse him."

"You had no right to tell him a lie!"

"Well, Thea, you can't afford to miss out on this opportunity. I was doing you a favour. The truth is, I've spent the past twenty years regretting the opportunity I turned down through my poor timing in rejecting Mr Granville." Aunt Minerva folded the parchment and tucked it between her ample breasts. "Perhaps you can give Mr Horne your acceptance just before we go to the celebration for little George tomorrow. I shall request the good doctor come to my apartments to massage my legs, as I fancy I may have a little walking to do." She clicked her tongue. "Goodness! Your cousin and her propensity for staging events outdoors that require a body to move will be the death of me. And did you know that Lady Quamby has insisted on the novelty of having a hot-air balloon? I can't imagine a more ridiculous notion than rising above the earth in a basket." She leaned forward, offering Thea a confronting view of her impressive bosom. "Did you know I once was forced to jump onto a footstool when a mouse ran across the room?" She leaned back with a self satisfied smile. "Well, that's as high as I'm prepared to go to save my life. Hot-air balloons? That's for adventurers who care nothing other than making the general public ooh and aah at their daring. Transient celebrity and nothing more! Now, how about a game of chequers?"

CHAPTER 21

AT last the day had arrived: the moment the child of a lowly Brightwell was officially acknowledged by the rest of the world as the heir to an earl.

Antoinette linked arms with her sister as they stood on the balcony and gazed at the enormous, colourful hot-air balloon that was slowly being inflated at the bottom of the grassy slope.

"Hasn't it all worked out so well?" She gave a happy sigh and dabbed at her eyes with a piece of lawn. "Who'd have thought I'd give birth to a little chap destined for such greatness? Quamby is over the moon to have the heir he thought he would never have. I overheard him promising his special friend of the moment, Francis Rind, that he'd take him on a journey to the moon to visit his heart's desire in that horrible looking hot-air balloon."

"To the moon? Well, I'm glad they're happy. And I'm glad you're happy." On one level she shared Antoinette's satisfaction that the two of them had done so well in the marriage stakes—she, through cunning and careful orchestration, and Antoinette through pure luck. She sighed. "I'm sorry we failed Thea."

"Yes, the poor darling. We gave them every opportunity, though, didn't we?" Antoinette squinted at the busy scene that accompanied the erection of the balloon. Tiny figures seemed to be scurrying everywhere, securing ropes to the basket while the canopy slowly grew, soon becoming enormous. Antoinette's tone changed from wistful to despairing as she turned back to her sister. "But even when Thea and Mr Grayling were pushed together in the coach and finally declared their true feelings and realised they each loved one another, it appears by his silence that Mr Grayling simply couldn't accept that they'd be happy without money, and I'm afraid I do agree with him. I just wish Thea didn't feel she has no option but to marry Dr Horne."

Fanny jerked her head around. "She can't make such a decision. Not yet, anyway! Of course there are other options! Bertram, tell me Thea has other options than to marry Dr Horne," she appealed to her brother, who'd just stepped out of the first-floor drawing room and onto the balcony.

Bertram ran his hands through his hair and adjusted his stock. He looked extremely agitated and Fanny wondered if he was about to confess to another loss at the gaming tables. She hoped not. Her lovely husband Fenton was the most patient and darling of men but even he was beginning to show more than the usual irritation at having to bail out her brother so frequently.

Finally Bertram managed to find the words that had eluded him as he grew increasingly red-faced and—which was even more concerning—elusive and cryptic. "Cousin Thea is not going to marry Dr Horne if George Bramley has anything to do with it." He ran his hands down his loud red and gold striped waistcoat.

"What are you saying?" his two sisters cried; and as he took a step back towards the double doors, Fanny had the very real fear that the mention of George Bramley's name meant that Bertram was about to furnish them with something even worse than his gaming losses.

Bertram swallowed. He truly looked like a man facing the gallows as he continued to address them with lowered eyes. "I thought I could fix everything and make it right." He began to pace, now running his hands up and down his pantaloons. "But truth is, I don't know what to do."

"What are you talking about, Bertram? Make what right? And what has this to do with George Bramley?" Antoinette sounded panicked as she gripped the balcony railing.

Bertram stopped and looked at her despairingly. "I tried to make Cousin Thea appear an enticing proposition to Mr Grayling—"

"Yes, by telling him she was dying. Well, that didn't work out, did it?" Fanny's tone was disparaging.

Bertram shook his head. "I'm not talking about that. I'm talking about afterwards, the other night when I tried to suggest a wager whereby Grayling would propose to Cousin Thea in a hot-air balloon. Well, before I knew it, someone had suggested that as they'd seen Cousin Thea slap George Bramley's face, then *that* ought to be the wager, as under such adverse circumstances it'd be so unlikely that a union between Thea and George Bramley would come to pass."

"Thea slapped Bramley's face?" Antoinette clapped her hands. "How perfectly marvellous," she crowed, but Fanny frowned. "So the wager is for George Bramley to entice Thea into the hot-air balloon tonight and propose marriage? That's ridiculous."

Bertram looked a touch confused. He

opened his mouth to speak then shut it again as he clearly reconsidered. Fanny pounced, her tone suspicious. "Tell us *exactly* the terms of this wager. The more we know, the more we can protect Thea."

Bertram scratched his cheek and screwed up his face, apparently trying to recall. *Dear Lord, could her brother not be trusted to get the simplest details right?* "George Bramley has wagered Lord Darington seven hundred pounds that he—George, that is—will somehow manage to encourage Miss Brightwell to step into a hot air balloon and fly away with her. And another seven hundred if—"

He shut his mouth quickly and raised his eyes to the sky, unable—or refusing—to continue with what he was about to say until Fanny threatened she'd tell their mother about his interest in the opera dancer he'd declared he intended to marry one night while in his cups.

Bertram's shoulders slumped. Gloomily he went on, "And George Bramley has made another wager that Miss Brightwell will..."

When he trailed off, both his sisters began to heckle him until he threw his hands in the air and cried, "Propose marriage but not only that, George Bramley has also bet Lord Darington that nine months later Miss Brightwell will joyfully give birth to a…child."

"Well, she's unlikely to give birth to anything else," Fanny muttered before shaking her head and adding, "Good lord, Bertram, do you mean to tell me you really began all this wager nonsense?"

"I didn't initiate any of *those* wagers!" Bertram defended himself. "The idea was completely taken out of my hands. You know I only wanted to help cousin Thea."

"Well, I think cousin Thea needs Antoinette's and my help right now. Clearly George Bramley has an evil plan, though I cannot imagine how he intends to carry it off."

"You don't think he can?" Bertram asked, hopefully.

Fanny tried to look more confident than she felt. "How can he possibly when there are so many people milling around the estate, getting things organised for the grand event, which is even now beginning?" The wager was preposterous. Thea would never willingly step into a hot-air balloon with George Bramley. Besides, Fanny would make sure she was by her side every minute of the festivities.

Antoinette nodded. "Even if he kidnaps her I don't know how he'd manage it. Thea is quick. She'd scream and struggle. There'd be too many witnesses. Goodness, but George Bramley is a very stupid man." She frowned, then added, "Besides, why would George want to marry Thea if he only had seven hundred pounds to gain? Or fourteen, even?"

Fanny was about to blithely agree to this when a look of horror crossed her face. "Oh, I think George would consider he'd gained a great deal more than just seven hundred pounds. Just think! If he compromised Thea so she in fact did feel she had to marry him, then he'd have secured the most wonderful revenge on us, wouldn't he?

Imagine how he could play us—blackmail us—to ensure Thea's continued happiness. Well, she'd never be happy but I mean…he'd make a sport of making her even more unhappy, just to spite us." She raised her eyes heavenward then said on a more pragmatic note, "Well, at least we know what George is up to. Now we just have to keep Thea close by to know she'll be safe from his sinister designs."

She was about to pass George to go inside when she hesitated on the threshold, turning to her siblings to ask with sudden dread, "By the way, where *is* Thea?"

<hr>

As the three siblings went in search of Thea, seemingly hundreds of guests were strolling about the beautifully landscaped gardens, standing in clusters to watch preparations for the ascent of the balloon from afar, or gossiping in groups.

"She's not here!" Fanny tried not to show her concern as she passed through knots of people, Antoinette having been held up by a garrulous admirer along the way.

"You don't really think George Bramley could succeed in something so outrageous, do you?" Panic cut through the insouciance Bertram was going to such pains to cultivate as he stumbled along in Fanny's wake.

"I wouldn't put anything past Mr Bramley," Fanny muttered, doggedly parting the crowd before adding on a sigh of relief, "Thank goodness, there she is!" as she rushed forward. "Thea, I've been so worried about you. Are you all right, dearest? You look so sad."

"I *am* so sad," Thea sniffed, pointing across a stretch of lawn to where a couple was walking at a sedate pace along the gravel path. Immediately Fanny recognized the tall, handsome figure of Mr Grayling and, at his side, Thea's slight, pretty but infinitely less appealing rival.

"I know he loves me and I certainly love him but he's going to ask Miss Huntingdon to marry him," Thea told her cousin in a small voice. "During the carriage ride he said he'd have to speak to his man of business to see if it were at all possible that matters might be arranged whereby a union between us might not be ruinous to his family. But here he is tonight and he's not even spoken to me. So I can only assume that he's received confirmation that it is as he feared all along. He needs a wife with a dowry and now he's about to propose to Miss Huntingdon. Do you think that's what he's doing right now?"

"Lord, no!" exclaimed Bertram. "He'd at least wait until tomorrow. Or until he'd spoken to you. Besides, Miss Huntindgon doesn't hold a candle to you, and that's the truth!"

Thea hiccupped on a sob. "That's hardly of any account, but thank you, Bertram. Miss Huntingdon has a handsome dowry and is mad for him, and of course Mr Grayling is no different from me in wanting to make a decent match that will secure his future. I just can't offer him what he needs to make him happy."

"Oh, Thea, if I only had the means to change it, I would." It was rare for Fanny to feel so helpless. "Do you really think he'd be so unheroic as to speak to Miss Huntingdon so quickly?"

Thea nodded. "I told him that's what he must do."

"What?" Fanny and Bertram looked at her in horror.

"What else could I say?" Thea choked on another little sob. "He might love me but I'd be a drain on his purse. He was very chivalrous in the carriage when his passions were aroused that he would get an answer from his man of business. But in the clear light of day one must be persuaded by practicalities. Certainly, Mr Grayling would be able to provide for me, but he couldn't for the rest of his relatives and if he and I had a large family. And you know how much I long for a large family. Yet how cruel it would be to put a daughter into the situation I'm in. I realised that and so I told him he should ask for Miss Huntingdon's hand if it wasn't practical to marry me." She pointed to the pair, deep in conversation by the bushes. "Yes, I'm certain that's what he's doing right now, though I confess that when that note was delivered late last night, my heart did leap with the hope that it *might* be from Mr Grayling and that he *might* be telling me he'd changed his mind and that he'd propose to me, instead. After all, *I* don't mind if we don't have money. I'm used to it."

She would have gone on, only Fanny stopped her. "What note, Thea? Did someone deliver you a note?"

"No, not to me, it was to Aunt Minerva. I don't know what was in it but it was addressed to her, and she would have me believe that Mr Granville had invited her to meet him for some secret assignation, which is why she'll soon no longer be able to offer me a home and I therefore must accept Dr Horne's marriage offer." Tearfully she added, "So that is what I'm going to do. I'm going to accept Dr Horne tonight, as Aunt Minerva has invited him to attend to her after the christening celebrations are over and that is what she's said I must do if Mr Grayling hasn't proposed—which, I have now accepted, he will not."

"You will do nothing of the sort!" Fanny and Bertram spoke in emphatic unison.

Fanny pushed back her shoulders. "It's

one thing to lose out on the love of your life but quite another to marry someone you have absolutely no feelings for." She bit her lip, before adding thoughtfully, "This note, though, sounds awfully odd. Are you sure it was from Mr Granville? I thought I saw him earlier talking to a young lady and her mother. Mr Granville is very dashing, I admit, but I have never seen anything to suggest he has a secret *tendre* for Aunt Minerva."

"No, but she's received letters from him before that make her go very flushed in the cheeks, so it must be true." Thea turned. "I really don't think I can bear watching Mr Grayling and his soon-to-be betrothed for much longer. Do you mind if I make my excuses and retire to my room, or...?" Her face lit up. "Perhaps I could go to the nursery and play with little Katherine and George?"

"That sounds an excellent idea!" Fanny looked at Bertram. "You must go with Thea, just to make sure she gets there safely."

"Of course I'll get there safely. I know exactly where the nursery is."

Fanny hesitated, unsure whether to say

more. "I'm just a little worried about George Bramley," she finally confessed. "He likes his revenge and I believe you slapped his face the other night?" When Thea, shamefaced, nodded, Fanny went on, "In that case, he will definitely be seeking retribution. Promise me you'll not venture anywhere near him."

Thea shook her head vehemently. "Of course not! But I think I saw him on his way to the Oriental Pavilion not far from where the balloon is going to take off. As I'm off to the nursery to play with the babies, I'll be quite safe."

Antoinette took Thea's wrist to stay her. "First we must interrupt Mr Grayling's romantic overtures." She looked determined. "We might not be able to stop him from marrying the wrong woman but we can at least make things a little harder for him."

Thea's heart felt ready to break in two. This was the worst evening of her life for it was true, she now realised, that she'd honestly held out hope, believing that if Mr Grayling really did love her he'd *somehow* find a means to marry her. Unable to extricate her fingers from Antoinette's, she allowed herself to be hurried down to the gravel path.

Antoinette greeted the couple, gaily. "I'm so glad to see you at darling baby George's celebration, Mr Grayling, Miss Huntingdon. Do you plan to take a ride in the hot-air balloon?"

Thea noticed the discomfort on the faces of both young people as they were descended upon by all four Brightwells who'd clearly interrupted something of importance.

Antoinette giggled and Fanny sent her a sharp look which did nothing to temper her next piece of outrageous behavior. Fixing the young man with an intense look, she tapped him on the shoulder with her fan. "Thea's going to marry George Bramley, did you know?"

Thea was pleased by the shock on Mr Grayling's face. He looked confused as he stared at her then towards the Pavilion.

"But I thought—" He broke off, shrugged, then after a long look at Thea, said, "I'm expecting my man of business to arrive here any moment—" He turned to Miss Huntingdon whose expression, which had been equally bleak, was suddenly transformed by hope. However, receiving no answering flare in Mr Grayling's expression her mouth turned downwards once more.

"At least," Antoinette went on as if she hadn't heard him, "Mr Bramley has wagered Lord Darington seven hundred pounds that he'll take Miss Brightwell up in the hot-air balloon to propose to her and as Thea has received no other offers to consider and her aunt will soon no longer be in a position to offer her a home, what choice does poor Thea have?"

Bertram, who'd been swaying on his feet while he downed the last of his second bottle of Madeira that night, interjected dolefully, "And he's wagered that nine months later Miss Brightwell will give birth to a beautiful—"

"Bertram!" his sisters cried out in horror though surely their horror was nothing compared with Thea's. Seeing Mr Grayling's anxious, then shocked expression, and aware also of Miss Huntgindon's doleful demeanour, she declared roundly, "Whatever my plans regarding matrimony, I would not get into a hot air balloon with Mr Bramley if he was the last man alive!"

Bertram looked at her approvingly. "Yes, well, I'm mighty glad to hear that, Thea, because of course Mr Bramley might be plump enough in the pocket after winning those bets to make him a likely prospect but I do agree that you'll be much better off marrying Dr Horne." He was about to add more when Mr Grayling interjected hurriedly, "I say, please excuse me, for there's Clunes, my man of business now." He took a step forward, stopped, then put his hand on Thea's shoulder, adding, as he bent his face close to hers, "Promise you'll not get into any hot air balloon or accept any doctor's proposals while I'm gone? I know you're angry with me, which is perhaps why you gave me no answer, but promise me you'll wait?"

"Wait?" Thea repeated as she closed her eyes briefly and savoured the feel of his sweet breath upon her cheek before opening her eyes to see him gone.

So, he *did* care for her. Yes, she realised she had been angry. No, more disappointed, but perhaps he really had not yet given her a *definitive* answer because he did not have one to give. With a jolt of fear—but of hope and anticipation too—she realised that the outcome of Mr Grayling's imminent meeting with Mr Clunes would be the decider of her fate. Both their fates. With beating heart she watched him cross the lawn as Miss Huntingdon murmured, "Congratulations, Miss Brightwell. Are you really to marry Dr Horne? That is a surprise."

"Poor Thea's got little choice," Antoinette replied, a touch tartly. "Aunt Minerva is expecting a marriage proposal tonight and says she isn't able to offer Thea a home after Mr Granville becomes my formidable aunt's husband. I expect their little assignation at the Pavilion is to arrange the final details."

Miss Huntingdon looked surprised. "Mr Granville intends to propose to Miss *Brightwell*? Miss *Minerva* Brightwell? I did not think they knew one another."

Miserably Thea explained, "He was a suitor in her youth whom she rejected more than twenty years ago. She was greatly upset by the fact that he was supposed to repeat his marriage offer only he didn't. And now, twenty years later, he has."

Miss Huntingdon's surprise turned to confusion. "I do beg pardon, but Mr Granville appeared greatly taken with my second cousin who is…well, a fair young lady with a substantial portion."

"What! Even fairer than the esteemed Miss Minerva Brightwell?" Bertram demanded as if he couldn't believe such a thing. "Well, it appears your second cousin is going to be disappointed since clearly Mr Granville has rekindled his romance with my aunt and intends to propose to her in the Oriental Pavilion."

***

SYLVESTER HAD HAD ENOUGH. ENOUGH OF his propensity for making excuses and of not being true to his heart and to his beliefs regarding what made for a good and worth-while life.

He wanted to feel worthwhile and right now, crossing the lawn towards where he saw Clunes in conversation with several gentlemen, he was more conflicted that he had ever been.

He'd felt a cad disappointing Miss Hunt-ingdon but it had been necessary to ease his conscience. Yet had he been premature? What was behind Miss Brightwell's mean-ing? Was she toying with him to test his feelings for her? It seemed out of character and, furthermore, extraordinary that after his note of last night to her, requesting that she meet him at the Pavilion, she should publicly inform him she intended accepting Dr Horne. Perhaps it was a ruse for the ben-efit of her cousins and Miss Huntingdon. Perhaps she was trying to throw them off the scent in order to meet him at the Pavil-ion, after all. It was confusing and Sylvester didn't like feeling confused.

That's why he liked Miss Brightwell so much. She didn't play games. She was com-pletely transparent and honest.

Which meant her words with regard to accepting Dr Horne were out of character.

Yes indeed! Miss Brightwell was the sweetest, most innocent creature he'd ever met and these were the qualities he esteemed: pure goodness and a complete lack of guile.

He was within hailing distance of Clunes when he heard a breathless voice from behind, calling for him.

"Mr Grayling! My Grayling! Wait!"

He hesitated, turned, then when he saw it was Miss Brightwell, was unprepared for the complete disorderly beat of his heart as he stepped a little off the path so they were partly concealed by several large saplings.

She reached his side, her expression intense as if she had something of great importance to say, her words labored as she burst out, "Whatever you have to tell me doesn't alter my opinion of you. My father couldn't afford my mother's...material needs and it made the whole family very unhappy. I wouldn't do that to any child of mine and I truly understand your feelings of honour and why you'd hold that as a very important factor when making your decision." Her smile was tremulous as she put her hand on his wrist, her look appealing. "We must both make decisions that may not be what we want but what are for the best; that is, when everyone else is taken into account."

He was touched by her sincerity. Her sentiments were so much as he'd have expected from her and that was why he loved her. She thought about everyone else before she thought of herself. She was too good for him but suddenly he was struck by the most earth-shattering realisation. By Gad he *was* going to marry her, regardless of what Clunes had to say. Or his mother. Or *anyone*.

With a quick glance behind her he gripped her shoulders, forcing her into the shadows, he whispered, "Will you kiss me in the seclusion of that small thicket over there?"

Wide-eyed, she nodded.

"You'd do so, even if I were to tell you news you might not wish to hear?"

Once again she nodded, adding, "But

only this once because I love you, Mr Grayling, and I'd have this to remember you by. And only if you had no other commitments to anyone else. You've not made promises to Miss Huntingdon?"

Warmth filled his heart as he shook his head. "No, my dear love, I've made no commitments to anyone else. Or rather, to no one except myself."

She smiled at the endearment, her gaze enquiring as he gently propelled her to the privacy he sought so he could truly convey his feelings to her.

"And since you're not asking what commitments I'm making to myself, I will tell you. Yes, regardless of what my man of business tells me I ought or ought not do, I intend to marry you, Miss Brightwell. Why? Purely selfish reasons, I'm afraid to say."

This time it was his turn to smile when she looked a little startled, but he stopped her question by touching his lips to hers, deep in the shadows of a spreading elm. But only for a second, only to whet her longing before he whispered, "You will make me a man I can be proud of. I truly believe that only you have that power."

And before she had time to answer, he kissed her more deeply, dipping his head to fuse his mouth to hers as he cupped the back of her head and caressed her waist, skimming her thigh which charged him with a lust so fierce he had to remember where he was.

After a moment or so, she drew back, perhaps for air, though also to murmur against his lips, "You don't need me to make you into anything, Mr Grayling. You're perfect as you are."

He had to kiss her again at this; and to feel her yielding, so willing, her gaze so tender and loving, was almost more than he could bear. In fact, her response was so rapturous it filled him with the sense that nothing could be more right and proper in the whole world than allying himself with this sweet angel.

Finally they both became conscious of the world around them; yet it was hard to break away. As they joined hands and gazed at one another, there was a new and shared understanding.

"I thought you had decided against meeting me in the Oriental Pavilion," he said, almost bashfully. Lord, he felt like a green boy in the throes of first love. And yet, this young woman was going to be his wife. He'd never felt happier in his entire life. Of course, he hadn't asked the question in the proper and formal manner he intended. But he would. Later. When the time was right.

She looked surprised. "Why should I do that? I..." She bit her lip and frowned. "I'm not a mind reader. You...you didn't send me a message did you?"

Surprised, he replied, "I sent a message last night making just such a request. I asked the messenger to wait for an answer which I received in the affirmative."

Miss Brightwell shook her head, wonderingly. "I received no such message though...Aunt Minerva did."

Surprised, he asked, "What time was this?"

"At about eight o' clock. She looked very

excited and then told me I must accept Dr Horne if you hadn't proposed to me by tonight."

They had returned to open ground by this point and when Sylvester raised his head to respond he instead exhaled on resignation. He knew he should not have been surprised to be confronted by all three Brightwell siblings but there they were advancing, en masse, towards them. They were a formidable team and the trick Bertram Brigthwell had played in deceiving him was deplorable. Yet he could not condemn him. Not for delivering him a lifetime of happiness.

"You look positively glowing, Thea!" cried Lady Quamby. "Do you have good news to report?"

Noting Miss Brightwell's embarrassment which was understandable since Sylvester had not stated anything in specific terms which she could in turn report to her cousins, he interjected, as forcefully as was polite, "I was hoping I might be allowed a few moments alone with your cousin in the Oriental Pavilion." He smiled fondly at his lovely bride-to-be, then returned his gaze to the Brightwell clan. "Then she *will* have something to report."

Instead of the delight he was expecting, Lady Fenton's brow clouded. "But that's where Aunt Minerva has gone."

"Indeed she has," his darling Miss Brightwell corroborated anxiously. "As I told you, she received a message last night from Mr Granville, requesting that she meet him there."

Sylvester stared from each questioning face before returning his gaze to his darling's. "I think, perhaps, she is mistaken. *I* sent a message to *Miss Brightwell* requesting her company at the Oriental Pavilion."

"To Miss *Thea* Brightwell?" Bertram clarified.

"Lord, not Miss Thea Brightwell." Sylvester sent Thea a stricken look. "Are you not the eldest young lady, the lady I was introduced to as Miss Brightwell?"

"Indeed she was, as you could hardly be on Christian name terms," Bertram said smoothly. "I say, it's an easy mistake to make, but rather a foolish one. Of course

Miss Brightwell—Aunt Minerva—would imagine any letter addressed to Miss Brightwell was for her. Not very clever of you, eh wot?"

Sylvester's anxiety grew as he directed an even more intense look at Miss Brightwell. "You say your aunt has been in receipt of a *number* of notes during the past two weeks?"

"Yes, Mr Grayling. I glanced at one of them and indeed, I can assure you that Mr Granville's growing interest is not a figment of her imagination. He apologized for his shabby treatment and begged for a sign from her to reassure him that she forgave him. This was just before the masquerade."

"The note was addressed to Miss Brightwell and signed with the initials SG?"

Miss Brightwell nodded.

Impulsively he gripped her hand, bringing it to his lips as he cried, "*I* wrote that note. In fact, I wrote all of them. But I addressed them to Miss Brightwell assuming they would be delivered to *you*."

Miss Brightwell gasped. "*You* wrote all those notes to Aunt Minerva?"

"No…to *you*, of course!"

"To me?" she whispered. Sylvester's apparent stupidity was then rewarded by a look of the utmost adoration.

Meanwhile Lady Fenton looked greatly discomposed. "I fear Aunt Minerva is on her way to the Pavilion for a secret assignation which she believes will be with her long-lost Mr Granville. As she would if she believes all the letters Mr Grayling intended for Cousin Thea were for *her*."

Bertram guffawed. "Just as well you didn't get there earlier and find yourself stuck with the old trout, Grayling old chap. Not that she won't be mightily disappointed to find nobody there, now."

Lady Fenton let out a resounding sigh. "Well, Thea is accounted for, and that's our greatest relief."

"I wonder where George Bramley is?" Bertam fiddled with the buttons of his waistcoat and Sylvester assumed he had a good deal of money wagered on something to do with the odious George Bramley. But with Thea Brightwell by his side, he felt easy. No, he was not going to let her out of his sight. Not tonight. In fact, he'd be there always to see to her best interests in case someone tried to put a wedge between them by making her feel at some time in the future that she and their growing brood of children—funny how he loved the idea!—might ever be considered a drain on his purse.

"I daresay he's somewhere near the hot air balloon since that's where he intends to win that stupid wager," the young man went on, "though he certainly won't now."

They all looked towards the Oriental Pavilion and, nearby, where the balloon had been tethered to the ground, its enormous brightly coloured canopy reaching for the sky.

"Really, I think the kindest thing right now would be to put Aunt Minerva out of her misery and tactfully explain that Mr Granville will not be making an appearance let alone any heartfelt declarations," suggested Lady Fenton.

At which Lady Quamby cried in stirring tones, "To the Oriental Pavilion, one and all!"

ALL WAS QUIET WHEN THEY REACHED THE Oriental Pavilion en route to their destination. However knowing that poor Aunt Minerva was waiting like a lovelorn damsel somewhere inside, they peeped through a section of uncovered window.

In unison they all voiced their horror before clapping hands to their mouths.

George Bramley was on a raised dais, strutting backwards and forwards as if addressing a rapt audience. Every now and again he'd stop, run his hands down his sides, flex his muscles, then throw his head back and laugh.

"He's quite mad, you know." Lady Quamby rolled her eyes. "And to think he imagined he might succeed in making Thea his wife."

The idea was so preposterous, Sylvester felt his stomach lurch. The moment he had the Oriental Pavilion all to himself he was going to ensure Miss Brightwell received the offer for which she was waiting so patiently. In fact, he could barely contain himself from blurting out his marriage proposal right now, just to ensure it was official.

"What is he doing?" Lady Fenton cried, squinting with greater concentration into the gloom. "Good God, who is that?"

The horrified squeals of the young ladies echoed in his ears and instinctively he gripped his true love's hand.

"Aunt Minerva has been made a prisoner to his antics!" cried Lady Fenton. "But… Heavens! I believe he cannot *know* it's Aunt Minerva."

A huddle of something large and trembling in the far dim corner, covered by a large black cloak, was settled across a tumble of cushions; human, and to Sylvester's discerning eye, most likely Miss Minerva Brightwell, judging by a pair of ruby slippers upon her feet that he recognised.

George Bramley continued to strut in front of her, conducting a monologue, it would appear, stopping every so often to contour his body as if to illustrate something. Something very unattractive, to Sylvester's mind. Something suggesting the manliness of his manly appendage. And this man sought to marry his Thea?

His Thea. Every sense revolted against such an idea and, surreptitiously, he tightened his grip on her hand in the dark. Her answering squeeze warmed his heart. True, he'd forsaken her only two days since with the heat of their kiss still burning his lips, grateful for her meek acceptance that she was not a suitable wife for him if he needed greater funds to wed.

Yet she'd entirely forgiven him.

Her ability to forgive only reinforced the temporary madness that had possessed him when he'd contemplated giving up the only true and pure love he'd experienced. Thinking of that was even more powerful than making sense of the prurient scene before them in which, clearly, an innocent woman was being held hostage to the rantings of a madman.

They must act, of course, but the crunch of footsteps on gravel made them all stiffen. Approaching from the trees on the other side of the building, a barrel-shaped man dressed as a gentleman but with the bearing of a peasant marched through the door of the Oriental Pavilion and before their very eyes, whisked up the black-cloaked figure that was assuredly Minerva Brightwell and tossed her quivering body over his shoulder. George Bramley looked like an excited monkey as he hurried alongside them, out of the front doors.

"We must do something!" cried Miss Thea.

The balloon was on the far side of the building, across the lawn, and together the they dashed around the side of the Pavilion to see what was happening and arrest George Bramley's villainy.

"That's right! Put her into the basket!" they heard Bramley call, clapping his hands before leaping in as the balloon tugged on its moorings.

"Stop!" Lady Fenton cried, rushing forward, as the rest of the party joined in unison. But their voices were drowned out by the sudden arrival of seemingly dozens, and then hundreds, of onlookers who were suddenly streaming down the hill.

"Cut the rope!" Bramley yelled at the top

of his voice just as Sylvester rushed forward and snatched the covering cloak from the prisoner…

Revealing Miss Minerva Brightwell, bound and gagged—and George Bramley's red, shocked face.

The crowd roared at the spectacle but Sylvester had had enough. Amidst the general hilarity, catcalls and equivalent mockery, he turned and clasped Thea's hands in his. "The Oriental Pavilion is quite deserted with all the action centred here. Will you come with me?"

"Alone?"

"Unless you'd prefer to have witnesses to what I have to ask you."

"No witnesses, thank you. Not for that, and not for when you show me…" Her delicious lips turned up in a wicked smile.

All the tension drained out of him and he laughed, bringing up her hands to kiss her knuckles.

"Maybe, in that department, it's best we should wait—"

She affected such a look of disappointment he wanted to hug and kiss her right there and then before indeed showing her exactly what it was she wanted him to show her.

Making a great show of pandering to her, he nodded. "Indeed, how else is Mr Bramley to win his wager?"

When she frowned slightly, he refreshed her memory. "I believe Miss Brightwell was to give birth to a bonny baby nine months after ascending in a hot air balloon." With a gentle tug of her hand he drew her a little away, setting his footsteps for the Pavilion. "You said you wanted lots of little ones, didn't you?"

"But you've not yet spoken to your man of business."

"Whatever he says is of no account when it comes to what you want in a family, my darling."

By the portico of the Pavilion just behind the privet hedge, he went down on one knee and took her hand, bringing it to his lips.

"It seems I have lost my desire for the larger expenses I thought were the lifeblood of excitement. No, Thea—if I can call you that now—I want nothing more than to have you for my wife, to live with you in mutual happiness and harmony and to have as many darling little ones as you wish, even if it means I have to cater to a brood as large as that belonging to our good Duke of Clarence."

Miss Brightwell's sigh of pleasure was audible and his own heart hitched in response.

He cleared his throat, emotion making his voice break as he murmured, quietly but with passion, "Miss Thea Brightwell, will you do me the very great honour of becoming my wife?"

Tenderly she touched his face, her tearful smile answer enough until she whispered, "Nothing would make me happier... Mr Sylvester Grayling."

He would have replied, except that a loud screeching was borne upon the air and they looked up in time to see the basket passing low across the moon, highlighting the horror on Bramley's face as he shouted, "I've been tricked!"

This was followed by Miss Brightwell's

shrill response, "It is *I* who has been tricked! Where is Mr Granville? What have you done with him?"

Across the lawn a flurry of shouts could be heard: "A thousand pounds if you ask her to marry you, Bramley!"

"Fifteen hundred!" shouted others.

"Two thousand if she says yes!" came another cry.

Sylvester had no desire to hear more but his conscience was ready to do business when Thea cried anxiously, "We have to rescue her! Look, the basket is dropping and there's the rope!"

And so Sylvester leapt to his feet, not because he was a hero, or had a particular desire to extricate Miss Minerva Brightwell.

Not for any reason other than that Thea made him remember what it was to be a good man. A better man. The best man he could be.

So he dashed forward when no one else was bestirring themselves and took hold of the rope which had enough slack that he was able to tie it to a tree.

And thus he became not only Thea's

hero, but also Minerva Brightwell's, who shortly thereafter declared she would favour Thea in her will as Thea had finally done the sensible thing by choosing a husband who clearly respected Minerva Brightwell as a woman of her consequence demanded.

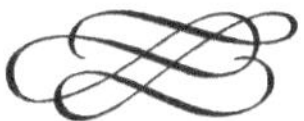

Ten Months Later

Thea stretched out an arm and gently caressed her husband's cheek as she opened sleepy eyes to find him watching her.

"You've been in a deep dream. A pleasant one, I think." He was leaning on one elbow, gazing at her intently, as if he'd been committing her image to heart. "Young Jamie has been waiting patiently for his morning feed."

Only then did Thea realize the infant was wailing fit to bring the house down as his nurse brought him out from the nursery. Thea had insisted on feeding the child herself, despite the disapproval of almost everyone, especially Antoinette who'd declared that Thea could not possibly have fun if she were so bonded with a creature that would make her his slave.

"I already am," Thea had replied, "and I wouldn't have it any other way."

Now she arranged herself comfortably and cleared her throat, deciding how to phrase what was so important to her.

"Maybe we should get James a playmate, Sylvester, darling."

Her husband's warm hand on her thigh, exploring higher made her realize he misunderstood. Especially when he complained that she was being awfully impatient and shouldn't she wait until she'd fed James and the nurse had taken him away?"

"No, I mean a little fellow he can play with in the nursery. Like a brother."

Sylvester frowned. "Foster a child?" he asked, and though his arms were just as warm and loving, the tone of his voice made clear his antipathy to the idea.

Thea snuggled against him. He was always at his most amenable like this. "No, not foster or adopt,' she said calmly. "Just invite a playmate to the house on occasion to keep James company."

Gently she began to massage her darling Sylvester's temples and immediately he closed his eyes to savour the sensation. Thea had learned the way to her husband's heart through gentle touch and persuasion, just as she'd learned to manage the household accounts with the same care she'd learned during the lean years growing up. Sylvester had voiced his wonder on more than one occasion that three seemed to be able to live just as comfortably as one. Yet now he'd made certain economies there was far more at his disposal than he'd realised.

"But he has his cousins, George and Katherine."

"True, but there's one little being in particular I can't stop thinking about."

Sylvester chewed on his lip as he stared at his beautiful wife who looked like a madonna, bathed in the sunlight that filtered through the bedroom curtains. He traced the corner of her mouth, his smile full of tenderness. "Oh my darling, it's that child your coachman nearly ran over the day we met, isn't it?"

She nodded. "Yes. Don't you think it would be appropriate to offer him something more than the dreary existence to which he's condemned? Clearly his mother was of good breeding and—"

"Got herself into trouble, which is what Aunt Minerva would call getting her just desserts. Can you imagine what your aunt would say to us taking in a foundling?"

"I can imagine it very well, but when have you ever taken account of anything my aunt thinks, though you're polite enough when we visit." She grinned. "Even if you do rile her with your constant references to letting George Bramley slip through her fingers just to make her turn puce."

"Poor Mr Bramley. What a terrible decision to have to let her go," he mocked. "He'd have made himself a fortune if he'd married your Aunt Minerva for she didn't seem entirely opposed to the idea. I'm glad there are no more unmarried Brightwells on whom he can have his revenge." He chuckled and looked about to continue with the topic of

Mr Bramley and his odious ways but Thea had not yet secured that for which she hungered: bringing a little happiness to a child who needed it.

"I don't mean taking in an orphan to live with us, but just occasionally to play with James. Please, Sylvester?"

He kissed her tenderly. "You know I can't refuse you anything, my dear. If that's what you wish, then by all means, go and organise it."

Thea pressed up against her wonderful husband and kissed him back with passion. "Thank you, Sylvester, darling," she whispered. "I thought I might suggest to Aunt Minerva that we visit the Foundling Home today to do just that. She's been wanting a girl to help with some of the things I was so useful at doing, like rubbing in her unguents and applying her smelling salts, so we'll be able to satisfy both needs: a playmate for James and a companion for Aunt Minerva." Thea smiled up at him, her heart warming as his expression softened even further. It was always so satisfying to persuade the man she loved of the rightness of something simply by appealing to his heart and reason. A novelty she'd never enjoyed with Aunt Minerva.

"No doubt your reference to a 'companion' for your Aunt Minerva really means another orphan you can somehow save from a life of drudgery." He stroked her cheek. "You really are a diamond of the first water, my darling Thea. To think how little value I once placed on a bountiful heart, being only concerned with the bounty my prospective bride could bring me."

If Thea had been a cat, she'd have purred with contentment. Instead she arched against him and whispered, "And to think how little I was ready to value the physical delights of the marriage bed, believing the act a burdensome means of begetting children." She ran her hand the length of his thigh and added in a whisper, "And since we are trying for a playmate for young James, I think I'd rather fancy a little more of what we got up to last night, eh, my darling?"

THE END

Will Thea and Sylvester's decision to foster the young foundling lad unite two star-crossed lovers in **The Wedding Wager**? (The Wedding Wager is Book 3, previously titled *Devil's Run*).

OTHER BOOKS BY
BEVERLEY OAKLEY

HEARTS IN HIDING Series
The Duchess and the Highwayman
The Bluestocking and the Rake
Duchess of Seduction

SCANDALOUS MISS BRIGHTWELLS Series
Rake's Honour
Rake's Redemption
Rogue's Kiss
The Wedding Wager
The Accidental Elopement

DAUGHTERS OF SIN Series
Her Gilded Prison

Dangerous Gentlemen
The Mysterious Governess
Beyond Rubies
Lady Unveiled: The Cuckold's Conspiracy

GEORGIAN MYSTERY ROMANCE Series
Wicked Wager
Her Valentine's Secret

FAIR CYPRIANS OF LONDON Series
Saving Grace
Forsaking Hope
Keeping Faith
Wedding Violet
Christmas Charity

ABOUT THE AUTHOR

Beverley Oakley, an Australian author who grew up in the African mountain kingdom of Lesotho, emigrated to South Australia when she was young, and married a Norwegian bush pilot she met while managing a safari lodge in Botswana's Okavango Delta.

Beverley writes historical romance laced with mystery, scandal and intrigue. She lives north of Melbourne (overlooking a fabulous Gothic lunatic asylum) with the same gorgeous Norwegian husband, two daughters and a rambunctious Rhodesian Ridgeback.

Browse Beverley's books, on Amazon.

Visit Beverley's website to sign up for her
newsletter (and receive a free book)
Join Beverley's reader group on Facebook

Follow Beverley

On Bookbub
On Goodreads
On Facebook